Critical Care

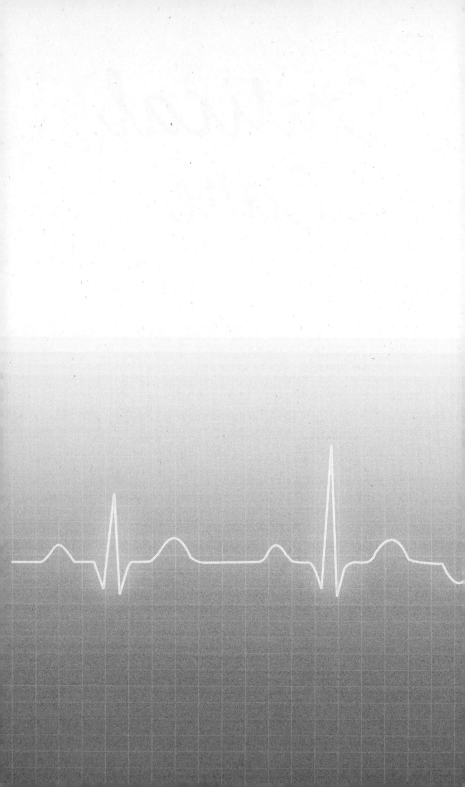

CANDACE CALVERT

TYNDALE HOUSE PUBLISHERS, INC.
CAROL STREAM, ILLINOIS

Visit Candace Calvert's Web site at www.candacecalvert.com

TYNDALE and Tyndale's quill logo are registered trademarks of Tyndale House Publishers, Inc.

Critical Care

Designed by Mark Anthony Lane II

Edited by Lorie Popp

Published in association with the literary agency of Natasha Kern Literary Agency, Inc., P.O. Box 1069, White Salmon, WA 98672.

ISBN-13: 978-1-61523-293-2

Printed in the United States of America

For Elizabeth Dewante
Artist, loving mother, and wonderful woman of faith.
You've blessed my life.

ACKNOWLEDGMENTS

Heartfelt appreciation to:

Agent Natasha Kern—for encouraging me to follow my heart.

Tyndale House editors Jan Stob and Lorie Popp—I'm honored to be part of the team.

Talented critique partner Nancy Herriman—your friendship and help . . . priceless.

Nurse Linda Roberts—"To get through it, you've got to go through it." Wise words, dear friend.

Barbara Jamieson, RN, and Tim Sturgill, MD—I appreciate your willingness to look over my medical scenes. Any inaccuracies are mine alone.

Methodist Hospital of Sacramento—my second home and special family for so many years.

Fellow nurses and medical professionals—inspirational heroes all. Hang in there; we need you.

St. Helena's Church, the awesome women's Bible study, and Community of Hope—thank you.

My incredible children and grandchildren—your enthusiasm and support mean so much.

My wonderful husband, Andy Calvert—you've made me believe in happy endings.

CHAPTER ONE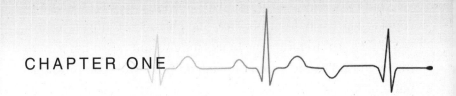

Don't die, little girl.

Dr. Logan Caldwell pressed the heel of his hand against Amy Hester's chest, taking over heart compressions in a last attempt to save the child's life. Her small sternum hollowed and recoiled under his palm at a rate of one hundred times per minute, the best he could do to mimic her natural heartbeat. A respiratory therapist forced air into her lungs.

Don't die. Logan glanced up at the ER resuscitation clock, ticking on without mercy. Twenty-seven minutes since they'd begun the code. No heartbeat. Not once. Time to quit but . . .

He turned to his charge nurse, Erin Quinn, very aware of the insistent wail of sirens in the distance. "Last dose of epi?"

"Three minutes ago."

"Give another." Logan halted compressions, his motionless hand easily spanning the width of the two-year-old's chest. He watched until satisfied with the proficiency of the therapist's ventilations, then turned back to the cardiac monitor and frowned. Asystole—flatline. Flogging this young heart with atropine and repeated doses of epinephrine wasn't going to do it. A pacemaker, pointless. She'd been deprived of oxygen far too long before rescue.

Logan pushed his palm into Amy's sternum again and gritted

his teeth against images of a terrified little girl hiding in a toy cupboard as her day care burned in a suffocating cloud of smoke, amid the chaos of two dozen other burned and panicking children.

"Epi's on board," Erin reported, sweeping an errant strand of coppery hair away from her face. She pressed two fingers against the child's arm to locate the brachial pulse and raised her gaze to the doctor's. "You're generating a good pulse with compressions, but . . ."

But she's dead. With reluctance, Logan lifted his hand from the child's chest. He studied the monitor display and then nodded at the blonde nurse standing beside the crash cart. "Run me rhythm strips in three leads, Sarah." After he drew in a slow breath of air still acrid with the residue of smoke, he glanced down at Amy Hester, her cheeks unnaturally rosy from the effects of carbon monoxide, glossy brown curls splayed against the starched hospital linen. Dainty purple flower earrings. Blue eyes, glazed and half-lidded. Tiny chin. And lips—pink as a Valentine cupid—pursed around the rigid breathing tube, as if it were a straw in a snack-time juice box. Picture-perfect . . . and gone.

He signaled for the ventilations to stop and checked the code clock again. "Time of death—9:47."

There was a long stretch of silence, and Logan used it to make his exit, turning his back to avoid another glance at the child on the gurney . . . and the expressions on the faces of his team. No good came from dwelling on tragedy. He knew that too well. Best to move on with what he had to do. He'd almost reached the doorway when Erin caught his arm.

"We've put Amy's parents and grandmother in the quiet room the way you asked," she confirmed, her green eyes conveying empathy for him as well. "I can send Sarah with you, if—"

"No. I'll handle it myself," Logan said, cutting her off. His tone was brusquer than he'd intended, but he just wanted this over with. "We need Sarah here." He tensed at a child's shrill cry in the trauma room beyond, followed by the squawk of the base station radio announcing an ambulance. "There are at least five more kids coming in from the propane explosion. We'll need extra staff to do more than pass out boxes of Kleenex. I want nurses who know what they're doing. Get them for me."

+++

Why am I here?

Claire Avery winced as a child's painful cry echoed up the Sierra Mercy emergency department corridor and blended with the wail of sirens. Almost an hour after the Little Nugget Day Care explosion, ambulances still raced in. Fire. Burns. *Like my brother. No, please, I can't be part of this again.*

She leaned against the cool corridor wall, her mouth dry and thoughts stuttering. Being called to the ER was a mistake. Had to be. The message to meet the director of nursing didn't make sense. Claire hadn't done critical care nursing since Kevin's death. Couldn't. She wiped a clammy palm on her freshly pressed lab coat and stepped away from the wall to peer down the corridor into the ER. Then jumped, heart pounding, at the thud of heavy footfalls directly behind her.

She whirled to catch a glimpse of a man barreling toward her with his gaze on the ambulance entrance some dozen yards away. He looked a few years older than she was, maybe thirty-five, tall and wide shouldered, with curly dark hair and faded blue scrubs. He leveled a forbidding scowl at Claire like a weapon and slowed to a jog before stopping a few paces from her.

"What are you doing?" he asked, grabbing his stethoscope before it could slide from his neck.

"I'm . . . waiting," Claire explained, awkwardly defensive. "I was paged to the ER."

"Good. Then don't just stand there holding up the wall. Let's go. The charge nurse will show you where to start."

"But I—," she choked, her confusion complete.

"But what?" He glanced toward sounds at the ambulance bay and then back at her.

Claire cleared her throat. "I don't know why I'm here."

He shook his head, his low groan sounding far too much like a smothered curse. "If that question's existential, I don't have time for it. But if you're here to work, follow me. Erin Quinn will tell you everything you need to know." He pointed at a crew of paramedics racing through the ambulance doors with a stretcher. A toddler, his tiny, terrified face raw and blistered behind an oxygen mask, sat bolt upright partially covered by a layer of sterile sheets. "See that boy? *That's* why I'm here. So either help me or get out of the way." He turned and began jogging.

Speechless, Claire stared at the man's retreating back and the nightmarish scene beyond: burned child, hustling medics, a flurry of scrubs, and a hysterically screaming parent. *Help or get out of the way?* What was she supposed to do with that ultimatum? And what gave this rude man the right to issue it?

Then, with a rush of relief, Claire spotted the Jamaican nursing director striding toward her. This awful mistake was about to be cleared up.

"I'm sorry for the delay," Merlene Hibbert said, her molasses-rich voice breathless. "As you can imagine, there have been many things to attend to." She slid her tortoiseshell glasses low on her nose, squinting down the corridor. "I see you already met our Dr. Caldwell."

Claire's eyes widened. *Logan Caldwell? Sierra Mercy Hospital's ER director?*

Merlene sighed. "I'd planned to introduce you myself. I hope he wasn't . . . difficult."

"No, not exactly," she hedged, refusing to imagine a reason she'd need an introduction. "But I think there's been a mistake. He thought I'd been sent down here to work in the ER." *Tell me he's mistaken.*

"Of course. A natural mistake. He's expecting two more agency nurses."

Claire's knees nearly buckled with relief. "Thank goodness. They need help. I can see that from here." She glanced at the ER, where patients on gurneys overflowed into the hallway. A nurse's aide held a sobbing woman in her arms, her face etched with fatigue. Styrofoam coffee cups, discarded cardboard splints, and scraps of cut-away clothing littered the floor. All the while, the distant cries of that poor child continued relentlessly.

"Yes, they do," Merlene agreed. "And that's exactly why I called you."

"But I've been at Sierra Mercy only a few months, and my hours are promised to the education department—to train the students, write policies, and demonstrate new equipment." Claire floundered ahead as if grasping for a life preserver. "I've interviewed to replace Renee Baxter as clinical educator. And I haven't done any critical care nursing in two years, so working in the ER would be out of the—"

"That's not why you're here," Merlene said. Her dark eyes pinned Claire like a butterfly specimen on corkboard. "I need you to assess my staff to see how they're coping emotionally. I don't have to tell you this has been one miserable morning." She studied Claire's face and then raised her brows. "You listed that in your résumé. That you've been recently trained in Critical Incident Stress Management?"

CISM? Oh no. She'd forgotten. Why on earth had she included that? "Yes, I'm certified, but . . ." How could she explain? Merlene had no clue that Claire's entire future—maybe even her sanity—depended on never setting foot in an ER again. It was the only answer to the single prayer she'd clung to since her firefighter brother's death in a Sacramento trauma room two years ago. Being helpless to save him left her with crippling doubts, sleep-stealing nightmares, and . . . She'd mapped her future out meticulously. The move to Placerville, a new hospital, a new career path, no going back. Everything depended on her plan.

Claire brushed away a long strand of her dark hair and forced herself to stand tall, squaring her shoulders. "I understand what you're asking. But you should know that I haven't done any disaster counseling beyond classroom practice. I'm familiar with the principles, but . . ." What could she possibly offer these people? "Wouldn't the chaplain be a better choice?"

"He's going to be delayed for several hours. Erin Quinn's my strongest charge nurse, so if she tells me her ER team is at risk, I believe it. They received six children from that explosion at the day care. Four are in serious condition, and a two-year-old died." Merlene touched the amber and silver cross resting at the neckline of her uniform. She continued, frowning. "Dr. Caldwell's working them ragged. An agency nurse threatened to walk out. Security's got their hands full with the media. . . . You're all I can offer them right now."

Claire's heart pounded in her throat. With every fiber of her being, she wanted to sprint into the northern California sunshine; fill her lungs with mountain air; cleanse away the suffocating scents of fear, pain, and death; keep on running and not look back. It would be so easy. Except that these were fellow nurses in that ER; she'd walked in their shoes. More than most people, Claire understood the awful toll this work could take. The staff needed help. How could she refuse? She took a breath and let it out slowly. "Okay. I'll do it."

"Good." Relief flooded into Merlene's eyes. She handed Claire a dog-eared sheaf of papers. "Here's our hospital policy for staff support interventions. Probably nothing new there." She gestured toward her office a few yards away. "Why don't you sit down and review it for a few minutes before you go in? You can report to me later after I make my rounds."

Before Claire could respond, the ambulance bay doors slammed open at the far end of the corridor. There was an answering thunder of footsteps, rubber-soled shoes squeaking across the faded vinyl flooring.

Logan Caldwell reappeared, shoving past a clutch of reporters to direct incoming paramedics. He raked his fingers through his hair and bellowed orders. "Faster! Get that stretcher moving. Give me something to work with, guys. And you—yeah, you, buddy—get the camera out of my face! Who let you in here?" The ER director whirled, stethoscope swinging across his broad chest, to shout at a tall nurse who'd appeared at the entrance to the ER. "Where are those extra nurses, Erin? Call the evening crew in early; a double shift won't kill anyone. We're working a disaster case here. Get me some decent staff!"

Claire gritted her teeth. Though she still hadn't officially met him, there was no doubt in her mind that Logan Caldwell deserved his notorious reputation. Dr. McSnarly. The nickname fit like a surgical glove. Thank heaven she didn't have to actually work with him—the man looked like he ate chaos for breakfast.

Claire turned to Merlene. "I'll do the best I can," she said, then drew a self-protective line. "But only for today. Just until the chaplain comes."

"Of course. Very short-term." Merlene began walking away, then stopped to glance over her shoulder. "Oh, a word of caution: Dr. Caldwell hates the idea of counseling. I'd watch my back if I were you."

Claire hesitated outside the doors to the emergency department. She'd reviewed the summary of steps for an initial critical stress intervention and was as ready as she'd ever be. Considering she'd never done any peer counseling before. *I'm a fraud. Why am I here?*

She shut her eyes for a moment, hearing the din of the department beyond. It had been stupid to put the CISM training on her résumé. She'd taken the course last fall and participated reluctantly in the mock crisis situations, mostly because it would look impressive on her application for the clinical educator position. But afterward Claire knew that she could never volunteer as a peer counselor. Never. It felt too personal, too painful.

Healing the healers, they called it, the basis for the work of volunteer teams that waded into horror zones after events like 9/11, the killer tsunami in Indonesia, and the devastating aftermath of Hurricane Katrina. *And a Sacramento, California, trauma room after a warehouse fire that killed seven firefighters.*

Claire fought the memories. Yes, the counseling teams made

sure that caregivers took care of themselves too, assessing them for burnout and signs of post-traumatic stress. Like difficulty making decisions, sleeplessness, nightmares, and relationship failures. Claire knew the symptoms only too well. She'd struggled with most of them herself these past two years, exactly the reason she'd run away from that Sacramento hospital—after refusing its offer of stress counseling—and never looked back.

But here she was at another ER door, peeking inside through a narrow panel of bulletproof glass. And now she was responsible for helping these people deal with everything she was trying so hard to forget and expected to offer the kind of counseling she'd never accepted herself. Beyond ironic—impossible and completely at odds with her plan.

Claire raised her palm and pushed the door inward.

Heal my heart and move me forward. She'd prayed it every single day.

So why was her life slamming into reverse?

The essence of Sierra Mercy ER hit Claire's senses like an assault. Sounds: anxious chatter, a burst from the overhead PA speakers, beeping of electronic monitors, inconsolable crying, and painful screams. Smells: nervous perspiration, stale coffee, surgical soap, bandaging adhesive, the scorched scent of sterile surgical packs . . . and of burned hair and flesh.

No, no. Claire's stomach lurched as she clutched her briefcase like a shield and scanned the crowded room for the charge nurse. *Find Erin Quinn. Concentrate on that.*

She took a slow breath and walked farther into the room, searching among the eddy of staff in multicolored scrubs—technicians, nurses, and registration clerks. She forced herself to note the glassed-in code room, a small central nurses' station and its large dry-erase assignment board, the semicircular arrangement of curtained exam cubicles with wall-mounted equipment at the head of each gurney, and the huge surgical exam lights overhead.

Claire tried to avoid the anxious faces of the family members huddled close to the tiny victims. Because she knew intimately how much they were suffering. No, much worse than that. *I feel it. I still feel it.*

When she'd agreed to do this for Merlene, she'd hoped this smaller ER—miles from the Sacramento trauma center and two years later—would be somehow different, but nothing had changed. Especially how it made Claire feel, the same way it had in those weeks after Kevin's death. Unsure of herself for the first time in her nursing career, she'd been antsy, queasy, and clammy with doubt. Dreading the wail of approaching sirens and jumping at each squawk of the emergency radio. No matter how hard she tried, she couldn't shake the irrational certainty that the very next ambulance stretcher would be carrying someone she loved, someone she'd be unable to save, and . . .

A cry in the distance made Claire turn. Her breath caught as the young charge nurse opened a curtain shielding a gurney.

A child, maybe three years old, rested upright in a nest of blue sterile sheets, tufts of his wispy blond hair blackened at the tips— some missing in spots—reddened scalp glistening with blisters. One eye had swollen closed, and his nose was skewed a little to one side by the clear plastic tape securing a bandage to his cheek. The other blue eye blinked slowly as if mesmerized by the drip chamber of the IV setup taped to his arm. An oxygen cannula stretched across his puffy, tear-streaked face.

Beside him, a stainless steel basin, bottles of sterile saline, and stacks of gauze squares sat assembled on a draped table. Burn care:

control pain, cool the burn to stop it from going deeper, monitor for dehydration, and prevent tetanus and infection. All the bases covered. *Unless the burns are horrific and complicated, like Kevin's. Unless there is profound shock, heart failure, and : . . No, don't think of it.*

Claire exhaled, watching as Erin Quinn pressed the button on a blood pressure monitor and efficiently readjusted the finger probe measuring the child's lung status. She made a note on a chart and moved back to the bedside as the child stirred and cried out.

"Mommy?"

"Mom's getting a bandage on her leg, Jamie, remember?" she explained gently, then caught sight of Claire and acknowledged her with a wave. She called to another nurse across the room. "Sarah, can you finish the ointment on Jamie's scalp? watch him for a few minutes?" After giving a brief report to the petite blonde nurse, she crossed to where Claire stood.

"Good, you found me," Erin said, noting Claire's name badge and offering a firm handshake. Strands of coppery hair had escaped from her ponytail, and her blue scrubs were splotched with snowy white burn ointment. She nodded as Claire glanced once more at the injured boy. "Second-degree burns. No explosion trauma, otherwise he'd be on a chopper ride to Sacramento. But Jamie's got asthma, and the smoke stirred things up. So . . ."

"He needs close observation," Claire finished. "I understand."

Erin smiled. "Hey, I really appreciate your coming here. We've had a horrible shift, and my staff are workhorses, but the Hester child was a real heartbreaker. We worked a long time to save her, but it didn't happen. And only last weekend we had the first drowning of the season. Junior high boy fishing on the river. Overall my crew seems to be coping fairly well, but today might be that last straw, you know? So I have a couple of issues I'd like to discuss with you. I can spare about ten minutes to fill you in. Will that be enough to get you started?"

"Yes . . . okay." Claire tried to recall the details of her review. How much could she offer here? One person couldn't do more than a brief assessment and let the staff know more assistance was available. At least she'd found the self-help pamphlets. "But first I should tell you that I left a message for the hospital social worker because if an actual debriefing is needed, then a mental health professional is required. That's policy." She swallowed, hoping she sounded more confident than she felt. "The debriefing should be done tomorrow or the next day."

"What?" Erin shot her a look that clearly implied Claire was the one who needed mental help. "Tomorrow? I called you here because we need help now. Didn't Merlene tell you that?" She pressed her fist to her lips. "Look, I've had a lab tech faint, the media's harassing family members in the waiting room, and an agency nurse threatened to walk out. Walk out, when I'm short-staffed already! I'm sorry if I seem testy, but I'm responsible for the quality of nursing care here. My team needs help, and I'll do everything it takes to make that happen. Merlene told me you were a trained peer counselor. Aren't you?"

She hated herself. Erin Quinn was right. Claire needed to do whatever she could for these people. Somehow. She reached into her briefcase and grabbed a sheaf of glossy pamphlets. "Yes, I've been trained. And I can start an initial assessment, get things going in the process. I promise I'll do as much as I can to help, and . . ." Her voice faltered as heavy footsteps came to a stop behind her. She fought an unnerving sense of déjà vu and impending doom.

"Help?" A man's voice, thick with sarcasm, prodded her back like the devil's pitchfork.

Claire turned, several pamphlets slipping from her fingers.

It was time to officially meet the newest threat to her plan, Dr. Logan Caldwell.

CHAPTER TWO

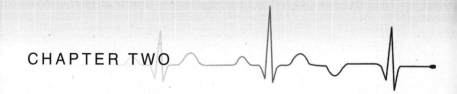

Dr. Caldwell knelt down a split second before Claire did, and their fingers brushed as they reached for the same pamphlet. She pulled back, her face flushing. "I've got them, Doctor. I . . ." Her voice failed as she met his eyes.

Logan Caldwell's eyes were impossibly blue. Intense, almost crystalline, like the still surface of Lake Tahoe after a first snow. Fringed with black lashes, they seemed mismatched with his dark brows, curly hair, olive skin, and wide-bridged nose. And now they were narrowing, with tiny crinkles forming at the edges, as he began to . . .

Laugh? Claire heard him chuckle deep in his throat. *He's laughing at me?* She clenched the handle of her briefcase.

"I guess you figured out why you're here," Dr. Caldwell said, his tone making it clear he recognized Claire from their earlier skirmish in the corridor. He held out the pamphlet, then tipped his head, trying to read her name badge. He skimmed her fawn linen business suit. "So what are you, a sales rep?"

What am I? Claire's lips pressed together. How dare he. He was leaning so close now that she could smell him—surgical scrub soap, coffee, and a trace of some woodsy cologne that ought to come with a surgeon general's warning. Masculine and intentionally knee-weakening, she suspected. Maybe. For any woman but her. Claire snatched the pamphlet and stood. "No. I'm a registered nurse with the education department."

He gathered the remaining papers and stood as Erin Quinn attempted introductions. She was interrupted by the loud squawk of the base station radio announcing incoming ambulance traffic. A cardiac patient? Hard to tell; the report was garbled by static.

"Claire Avery," Erin continued, "this is Dr. Caldwell, our ER director."

"Logan," he said, shifting the stack of pamphlets to one hand and extending the other toward Claire. "I'm not much on formality."

"Logan, then." Claire felt his hand engulf hers as she looked up—way up—into his face. The man was huge, easily towering over her own five feet eight inches and making her feel small for the first time in a long while. She hated it.

She straightened her shoulders, lifting her chin and stretching taller. Then pulled her hand away. "I'm here because I was told you needed some help." *As quickly as I can; then watch me run the other way, Goliath.*

Logan lifted the sheaf of pamphlets and scanned a cover. His dark brows furrowed and he searched her eyes warily. "'Healing the Healers'?"

Erin intervened. "She's with the CISM team. I told you I requested that." She glanced at the treatment cubicles and then toward a closed door marked Do Not Enter at the far end of the trauma room.

Claire's stomach sank. No doubt it was a temporary morgue, where they'd placed the little girl who'd been killed. It reminded Claire of the painful realities of every ER—body bags, lists of personal belongings, and impossible explanations to family members forced to wrap their arms around the clinical facts of death instead of around their loved ones. *Don't make me do this. Not again.*

Erin nodded with certainty. "I'm asking for Claire's help with our staff. Because this day care incident's been tough on all of us."

Claire studied Logan's expression and knew Erin was wasting her energies. She'd dealt with this kind of hard-driving, unbending, and callous physician before. Like the doctor who'd repeatedly questioned her competency in the weeks after Kevin's death.

"Tough?" Logan shook his head. "This is what we do, Erin. Tough comes with the territory. And death is always a factor. Do you see me crumbling here?" He smacked the pamphlets against the leg of his scrub pants and frowned. "The only kind of help we need here is more staff, more warm bodies. Real nurses. Not administration's attempt at some . . . touchy-feely counseling."

Touchy-feely? Real nurses? Claire dug her nails into the leather of her briefcase. She reminded herself she'd soon be back in the education department and out of here for good. Otherwise, she'd have to make this man, giant or not, eat his words.

"Here," he said, handing Claire the pamphlets, then rubbing the side of his jaw. The hollows of his eyes were shadowy dark. He looked suddenly weary, a caregiver nearing the end of a bruising shift. If he'd been someone else—anyone else—Claire would have felt compassion. She'd been in that situation herself plenty of times. "I'm sorry, but we just don't need—"

The base station radio crackled with static and then shrilled an update on the incoming ambulance traffic. Four minutes. Sixty-year-old female in full cardiac arrest.

Erin widened her stance, and Claire half expected her to raise her fists like a boxer awaiting the first-round bell. Claire smiled, feeling a rush of admiration for this feisty redhead so competent at running her ER . . . and determined to handle its stubborn director.

"I'm showing Claire around for a minute," Erin told him, "and then I'll be there for the cardiac code. We need this help."

Logan's mouth twisted into a smile, and the corners of his tired eyes crinkled again. "Sure. Why not? Keep the educator around. Maybe her pamphlets double as defibrillator pads." He chuckled and began walking away.

He stopped to look over his shoulder, his changed expression leaving no doubt that his amusement had vanished. "But have her start with the registration staff. I can't afford distractions right now."

The registration office, which looked out onto the emergency department waiting room, was a cluster of windowed cubicles filled with computers, copy machines, and incredible stacks of clipboards destined for avalanche.

Claire headed to the first open door, trying to convince herself that she hadn't been thrown out of the ER by Logan Caldwell. CISM policy clearly indicated staff contact was to be made away from the action, so this sequestered niche—which smelled blessedly like coffee and printer ink instead of soot and scorched hair— might be the best place to get her feet wet in the staff assessment process. It was a long way from the horror and heartbreak. Far safer. And that suited Claire just fine. All she had to do was let these office people know that help was available. Though she couldn't imagine they'd be at risk for traumatic stress.

"Hello?" she called, peeking around a column of wall-mounted plastic files labeled HIPAA, Emancipated Minors, Dog Bite Reports, and Workers' Comp.

"Come on in."

Claire stepped inside the cluttered space, then smiled at the sight of a tiny clerk leaning back in her chair, feet propped on a stack of copier paper boxes, and holding a Tupperware bowl. Her gray-streaked black hair was looped in long braids across her head and sported at least three ink pens, one topped with a jiggling plastic Cookie Monster. On the desk beside her computer a collection of framed photos of children flanked a ribbon-tied canning jar overflowing with mustard flowers. The clerk's name tag, studded with service pins, read *Inez Vega*.

"I hope I'm not disturbing you. I'm Claire Avery, and—"

"No, no," Inez said quickly, sitting upright and setting her food aside. "Erin said you were coming. And it finally settled down enough so I could take a little break." She smiled, revealing a glimpse of a gold-rimmed front tooth. "Been quite a day. I feel so bad for the nurses and Dr. Logan. I'm glad you're here to help them."

Claire looked past her into the sparsely populated waiting room. A woman rose from her chair to push an elderly man in a wheelchair to the adjacent registration cubicle. "But things are better now?" she asked, knowing from the looks of the waiting room that it had to be true. And sensing, for the first time in an hour, that this wasn't going to be so bad after all. Maybe Erin had underestimated her staff. "No more injuries from the day care?"

"Oh no. That's finished. There's nothing serious waiting right now." Inez glanced at her computer screen. "Just a lady who tore her acrylic fingernail, that old gentleman with gout, and—"

Before she could finish, a middle-aged woman appeared at the window and tapped anxiously.

"Oh, dear, excuse me." Inez opened the window.

Claire stepped back to allow them privacy, but she could see that the woman was distraught. Her mascara was streaked, clothes rumpled, and her reddened and swollen eyes fixed on Inez like she was her last sliver of hope in the world.

"I'm sorry to bother you." The woman placed a small satin-trimmed lavender blanket on the counter in front of Inez. "You probably don't remember me."

"I do, Mrs. Hester," Inez said, one hand moving discreetly toward a box of Kleenex.

Hester? Claire's breath snagged. The dead child's name.

"But I thought you'd gone home." Inez's voice lowered to a whisper. "After your family . . . spent time with Amy, I thought you went home. Do you want me to call the nursing director?"

"No, don't bother her. You can help me." Mrs. Hester lifted the blanket and clasped it to her chest for a moment, her eyes filling with tears. "This is my granddaughter's blanket. She calls it her baba, and—" a tear slid down her face—"she can't sleep without it."

Claire's chest squeezed tight.

"She usually takes it to day care, but I was replacing the satin trim—purple's Amy's favorite color." Mrs. Hester raised the blanket to her face, and a low sob escaped her lips. "It smells . . . like her. Oh, please. Please, she needs this. Will you make sure she gets it?" Before Inez could answer, the woman reached through the window and grasped her hand. "They're sure she's dead?" she whispered, her voice raw with desperation. "My baby's so still when she sleeps. They're sure?"

No . . . Claire swayed against a wave of dizziness, clutched her briefcase to her stomach, and backed out of the office and into the hallway. She leaned her shoulder into the cool, enameled wall, squeezing her eyes shut against a rush of agonizing images: her mother standing beside Kevin's body, his leather-strung cross dangling from her fingers; her father's confusion, repeated questions, and finally his guttural, anguished sobs . . . stunned disbelief morphing into terrible, final truth. *"My son's . . . gone?"*

Claire opened her eyes and scanned the hallway, desperate to leave but knowing she couldn't. She took a slow, halting breath, then pulled the pamphlets from her briefcase. *Why am I here? I don't have a plan for this.*

After contacting every staff member from the list Erin supplied, Claire reviewed her CISM notes. She nodded. Peer counseling, if performed within several hours after a critical incident, might mitigate the effects of post-traumatic stress. And it was voluntary; she could offer assistance but not insist any staff member accept it.

Claire dragged her pen under several key words, underlining them three times with the same red ink she'd used on her lists of career plans. She was relieved that so far the staff—from the physician's assistant in the adjacent urgent care clinic to the admitting clerks—seemed to be in fairly good shape, considering. Even Inez Vega, who'd thanked Claire for the pamphlet and put the baby blanket into a bag to give to the nurses. She'd sighed with relief, along with Claire, when the Hester family's pastor hurried through the waiting room doors.

The laboratory technician Erin said had fainted had admitted, with some embarrassment, that her swoon had been caused by a newly diagnosed pregnancy, not emotional trauma. And the agency nurse who'd threatened to abandon her shift hadn't. But she'd told Claire in no uncertain terms that she would be speaking with her supervisor regarding unacceptable working conditions at

Sierra Mercy Hospital. Hinting, of course, that the conditions had everything to do with one Dr. Caldwell.

Claire glanced away from her makeshift desk in the ER utility room and toward the open door of the code room only yards beyond. The resuscitation had been continuing for more than forty minutes, and even from a distance Logan looked powerful and in control. She watched his big shoulders hunch abruptly, his head lowering as he leaned over the waxy, still body of the unconscious woman on the gurney. Grade school teacher, an admitting clerk said. Collapsed on a playground full of kids. Claire's throat tightened, thinking of Kevin's fiancée, a school counselor. Gayle. Who'd dressed for a funeral instead of a wedding.

Logan pressed his fingertips against the side of the teacher's neck, checking for a carotid pulse as he watched the rhythm on the cardiac monitor. He grabbed the paddles of the defibrillator, pressed them against her chest, and delivered a shock. Her body jerked and was still; then he checked the pulse again, nodded, and waved his arm.

There was a corresponding flurry of scrubs as nurses and technicians responded, pulling medicine vials from the crash cart, running monitor strips, and tearing open bags of IV fluids. Claire didn't have to hear it to know Logan was shouting orders or that this woman's life hung by a slender thread. Just as Kevin's had that awful day.

Images rushed back faster than Claire could filter them. Sounds too. The ones that still filled her nightmares: sirens, clattering buckles on an ambulance stretcher, the stuttering rip of trauma scissors against a hopelessly charred uniform, and a futile hiss of oxygen. Her escalating horror in searching for her brother's heartbeat—wrist, neck, finally by pressing her stethoscope against his blistered chest—and finding none. Then her own voice screaming, screaming . . . *Oh, please. No.* This department was stirring too many memories; she had to get out.

Claire forced herself to her paperwork and wrote some notes for Merlene Hibbert, the chaplain, and the social worker. She looked up as someone spoke from the doorway.

"Claire?"

"Yes, come in." Claire smiled at a petite woman in her mid-twenties wearing a rumpled scrub dress printed with angels. Her shoulder-length blonde hair was tucked haphazardly into a huge clip, and freckles dusted the bridge of her nose. Her fair lashes were barely visible, making her look wide-eyed and childlike. Claire had noticed her taking over Jamie's burn care and then again in the code room. A nurse—an incredibly efficient one from what she'd seen. Thankfully she was the very last person on the interview list. This nurse was Claire's ticket out. "You're Sarah, right?"

"Sarah Burke," she answered, extending her hand. Her fingers trembled slightly as they met Claire's and then steadied into a firm grip. Her other hand clutched a Diet Coke can. Caffeine, emergency department lifeblood. Claire understood. "I know you were looking for me earlier, but . . . I haven't had time for a break." She gave a short laugh and patted the pocket of her scrub jacket. "Good thing I'm packing M&M'S."

"You bet." Claire knew all too well the demands of a busy shift and how things like meals and even bathroom breaks got pushed way down the priority list. Adrenaline was a rugged enough taskmaster without the infamous Dr. Caldwell. "So how did things go with the resuscitation?" Claire asked, moving slowly according to protocol. She'd start with the current situation and feel her way toward the critical incident with the day care children.

Sarah sighed. "She's on a ventilator, but the heart rhythm finally looks decent. It kept going back into pulseless V-tach, so we gave a bunch of meds: epi, amiodarone, magnesium . . . bicarb. Shocked her a lot. She went to CCU on an amiodarone drip." She glanced down at her slim fingers and shrugged. "Out of our hands now."

Claire turned toward the code room, eerily empty now that the resuscitation team had moved the patient to the CCU. An elderly housekeeper wearing a knee brace over purple denim scrubs pushed a broom to clear the residue of lifesaving procedures: discarded tourniquets, syringe caps, iodine swabs, gelled defibrillator pads, and monitoring electrodes. The patient's clothing, snipped from her body by the paramedics, lay in a heap in the corner of the room. It looked like a soft pink tweed pantsuit, carefully chosen for a day ending in a way this teacher would never have dreamed.

Claire looked away, fighting the image of Kevin's uniform suspenders and his pewter cross on its knotted leather cord lying on a sooty pile in that Sacramento trauma room.

"I know you want to help us," Sarah said. Her voice was husky, soft. "But I don't have time for—"

The PA crackled overhead and Sarah jumped, startling as if stung and sloshing her Coke onto her scrub dress. The system droned a simple page, and her shoulders relaxed. "Sorry," she murmured, her face coloring as she turned back to Claire.

Sarah set the can down and reached for the paper towel holder on the wall, snatching a handful and mopping at the front of her scrub dress. "Really. I'm already late for my overtime shift upstairs. Besides, I'm fine. Did someone say I wasn't or something? Not Dr. Caldwell?"

"No," Claire said quickly, reminding herself that peer counseling was free of fact-finding or implied blame. Not that there had been anything amiss. It was simply a release valve for staff, a pulse check for the caregivers. *Acknowledge, validate, reassure.* "I'm just here to see if there's anything I can do to help any of you." She paused and smiled gently. "The explosion at the day care, the injured children, and the one who died . . ." She watched Sarah's eyes for a reaction. "It's normal to feel strong emotions related to that, even days afterward, so I'd like to offer—"

"I'm fine," Sarah interrupted, reaching for her drink. "I've been in the ER for a couple of years now. Nothing gets to me much anymore." She took another halfhearted swipe at a soggy angel before folding the towel and pressing it to her forehead. "Can I just go now?"

Claire touched her notes, making certain she'd covered all the bases. "Would you mind telling me what your part was in the day care incident today?" she asked, knowing that having a person retell the event allowed the related emotions to surface in the process. Exactly why she never talked about Kevin—to anyone. "Were you assigned to the child who died?"

"Yes," Sarah said, her eyes meeting Claire's directly for the first time. "But I was also part of saving the kids who lived. That's what I'm remembering. Only that. Look, I'm a nurse." She shrugged and tossed her empty can in the wastebasket. "I do what needs to be done. Then I come back the next day and I do it all again. Except for those lucky days when I get to do it for two shifts in a row. And that's today. Honestly, I'm fine and I've got to go." She smiled ruefully. "Literally. I'm heading to the bathroom next door."

Claire smiled back, despite a sinking feeling that she'd done nothing to help this woman. Offered her exactly . . . zip. But Sarah seemed to be made of stronger stuff than most. Some people were. What was it that Logan Caldwell said earlier? "Tough comes with the territory"? Yes, and maybe Sarah was simply asking the same thing he had: "Do you see me crumbling here?" It was possible that Sarah Burke and Logan Caldwell were simply two tough cookies. Who was Claire to argue with that?

"May I at least offer you a pamphlet?" she asked. "Maybe some tips for taking care of yourself: exercising, eating right, avoiding alcohol?"

"No thanks." Sarah gave Claire a thumbs-up. "I'm good."

"But . . ." Claire waved the trifolded paper at the nurse's retreating back and watched until the angel scrubs disappeared down the hallway.

It was her farewell salute to Sierra Mercy ER. Back to the plan for her future.

Half an hour later, Claire finished her notes and gathered her notebook and papers, realizing as she tucked them into her briefcase that she was totally exhausted. Bone-deep, like she'd just finished one of her long runs through the oak-studded foothills. Nerves, she supposed, from being in an ER after dreading it for so long. Still, she hadn't done so badly, had she? It was after four o'clock, and all that was left was to leave a reassuring voice mail for the hospital chaplain. She could do that from the education department.

An earlier conversation with Merlene made Claire fairly certain she'd scored points by going the extra distance in ER. Not that she was going to make it a habit. But the director of nursing's opinion might help in Claire's bid for the full-time clinical educator position. In truth, it could all dovetail nicely with her plans.

Claire turned toward the sound of footsteps, which was followed by the rich, enticing aroma of coffee.

Erin Quinn stood in the doorway. "Figured you could use this," the charge nurse said, stepping in to hand her a plastic-topped cardboard cup. "Raspberry mocha."

"Wow, wonderful. Thanks." Claire noticed that Erin's ponytail was gone, allowing the nurse's copper hair to spill casually across her shoulders. She'd pulled a zip-front white hoodie sweatshirt over her scrubs and carried a red stenciled canvas tote over her shoulder. End of the day for Erin too.

Claire spotted the familiar green label on the coffee and grinned. "Starbucks? Where'd you find something like that in a joint like this?"

"Gift from an ambitious pharmaceutical sales rep," Erin explained, then shook her head. "A real sales rep. Look, I'm sorry Logan called you a rep and made fun of your pamphlets."

"Not a problem," Claire fibbed with a wave of her hand. The last thing she wanted now was a discussion about Logan Caldwell. She'd survived her first brush with Dr. McSnarly relatively unscathed and was finally just minutes from her last walk through this department. "It all worked out," she reassured Erin with a genuine smile. Then she tipped her head sideways, studying the artsy stencil on Erin's tote bag. It was sort of like a genie lamp—no, more like the old Florence Nightingale nurse's lamp but with the symbol of a cross in the handle. "What *is* that?" she asked, pointing to the white design.

"Huh? Oh, this." Erin slid the strap off her shoulder and turned the bag so Claire could see. "I designed it myself. Sketched my grandmother's graduation lamp. I've even put it on some T-shirts."

Claire looked closer. A Florence Nightingale lamp overlaid with a cross.

Erin pointed to the design. "It says, 'Faith QD.' You know, medical shorthand for 'every day,' the way medicines and treatments are ordered. Kind of a play on words."

"Pretty ingenious," Claire said, impressed. "But what's it for?"

"It's a new idea I'm trying out," Erin answered, her green eyes lighting up. "A nondenominational Christian fellowship group for nurses, aides, techs, doctors, anyone really. Nothing that could be viewed as pushy or preachy. But something to sort of jump-start our days. Anyway, we've been meeting in the chapel fifteen minutes before our shifts start. Logan calls it my God huddle, but—" She glanced at her watch. "Oops."

"Gotta go?"

"Brad's picking me up. New guy, and he doesn't get it that a charge nurse's shifts don't run like clockwork. I'm breaking him in gently." She touched Claire's arm. "Hey, I appreciate your doing the peer counseling today. Really. And if you want to stop by Faith QD, you know where to find us. Just say the word and I'll order you a T-shirt." She hoisted the tote over her shoulder and strode away, leaving Claire feeling suddenly very alone.

She took a sip of her coffee, savoring the berry-sweet cocoa flavor and wondering how this gutsy and dedicated charge nurse's idea for a hospital fellowship would play out. Claire frowned at Logan's cynical and sarcastic remark. *God huddle.* But then, Claire already knew Erin well enough to believe she'd move ahead with it, no matter what the insensitive ER director thought.

And Claire was just as sure that she wouldn't be joining the Faith QD gatherings. No need to gird your loins to write policy manuals or help develop nursing procedures. Thank heaven she was on her way back to those tasks right now. Out of the ER and away from Logan Caldwell. A winning combination.

As Claire stepped out of the utility room and walked past the temporary morgue, she noticed its door was ajar. It was only a crack and barely wide enough for a faint light to escape from the inside, a quiet vacuum now. The Do Not Enter sign was still in place, but no doubt the poor child had finally been moved. That would help put things back to normal for the staff, if there ever were such a thing as normal in ER.

Oh, great. Claire stopped short in the trauma room as she recognized him.

The ER director, seeming even bigger if possible, stood there in street clothes, chambray shirtsleeves rolled back over tanned forearms, faded jeans, cowboy boots, and a pair of sport sunglasses dangling from a blue cord around his neck. His dark hair looked damp, like he'd just showered. Logan Caldwell, standing beside the gurney of Jamie, the little burn victim with asthma.

He glanced up from the sleeping child, his impossibly blue eyes meeting hers. "Hi, Educator," he whispered. "Got us healed yet?"

CHAPTER THREE

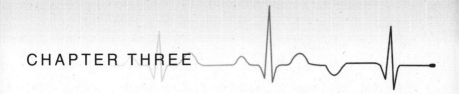

Claire hated it that her feet carried her forward as if she had no will of her own, a moth headed for a complete and thorough scorching. Tired or not, she wasn't about to let Logan have the last jab without putting up a struggle. She stopped at the side of the gurney opposite him and bit back a sigh. It would be easier if he weren't standing there with a little boy's fingers holding on to his. And far less distracting if this medical director didn't look like he'd just walked off an action-hero movie set.

"I thought you went home," Claire said, noticing a smear of burn ointment on Logan's muscular forearm as he slid his fingers from Jamie's.

The child dozed, lashes feathery against his cheeks, his breathing mercifully peaceful and rhythmic. His blond hair was still dark at the tips, damaged from the fire's intense heat. Claire's chest tightened as she remembered the story of the fire captain who'd carried this boy from the burning day care. Firefighters. Heroes— *my biggest hero*—always.

"I stopped by the CCU. To see that patient, the teacher." Then Logan answered Claire's next question before she could ask it. "She's awake. And giving orders." He shook his head. "Told me to get a haircut."

Claire smiled, equally pleased with the teacher's clinical improvement and her feistiness toward the imposing Dr. Caldwell. Not that he looked so imposing standing watch at a child's bedside.

"I thought I'd stick around until Jamie is moved to the room upstairs. He only has his mom, and she was at the day care too. She's been admitted already." Logan glanced at his watch and frowned. "But looks like Jamie won't see her until the new shift finishes report. I want to be sure he's got humidified oxygen at the bedside and respiratory therapy available in case his asthma flares up." He leaned over the bed, closer to Claire, and smoothed the child's sheet.

Claire watched him, more than a little surprised at the act of tenderness. Could this be the same man who'd so dispassionately said, "Death is always a factor"?

"Why the delay?" Claire asked. "This boy's stable and comfortable. Shouldn't he have gone to his room long before now?"

Her question was met with an awkward silence. Then Logan gave a short, brittle laugh. "Yes, Sarah Burke was all set to take him upstairs before her shift ended. But she—" he paused with a faint smirk—"was delayed by peer counseling."

Claire bristled but found herself strangely relieved to be back in familiar territory. Just because he was concerned about an injured child didn't mean the man had been reformed. "Look," she said, lowering her voice as a nurse guided a patient to an adjacent cubicle, "administration threw me in here today. No warning. No choice. I wanted to be here about as much as you want me here."

Logan said nothing for a moment while he studied her, almost as if he were seeing her for the first time. Claire wasn't sure, but there may have been a smile playing at the edges of his mouth. She brushed a tendril of hair from the side of her neck, suddenly self-conscious as Logan's gaze followed every millimeter of the movement.

"Good," he said finally, the suggestion of a smile gone. He nodded as if they'd sealed a deal. "Then we're in agreement after all."

"Agreement?"

"That this CISM business is counterproductive."

She stared into his face, wanting nothing more than to nod furiously and retrace her steps out of this place. Back to the education department, where she had protocols to write and a procedure demonstration to outline, tasks that would take her closer to her goal of being hired to a full-time educator position. Not add to her bouts of insomnia. Logan was actually making it easy for her. Wasn't he?

He leaned toward her again, his whisper conspiratorial. "So what would it take?"

"What do you mean?"

"To satisfy administration. Sign us off here." Logan sighed. "I'm all for doing whatever it takes to make my team the best it can be, but in my experience, there's nothing worse than dwelling needlessly on tragedy."

Claire saw a fleeting look, almost like a memory of pain, flicker in his eyes.

He pressed his palm against the side rail of the gurney. "It's like this: you go around telling people that they need to explore their feelings, all that sort of shrink-to-fit nonsense, and then the team starts falling apart." He jabbed a finger in the air. "The links weaken."

Weaken? Claire's stomach twisted into a familiar knot as the thought struck her. That's probably what the Sacramento doctor had labeled her in the weeks after her brother's death, when despair left her numb and immobile and barely able to function. *A weak link.*

"I'm not saying that this isn't killer work," Logan continued, his voice fervent. "I'm just saying there are better ways to deal with it, that's all."

The knot in her stomach turned to anger, and Claire raised her chin, refusing to blink as she stared him in the eyes. "Oh?" she said, daring—maybe even needing—Logan Caldwell, of all people, to offer something that finally made heartbreak bearable. "And how do *you* deal with it, Doctor? Personally, I mean." She walked around the end of the gurney to stand directly in front of him and crossed her arms. "Go ahead, enlighten me."

"I . . ." He hesitated, unsure of his answer maybe or shocked by her nerve.

Claire waited, trying not to think about the hospital's chain of command. How much influence did Goliath have over the education department? Could he block her promotion? get her fired completely?

Logan laughed softly and ran a hand over his dark hair. His face grew serious, and once again his fatigue was very apparent. When he spoke, his voice sounded far away, almost vulnerable. "Speeding, maybe? Sure. My motorcycle on a mountain road, fast as it goes. To any place where nobody needs anything from me and where time just passes. Instead of being measured as seconds lost on some unforgiving code room clock. Trees and quiet."

Claire wished she could take the question back. All at once this felt too personal, too awkward.

"Or pizza," Logan added, a surprisingly boyish grin crinkling the corners of his eyes. "Pepperoni pizza and country music. That'll put things in perspective pretty fast."

They both turned as a woman's voice wailed in the distance.

"Where's that coming from?" Claire tensed as the painful and wrenching sound repeated.

"The storage room," Logan answered.

The nurse at the next bedside began jogging in that direction.

The temporary morgue. Hadn't Claire seen a light in there when she passed by a few minutes ago? Yes, and it had been quiet. "But didn't they take that little girl away?" she asked, filling with dread as she remembered the face of the anguished grandmother.

"No," Logan answered. He turned and broke into a trot, calling back over his shoulder, "We got the okay to remove the tubes, but we're still waiting for the medical examiner's deputy to arrive for transport."

Memories and images from another temporary morgue in Sacramento intruded into Claire's consciousness, and she struggled to keep them at bay. Then, against an urge to run the other way, she followed Logan toward yet another haunting wail.

When they arrived at the doorway, she saw the nurse slip an arm around a tiny, dark-haired woman's shoulders. Claire took in the scene in the dimly lit room, her eyes widening as she recognized the woman. Inez Vega, the registration clerk. Sitting in a chair beside an empty gurney, a plastic body bag crumpled at her feet and holding . . . Claire's breath stuck in her chest. Inez held Amy Hester, the child's face still and pale, like an earthbound angel. She'd wrapped the toddler in the lavender blanket and was gently rocking her. A rosary dangled from Inez's fingers and her lips moved silently. She stared up at the ER nurse over Amy's tousled curls, then over at Claire and Logan.

"This baby's *abuela*—her grandmother—wanted her to have this blanket," Inez said, tears streaming down her face. "Purple's her . . . favorite color. I didn't mean to break any rules, but it seemed wrong not to wrap it around her. I keep thinking about my own grandbabies and . . ." Her words faded into a mournful sob as the nurse lifted the child gently from her arms, laid her back on the gurney, and returned to Inez's side.

More than anything, Claire wanted to let the staff nurse handle things now, be done with her unexpected and unwelcome responsibility to these people, but . . . She turned to Logan and grasped his arm, a rush of tears blurring her vision. "This is your team. I know how you feel about counseling, and I know you want me to just sign off and satisfy administration. But I can't. These people are hurting, and they need help."

She let go of his arm and took a deep breath, looking once again at Inez. How many times had this woman quietly ached, after how many shifts? As a peer counselor, Claire couldn't offer the kind of help Inez needed, but she knew how to make it happen. "I'm calling the social worker to request a full debriefing for your department. Whether you like it or not."

+++

Running was always a balm for what ailed her. And it was working; Logan Caldwell was fading away. Claire closed the cabin door against the night air and slithered out of the soaking, oversize T-shirt, deliciously dizzy for a moment. A rivulet of sweat trickled between her shoulder blades as she raised her arms to weave her fingers through the long strands of damp hair, lifting them away from her salty skin. Her head floated, disembodied, and her lips tingled as goose bumps rose and drew a shiver. Runner's high. Endorphins.

She leaned against the wooden door in her racerback tank and running tights, closing her eyes and welcoming the familiar release. Her heartbeat whispered in her ears like the ocean trapped in a seashell. Endorphins were a blessing. Better than music, gooey chocolate, California sand under bare toes, or even the comfort of a warm and snuggly—

Oh, good grief. Claire opened her eyes, then wadded the T-shirt into a ball and hurled it across the cabin's living room like she was battling an intruder. Why on earth did the thought of being hugged—held, after such a long time—suddenly summon the unlikely image of Logan Caldwell?

She bit back a laugh as the wadded shirt bounced off the wall and onto the scruffy black cat sleeping on the suede couch. He yowled and jerked upright, his only ear flattening out sideways, tail twitching, glaring at her. As usual. Great, a skirmish with Goliath and Demon Cat all in one day. Claire could run to New Jersey and back and not brew enough endorphins to cover that.

"Sorry, Smokey. I'll fix it. Don't bite me—I feed you." Claire crossed the room in two strides, her Nikes scrunching on the plank floor. Unexpected tears threatened as she knelt to gingerly lift her brother's engine company T-shirt off his cat. The truth was, neither fit her. Not the shirt, not the cat. No matter how much she wanted them to.

She glanced around the living area of the rustic, four-room A-frame: cedar paneling, woodstove, Mexican blanket rug, and a vase of yellow silk daffodils, her one pathetic attempt to add a feminine touch to what would always be a man's house. Maybe her parents were smarter than she'd been. It didn't take a shrink to guess that accepting a transfer to Arizona had less to do with old friends in Phoenix and a lot more to do with the pain of their only son's death. Or to guess it was that very same thing that moved Claire into her brother's house.

Her gaze traveled to the rough-hewn oak mantel on a wall of river rock behind the freestanding woodstove, topped by a collection of photos she hadn't had the heart to pack away. The firehouse photo with Kevin mugging for the camera in a Superman T-shirt and red suspenders. Claire and Kevin with their parents at Lake Tahoe for their twenty-fifth wedding anniversary. Claire's eyes moved to the next photo—framed in hammered tin and draped with her brother's cross—a grainy black-and-white snapshot of Kevin with his fiancée, Gayle, on the church mission trip to Mexico. Her brother had one arm around Gayle and the other around the shoulders of a dark-eyed orphan. The last frame held Kevin's favorite Scripture carefully stitched onto vintage family linen by his beloved Gayle:

"For I know the plans I have for you," declares the Lord,
"plans to prosper you and not to harm you, plans to give you
hope and a future."
Jeremiah 29:11

It had been an engagement gift. Claire looked away, the familiar ache making her swallow.

Since Kevin's death, Claire had attended church infrequently; she couldn't bear sitting there without him. It seemed easier to read her Bible alone, avoiding inevitable questions about how she'd been coping. Like those questions in recent letters from Gayle, who was apparently moving on with her life. Claire sighed. She was glad for Gayle, but for right now, Claire was better off alone. With her lists and her decisive red pen.

Heal my heart. Move me forward. God knew her plan.

Claire stroked a fingertip warily over the fluff where Smokey's other ear should have been. Poor beast, he never purred. One of the firefighters figured that a raccoon attacked him, a common confrontation in the California foothills, but nobody would ever really know for sure how Smokey lost that ear and became so skittish.

Kevin couldn't have known, either, that shortly after adopting Smokey he'd be gone, leaving his sister with the demented cat, a house in the woods, and just enough insurance money to help fund her bachelor's degree in nursing education and pave her way out of the grim reality that was the ER. For a job opportunity that was still on hold because she'd been derailed by . . .

Claire hugged the damp T-shirt against her chest. The irony struck, making her stomach churn. Despite all her hard work and after endorphins by the quart, none of her troubles had faded away. Not a one. She'd simply run full circle. Back to the ER and smack into new turmoil with Logan Caldwell.

At 10:30 p.m., Claire picked up the phone, touched the first three numbers, then hit the End button and set the phone down. It was the second time she'd done that in half an hour. She took a sip of her chai tea and swung her legs up onto the bed. It was far too late to page the social worker again. The staff debriefing was scheduled, and it was best to leave things the way they'd been arranged.

"Right, Smokester?" Claire nodded at the lanky cat stretched across the foot of the double bed.

He raised his head and quit his silent kneading of the snowy comforter. His yellow eyes fixed on her big toe, and Claire gave it a risky wiggle, proving beyond a shadow of a doubt that she'd traded endorphins for insanity. Which would explain the continuous intruding thoughts of Logan Caldwell.

She groaned. She was acting like she was . . . what exactly? Attracted to him? Claire pressed her palms against her eyes. No.

The last thing she needed was any more confusion in her life, any risk of losing the equilibrium she was fighting to maintain. And—

"Hey!" Claire jerked her foot away as she felt the dangerous brush of Smokey's whiskers against her toe.

She shook her head, and her just-washed hair trailed across the shoulders of the pink pajama top. Close call—she'd almost been bitten. Good point: she needed to be just as careful about the medical director. Logan did nothing but dredge up painful reminders of Kevin, her humiliating last days as an ER nurse, and even her pitiful track record with men. It was best to avoid him, and that would be easy now that Social Services was taking over.

She reached for her shell-embossed teacup, and her gaze dropped to the business card next to her open Bible. It was for the social worker who would lead the debriefing tomorrow afternoon. Claire would take a minor role this time, letting Social Services and the hospital chaplain handle the real guts of the process. The nagging doubt resurfaced and Claire glanced at the phone again. She swallowed a sip of the creamy sweet tea, waiting for the feeling to pass. It had been pestering her for the last several hours. *Am I making a mistake?*

No. Absolutely not. Logan didn't have to be at the debriefing. Wasn't that what she'd told the social worker earlier? She'd been right. The people most affected by the injured children—the ones at risk for post-traumatic stress—were the nonphysician staff, nurses, aides, and technicians. And Inez Vega.

Claire rested the warm cup against her cheek. Her breath escaped in a soft sigh. As much as she'd tried not to, she kept seeing the image of that poor woman crying in the dim light of the temporary morgue. She wondered about the kind of person who cared enough to leave her normal world, the safety of an office cubicle, to venture into a place so full of chaos and pain. About the risk it was, the heart it took, to wrap a blanket around a dead child.

Then she thought of Logan Caldwell riding his motorcycle as fast as he could away from all that. And the way he'd talked about "shrink-to-fit," touchy-feely counseling, about being tough and priding himself on not crumbling. But mostly Claire kept replaying over and over in her mind what he'd said about . . . weak links.

It had taken guts for Erin Quinn to defy him and call for peer counseling to help her staff. The same kind of dedication prompted the already exhausted Sarah Burke to volunteer for an extra shift, and Claire knew in her heart that Inez Vega was no weak link.

She swallowed the last of her tea and picked up the phone. Her foot tapped nervously against the down comforter as her call was transferred to voice mail.

"I'm sorry to be calling again so late," she said, her stomach sinking faster than her foot could tap. "But I was wrong earlier. The medical director needs to be at the debriefing tomorrow." Her foot tapped faster as she pictured herself squaring off with Goliath. "It's his day off, but have administration page him and say Claire Avery insisted."

She smothered a yelp as Smokey bit into her toe. "Dr. Caldwell is a big part of the problem."

CHAPTER FOUR

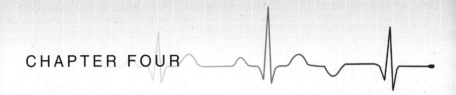

Logan nosed the Harley into a physician's parking space, then let his boots slide from the pegs and down to the asphalt, straddling the idling engine.

As he peered through the visor of his helmet at the brick and stucco back entrance to Sierra Mercy Hospital's ER, he weighed his options. Cell phone messages failed, didn't they? Who could prove he'd ever received notification of this Critical Incident Stress Debriefing? If he'd been thirty minutes deeper into the Sierra Mountains, he'd be out of phone range and on the threshold of granite slabs, roaring waterfalls, towering pines, and quiet escape.

It was his first day off in seven, and he shouldn't be here. The week had been brutal and not only because of yesterday's day care incident. Logan's throat tightened at the thought of the toddler he'd worked so hard to save and the always awful moment of telling parents a child was gone—*no, you had to say the word* died *to make it real, final. To leave no merciful hope.* "I did everything I could, but Amy died."

And he had done everything, even taken over the cardiac compressions himself, pressing the heel of his hand over and over against her little chest, willing the child to survive. Not wanting to quit, all the while knowing that was irrational. Even if he could have started her heart, she'd been robbed of oxygen too long to survive without devastating brain injury. Logan grimaced, remembering the stricken faces of the child's mother and grandmother and the way the young father slammed his fist against the wall, his cry like a tortured animal. *Ah, man.*

He swallowed hard, pushing aside the memory. On his way back to the hospital, he'd passed the charred Little Nugget Day Care, its fence now adorned with flower bouquets, letters from children, stuffed animals, and at least a dozen purple balloons. But it wasn't only the day care incident that was weighing on him. It was the continuing frustrations of limited staffing, the song and dance it took to get money budgeted to replace outdated equipment, and the need to jump through ridiculous hoops to comply with every new federal, state, and HMO mandate. He'd become a doctor to help people, make a difference in lives, and that shouldn't take a backseat to anything.

Logan gave the throttle a twist and felt his bike respond, proving its readiness to transport him away. The political problems weren't any worse than the personnel issues coming across his desk this week. Complaints: that agency nurse threatening to walk out yesterday because . . . What had she said to Erin? *"Dr. Caldwell is a slave driver and an inhuman beast."* Not his first complaint. Nor his last. It took time and effort to shape an effective medical team, and there would be a certain attrition rate. So be it.

Reaching down, Logan cut the bike's engine. He pulled off his helmet and shoved the keys into the front pocket of his jeans. His fingers brushed against a worn and folded sheet of stationery. The invitation to Beckah's wedding. Only a couple of weeks away now. Another reason he needed to escape today.

But instead of pines, fresh air, and solitude, he'd be sitting in a dank staff conference room. With hospital coffee and tense, nervous chatter. Being debriefed, for what that was worth. Maybe he could head some of it off at the pass and keep the inevitable psychobabble down to a dull roar. He'd meant what he'd said to that educator about dwelling needlessly on tragedy; it only made matters worse. Logan knew that better than most people.

Claire Avery was the one who'd insisted on his attending this meeting, and she'd be there. For some reason, that made the next hours seem almost bearable. He smiled, remembering the beautiful dark-haired woman and the way she'd gone toe-to-toe with him in the ER yesterday, with that determined lift of her chin when she faced him and the flush rising to her cheeks. Logan's smile faded as he recalled the incident afterward in the temporary morgue. Inez and the toddler. Claire's eyes filling with tears, followed by her decision to call for a staff debriefing.

He had no doubt she felt she was doing the right thing, just as Erin did with her efforts to support staff with the Faith QD meetings. The problem was that those things, no matter how well-intentioned, didn't work. He'd learned the hard way that there was no pamphlet and no prayer with the answers. When bad stuff happened, you had to tough it out and soldier on. Simple.

That and keep Mountain Mike's Pizza on speed dial.

+++

Claire took one look and knew Logan had been out on the bike. He arrived in the conference room at the last minute, wearing a black leather jacket, motorcycle chaps over his jeans, sunglasses, and the shadow of a beard. Along with a barely suppressed smirk aimed directly at Claire. He sat down in the empty chair directly opposite her.

Great. Cat bite on her big toe and Goliath within spitting distance.

"I'm sorry," he told the social worker with a smile. He dropped the sunglasses into his helmet. "I was halfway to Yosemite when I got the voice mail." He stared into Claire's eyes.

Yes, my fault—deal with it. Claire lifted her chin and stared back, willing herself not to blink. Today was about doing what she could to help coworkers at risk, then bidding farewell to this whole mess. She'd shrink her world down to a comfort zone again, where the worst that could happen was insomnia or a joust with a one-eared cat that never purred. And then she'd move forward with her master plan.

The heavyset social worker, Elaine Best, rose from her chair, and Claire glanced around the table. All the involved ER staff was here, including a security guard, Erin Quinn, Merlene Hibbert, Sarah Burke, and Inez Vega. The registration clerk, her hair in a single braid today, looked nervous but so much better than she had last night. It was a relief to know she'd talked with both her priest and a hospital social worker before she left the ER. Claire was surprised to see her shyly wave at Logan Caldwell. And even more so to see his return wink and warm smile. What was that all about?

"We are here because of the Little Nugget Day Care tragedy," Elaine began after introducing the CISM team, including Claire and the hospital chaplain, Ric Estes. "This process is not intended to be psychotherapy or to prevent and treat symptoms of post-traumatic stress. It is simply designed as a discussion to provide emotional support."

Claire stole a glance at Logan. His expression was unreadable, but his fingers drummed soundlessly on the tabletop, like a man who'd rather be anywhere but here. He looked up, and Claire refocused on the social worker.

"When a critical incident involving a child occurs, 85 percent of the personnel affected will develop symptoms of stress within twenty-four hours," Elaine said, her gaze traveling the room. "Some of you feel you can deal with this by yourselves. Maybe so."

Sarah Burke nodded over the rim of her Coke can. She was in scrubs again, and Claire wondered if she ever took a day off.

"However," the woman continued, "we've learned that people who try to handle everything alone take longer to do it. On the other hand, people who talk about a bad incident eat better, sleep better . . ."

Sleep. Claire's stomach tensed.

". . . remain healthier, stay employed longer, and have fewer problems in their home life as well as in other relationships," Elaine finished.

Logan began to doodle on a paper as Chaplain Estes, a balding man with a neatly trimmed beard, took over. "No one has any special status during this session. We are all just folks struggling through a rough situation." He smiled gently. "So forget your rank and be a human being first."

Claire looked over at Logan and heard him sigh. The corners of his mouth drew downward, and his expression read "touchy-feely . . . shrink-to-fit."

He met her eyes before penning something on the paper. And underlining it.

Chaplain Estes cleared his throat. "The next phase of Critical Incident Stress Debriefing is about to begin. We'll ask each of you to tell us who you are, what your job was at the scene, and what happened there."

Suddenly the room felt warm, and Claire thought about taking off her jacket. It was lightweight but she was still perspiring. Was the heater on? Her breathing quickened and she shifted uneasily in her chair. Her throat constricted. Then, without warning, she started remembering the Sacramento trauma room, hearing the sirens, smelling the smoke, the sickening sweet scent of burned flesh and . . .

Her pulse began to pound in her neck and her mouth went dry. She grasped the edge of the table, fighting a wave of dizziness. This was a huge mistake. She shouldn't be part of this team. How could she get out of here?

The chaplain's voice seemed to echo from a tunnel, and Claire struggled to hear, filled with a dread she couldn't name. "We also ask that you recall your first thought during this tragic incident once you stopped functioning automatically."

First thought. My first . . .

Claire closed her eyes, but the horrible image of the hopelessly burned firefighter remained. Along with the clear memory of her first anguished thought: *Oh no, that's my brother!*

The session took more than two hours, and Claire made it to her final pamphlet-dispensing duty with the help of a hasty bathroom break. Today was proof she'd been right. She needed to stay away from the ER and all the memories it stirred up. As soon as things ended today, she'd be out of there. For good.

Elaine smiled at the ER staff. "Please remember that most reactions to stress are normal. Don't try to hold yourself to impossibly high standards—give yourselves permission to feel lousy for a while." She nodded. "But remember that your employee benefits include counseling services if that need arises. And please look through the pamphlet. It has some great tips for dealing with the first forty-eight hours: exercise, keep busy, write down your thoughts, listen to music, eat regular meals even if you have to force yourself. Do the things that feel good to you."

Claire glanced across the table at the sound of Logan's fingers drumming on his motorcycle helmet. Then, with what looked like a smug smile, he folded the paper he'd been writing on into crisp quarters.

"I want to remind you about the 4-H fair and rodeo this weekend," the chaplain added, standing. "The hospital is manning an information and nurse recruitment booth. I think Claire's going to be volunteering there?" He acknowledged Claire's nod and then continued. "Take your families, why don't you? Pet the sheep, eat a corn dog, enjoy the music, dance, and laugh. Laughing is good for our souls."

The room emptied and Claire gathered her things, scooping up her folders but leaving the CISM pamphlets in neat stacks on the table. She wasn't going to need them anymore. All that was left was to—

Oh, boy. Logan was walking toward her. Claire's heart slammed against her ribs, completely without warning. He stopped in front of her. His dark brows scrunched, and he exhaled softly. There was nothing brash about his expression, no hint of any biting sarcasm to follow. And for some reason Claire felt an unexpected wave of sadness. This was likely the last time she would see more than a glimpse of him. She held her breath.

Logan's eyes were soft, almost vulnerable. He took half a step forward until he was so close that she could smell the scent of leather mixed with a trace of the familiar cologne. His nearness seemed to warm the air between them, and when he leaned toward her, Claire's heart rose to her throat. For a dizzying instant she imagined what it would be like to be held in his arms.

"Claire!"

As she turned, Claire heard Logan's low grumble.

Erin strode back through the doorway, grinning and holding out a bakery box. "Krispy Kremes. Snagged them from a sales rep," she said, a little breathless as she arrived to stand beside them. She lifted the lid and prodded the donut glaze with a fingertip. "I'm giving myself permission to feel lousy to the tune of a zillion calories. Anyone care to join me?"

Logan shifted his weight beside Claire. The motorcycle leathers creaked with the movement. He shook his head and gave a short laugh. The cynical edge reappeared as he spoke, but Claire was sure she heard an undercurrent of regret. "Actually," he said, glancing at Claire, "I'm more interested in those ways to feel good."

A flush crept up Claire's neck, and she was grateful to see Erin still inspecting the donuts.

"Well, be a party pooper, then." Erin leveled a look at Logan and chuckled. "Of course, now we know you're more of a strawberry-milkshake-in-the-park kind of guy."

What's this? A stab of jealousy surprised Claire. Logan and Erin? Didn't she already have a boyfriend?

She shook off the thought as Erin tugged at her sleeve. "But Claire has to at least split one with me. Because this is the closest we get to cake, and it's your last day, isn't it?"

Last day. Claire felt the strange sadness again. It made no sense and was even more confusing as she looked at Logan. He'd asked the same question. "Yes," she answered with as casual a shrug as she could muster. "I'm finished. Unless anyone wants another pamphlet?"

"No way." Logan glanced at the dry-erase board just beyond,

where the social worker had written a last suggestion for the ER staff in bold letters: *The most successful way to deal with traumatic stress is to face it. Feel it and heal it.* He frowned, and his voice emerged sharp and surprisingly bitter. "No more of any of this. I've already had way more than I can stomach." His eyes seemed dark, his gaze far away.

Claire's mouth opened, but no words came. Only the sickening feeling that she'd been right all along about this insensitive man. He didn't care about his staff or anybody but himself.

"Logan, what's wrong with you?" Erin's eyes widened. "Claire's worked hard to try and help us, and your attitude is—"

Claire stopped her before she could continue. "It doesn't matter. I know how Dr. Caldwell feels about this process. It was obvious from the start." She couldn't resist a jab. "And now look, I've gone and ruined his day off." *Back at you, McSnarly.* She was glaring and she didn't care; after all, she wasn't going to have to deal with him anymore.

Logan glowered at Claire. "That's right. You did. And I could handle that, if your people hadn't just tried their best to convince half my team to call in sick next week. Who's going to replace them?" He pointed at her. "You?"

Erin tried to step between them, but she wasn't fast enough.

Claire pressed forward until Logan's pointing finger brushed her collarbone. She jutted her chin and glared at him, trembling with anger. "Oh? You mean you can't fix them all with country music and pizza?"

+++

From the hospital patio, Claire heard the distant rev of a motorcycle engine. Like the warning growl of a Sierra mountain lion before it sprang away. Her breath escaped in a sigh of relief. *Good, he's going.* The donut was working too; if she could have eaten it while running a 10K, it would have been perfect. Endorphins and donut glaze could melt Logan Caldwell away faster than a bucket of water on the Wicked Witch of the West.

But maybe it had been good to see his true colors. He was insensitive, self-involved, and heartless. There was nothing attractive about a man who couldn't dredge up some empathy for his coworkers. Claire had been a target of a physician's callous disregard in those awful, vulnerable days after Kevin's death. How could she forget that? She looked across the small stone table at Erin.

"Better now?" Erin asked. Late afternoon sun slanted through the courtyard oaks, turning her hair to burnished copper. She handed Claire a napkin.

"I'm so embarrassed about the way I acted in there." Claire wiped the napkin across her lips. "I'm afraid that guy makes me crazy."

Erin laughed. "No big deal. Unfortunately Logan has that effect on some people." She tucked a tendril of hair behind an ear. "He jokes about the Reno nurses forming a lynch mob before he left there a few years ago, says he was written up more than once."

Claire gaped. "Logan was fired?"

"No. He said he needed a change. I'm guessing it had something to do with his wife."

Claire nearly dropped her elbow into the box of donuts. She blamed a rush of dizziness on sugar overload. "He's . . . married?"

"Was married," Erin explained. "I'd never ask details, but he's mentioned that it ended around three years ago."

"Oh." Claire felt a wave of sympathy and then an irritating sense of relief.

Erin's brows drew together for a moment. "The debriefing covered that subject too. The effect our work has on relationships. I don't doubt that."

"So do you think the debriefing helped at all? Or was Logan right? Did I really make things worse?"

"Hey, wait a minute." Erin reached across the table and placed her hand over Claire's. "Don't even go there." Her expression was warm and sincere, and Claire knew that this nurse could be a real friend. She hadn't realized until just this moment how much she missed the girlfriends she'd pushed away over the past two years.

"You absolutely helped us," Erin reassured. "You saw the way the staff opened up and how supportive they were of each other's feelings." She laughed. "We can't all be Super Nurse like Sarah. Even if Logan's right and half the staff call in sick, it wouldn't matter. Sarah could do it all by herself. The day that girl misses a shift, we'd better start building an ark!"

"And Inez?" Claire asked, watching as Erin began to gather her things from the tabletop. The whole debriefing process—even her own ghastly reaction—would be worth it if it had done something to help that tenderhearted grandmother. "I know she's starting counseling. But do you think today's session helped?"

"Oh yes." Erin stood and grinned at Claire. "But I'm not sure how much of it was the debriefing and how much was the result of well-timed milkshake therapy."

"Huh?"

"Yep. It seems that our medical director wrote a little prescription of his own last night." Erin's grin widened. "Imagine Inez Vega in a motorcycle helmet. I'm serious. Cross my heart. She said that after she'd talked with her priest and the counselor, Logan loaded her on the back of his bike, bought two strawberry milkshakes, and then drove down to Gold Bug Park. The woman can hardly close her wallet over that stack of grandkid pictures. Logan looked at every one."

+++

Claire set her purse and folders down on the coffee table, her mind so preoccupied that she barely dodged a swipe from Smokey's paw. She couldn't stop thinking of the strange mix that was Logan Caldwell: skilled doctor, thick-skinned taskmaster, and former husband. A man who offered strawberry milkshakes and—*Whoops, what's that?*

A paper, creased neatly into quarters, fell from between Claire's CISM folders. She must have picked it up from the conference table by accident. She slid the dusty vase of fake daffodils out of the way and flattened the paper out on the table.

Logan had doodled a motorcycle and a mountaintop, all crossed out with an exaggerated X. Beneath it was a short note, the words underlined: *Educator, you owe me an afternoon.*

Claire lifted the paper, stunned for a moment. That awkward, interrupted conversation they'd had after the debriefing—was he trying to ask her out?

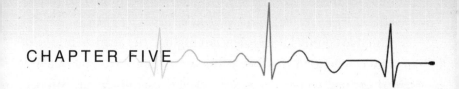

CHAPTER FIVE

Erin Quinn searched through her Faith QD tote bag again, her mouth dry with anxiety. *The money has to be here. Somewhere.*

It was in an envelope clearly labeled "Little Nugget Victim Fund." Erin had put it in her bag last night, planning to get it to the bank during lunch break today. She'd even reinforced the envelope with strapping tape, so the loose change—a quarter, two nickels, a dime, and a penny donated by Merlene Hibbert's little granddaughter—wouldn't tear through the paper when she transported it. Yesterday alone she'd collected $607.46 in cash and a few checks. And promises of more, come payday.

The Sierra Mercy staff was eager to help mostly because of Jamie, the blond three-year-old they'd treated for burns in the ER. His brave smile beneath all those bandages had stolen hearts throughout the hospital. His single mother, Carly, would need financial help until the day care insurance was settled. If it was settled. There were rumors the policy had lapsed, and Jamie's mother had no insurance of her own. With her own injuries and the home care of her son, it might be weeks before Carly could return to work. Every penny of the donations would seem a godsend. If only Erin could find those pennies.

She dumped the contents of the tote bag onto the nurses'

lounge coffee table. Protein bars, makeup pouch, Bible study workbook, copies of her staff schedule, CISM packet, and the valentine from Brad. But no money envelope. How could that be? She pressed her fingers against her eyes and forced herself to think, backtrack. *Please let me remember. This money is for Jamie.*

Erin had counted the money last night at her apartment; she'd put the envelope in the tote at the same time she'd laid out her scrubs and packed her lunch. She ticked the sequence off with her fingers. She'd driven to work, attended the Faith QD meeting, and gone on to the emergency department, putting the tote in her locker. Erin's breath caught, and her gaze flew to the battered metal lockers clustered along the wall. *Did I lock it?*

Guilt stabbed her instantly; only ER staff used this room, and they'd never had a problem. The nurses were like family.

Sarah entered the lounge, hoisting her Diet Coke in a mock toast. Though fatigue cast faint shadows beneath her eyes, her voice was hearty and teasing. "Here's to my heroic handling of another earwax crisis. You owe me big-time." She wrinkled her nose and watched as Erin restuffed her tote bag. "So what did you decide about lunch? You or me first?"

Erin forced herself to breathe in, breathe out. *Stop worrying.* Then she smiled warmly at Sarah. Her response held a soft chide. "Considering that you're supposed to be *off* today, I'd say you should go. What is this, nine shifts in a row for you?"

Sarah shook her head. "Seven, with yesterday's in Sacramento. But those nights in the nursery hardly count as work. Rocking babies. I should pay them."

Though Sarah was smiling, Erin thought she heard regret in her voice and maybe a hint of something more. Sadness? It occurred to her that though she'd worked side by side with Sarah for over a year, she really knew very little about her personally except for the fact that Sarah was single and appeared to be powered exclusively by Diet Coke. She felt a pang of guilt. Some charge nurse she was. Maybe she should suggest getting together for coffee sometime.

"So?" Sarah asked, pointing toward the door. "You or me in the trenches? I know you wanted to run to the bank."

Erin's stomach sank. *The money.* Where was it? "No hurry on that. You take a long lunch. I'll handle the ER." She winked at Sarah. "And Dr. McSnarly."

Sarah's laugh ricocheted off the top of her uplifted Diet Coke can. "No worries. Logan's gone. He got the on-call doc to take the rest of his shift."

"Really?" Erin clucked her tongue and then nodded knowingly. "Back to Yosemite, I'll be willing to bet."

"And you'd lose. He said he was going upstairs to visit Jamie. Then he was heading out to the 4-H rodeo."

+++

The Cajun band, its fiddle backed up by the *brush-thump* of a washboard, drew the rodeo crowd. Families with the season's first sunburns clapped along, relaxing from the day's activities: gold panning, mutton busting, face painting, and the win-a-goldfish ball toss. They wore blue jeans, T-shirts, and glittery yards of Mardi Gras beads, while devouring mustard-squiggled corn dogs.

Corn dogs . . . and sheep. The chaplain's rodeo therapy. *Sure.* Claire sighed and stretched her jean-clad leg across the bale of straw she was using as a chair. The spring sun seeped through her embroidered T-shirt, warming her. What did Chaplain Estes say about the therapeutic value of petting a lamb and munching a corn dog? Maybe it was true—these people were smiling. But the rest of his prescribed remedy simply wasn't going to happen. *Dance and laugh?*

She rolled her eyes behind her sunglasses. There was about as much chance of dancing and laughing as there was for Smokey the Demon Cat to purr. The same chance that she would . . . go back to the ER. Her stomach fluttered at the crazy, recurring thought. *Go back?*

Claire slid her sunglasses off and peered at the huge "Dare to Care: Face Your Future as a Nurse" poster stapled to the front of the recruitment booth. Its trio of scrub-suited nurses—African American, Hispanic, and Asian—looked convincingly heroic, bigger than life. Ready to glove up and face anything life had to dish out.

She groaned. The only thing she was facing these past few days was the very real possibility she was losing her mind. It was the only way to explain why the walls of her tidy office in the education department had begun to close in. Why its quiet order made her edgier by the hour until she wanted to string paper clips into a lasso, whirl it overhead, and holler like a demented cowboy. And, worse still, why the sirens and stat pages—sounds that had made her cringe for two years—now strangely drew her. They had even caused her to leave the safe haven of the office to wander across the hospital campus toward the doors of the emergency department, the setting of every single one of her nightmares—nightmares that had worsened in the past week.

She'd been telling herself it was only normal to want to check on Inez. See how she seemed now that she was receiving employee counseling. Or because of the camaraderie she'd begun to feel with Erin. Or, very likely, her concern after hearing that the staff had dealt with another near drowning. In fact, Claire almost convinced herself that all those reasons were true and that every instinct was selfless and purely professional. Until yesterday when she'd caught a glimpse of a familiar pair of shoulders beneath a head of curly dark hair. Her knees went so weak so fast that she could barely make it back to the safety of her office. That combination—Logan Caldwell and the ER—would be her undoing; she'd chain herself to her desk if that's what it took to avoid them.

Claire leaned down to grab her purse. The cleanup crew would take down the booth. It was obvious she wasn't going to hand out any more nursing recruitment brochures. A smile teased her lips. Everybody who had a life was probably out laughing or dancing.

She could still get in a nice, long run before it got dark. Maybe throw some chicken on the mini grill to share with Smokey. Claire sighed; right, like he wouldn't just drag it under the table and growl at her. At least her parents would be glad to hear from her. She'd give them a call later and hear the newest list of reasons why she should move to Phoenix. Frankly, right now cactus sounded pretty good.

"Hey, Educator."

Claire jumped at the voice, her heart climbing toward her throat as she looked up.

Logan was wearing Levi's with a Western belt, boots, and a well-worn red Henley. The shirt had faded to a deep rose color and was open at the neck, its sleeves pushed up his tanned forearms. His dark curls were windblown and backlit by the sun as he walked toward her.

"Sorry," he said, coming to a stop in front of her. "I didn't mean to scare you." A slow smile spread across his face as he glanced at the poster and stacks of brochures. He chuckled, the familiar crinkles appearing beside his eyes. "Good. Recruit away. Don't let me stop you. I'm short-staffed."

Claire's face warmed as she stood, feeling once again small beside him. Her heart was racing as she opened her mouth, scared silly she was going to bleat like one of the chaplain's therapeutic sheep. *What's he doing here?* "I . . . um . . ." Claire stopped, grateful for the reprieve when Logan raised his palm.

"Wait," he said, all the teasing gone from his voice. "I'm here because I owe you an apology, Claire."

Her skin prickled as she remembered his undelivered note. *And I owe him an afternoon?* She found herself staring at his lips, realizing this was the first time he'd ever said her name. It made her feel ridiculously giddy.

"I acted like a real idiot," Logan explained. "A few days ago, after the debriefing. I'm sorry."

She wasn't sure what to say, but the look on his face, like a little boy in trouble, made her smile. *Goliath disarmed?* Claire tried not to laugh and struggled to resist a crazy urge to hug him.

She was rescued from the impulse when a loudspeaker squawked, a recital of the team roping times and a reminder about the evening's dance.

The Cajun band resumed, and Logan raised his voice to be heard. "So anyway, I want to make it up to you." He nodded like he was coaching her answer and then stepped closer, tilting his head to look down into her face. He swallowed.

Claire breathed in a trace of woodsy cologne and soap. Her rational mind warred with her senses . . . and lost.

"Well?" he whispered.

"Fine," she said, taking a step backward. She crossed her arms and lifted her chin. "What are you offering? Willie Nelson and pizza?"

Logan laughed. "No. Flowers. I'm giving you Daffodil Hill."

Claire's stride lengthened, calves stretching as her short boots navigated the leaf-strewn, red clay trail. Crisp pine air and dappled April sunshine. It was the perfect escape if it weren't for her stupidity and the resulting effect that right behind her was—*oh, boy.*

"Hey." Logan grasped Claire's elbow from behind, his fingers sinking softly into the thin cotton poncho she'd thrown on at the last minute. He was breathless, but he smiled as she slowed her pace and turned to look at him. "Whoa, there." He shifted his backpack over his shoulder as he caught up with her. "I'm thinking that the daffodils aren't going anywhere. Bulbs, right? Stuck in the dirt?" He fell into step beside her. "You've been covering ground like a gazelle since we left my Jeep. Are you trying to lose me?"

"I . . . of course not." Sure she was, and the only thing that could have made her more panicky was if he'd brought the motorcycle, forcing her to ride twelve curvy miles up Highway 49, hanging on to him for dear life. Could have happened. Easily. Why in the world had she agreed to come? She wasn't good at this. Claire forced a smile, avoiding his eyes as they neared the trail's end. The hand-carved sign ahead read, *McLaughlin Farm 1887, Daffodil Hill.* "I'm just anxious to see them, I guess. I mean, four acres of flowers and—oh, Logan, *look!*"

Claire stopped at the end of the trail, grabbing his arm without thinking. Her breath caught and her eyes widened, transfixed by an endless sea of green and yellow and white. Blossoms, some delicate, some buttery bold with orange centers, fluted like nature's champagne glasses, rose tiptoe on slender stalks just high enough to dance with the breeze. She faced Logan, speechless.

"Three hundred thousand of them, I heard," Logan whispered like he was in church. "Hundreds of varieties." He gazed at Claire, his expression as hopeful as a boy presenting a homemade gift. "You're happy I brought you?"

"Oh yes," she answered, letting go of his arm and at the same moment wrestling another impulse to hug him. "Thank you." She blinked, suddenly horrified that she might actually cry as she remembered the dusty silk flowers on her brother's table, a failed attempt to bring sunshine into that grief-darkened space. The sight of these real blooms—the hopeful life in them—was almost more than she could bear. Claire smiled at Logan despite the ache in her throat. "I don't think you could have done anything nicer."

He touched the tip of her nose and winked. "You ain't seen nothin' yet."

They wandered the grounds for nearly an hour, dizzied by hill after hill of daffodils nestled amid weathered outbuildings and rusty farm equipment. They shook their heads at the thought of the owners rolling out this amazing carpet of blooms for decades, free of charge, just for the love of it.

Finally Logan shooed away a trio of speckled chickens and plunked himself down on the grass to rummage through his backpack. "If we don't eat this," he said, gesturing for Claire to join him, "I'm going to throw my back out from lugging it."

She knelt, disarmed by the man despite her lingering misgivings. After all, he opposed what she'd done for his department and saw no value in procedures set up to protect his staff from the effects of stress. McSnarly. It still suited him.

Claire settled on the grass, hiding a smirk as she remembered an old adage. How did that go? *"When you sup with the devil . . . use a long spoon"?* Logan had been called that too. "What's in there?" she teased, watching him produce a small zippered cooler. "Buffalo wings, beer nuts . . . chewing tobacco?"

"No," Logan said, opening the lid and making a show of presenting it to her. He feigned a scowl. "I'm hurt you think so little of me."

I know nothing about you. Claire studied the artfully wrapped California rolls, little strips of ginger, and the creamy green mound of wasabi—all packaged for takeout by a Japanese restaurant she frequented whenever she could afford it. "Sushi? You brought sushi to a rodeo?"

"I heard you liked it," he said as he produced two glass bottles of spring water from the depths of his pack. "Besides, this isn't a rodeo. It's a date."

Date. Claire's face flushed. And there was no way that Logan could have missed the reaction.

He shrugged, his voice graciously casual. "But I'm afraid you're going to have to deal with paper plates. And since I didn't think of something as civilized as a tablecloth, you'll need to find a spot without chicken droppings to sit." He handed her the California rolls, then busied himself with uncapping the drinks.

Claire's lips sank into the cool, sweet combination of rice, avocado, and crab, and she followed it with a sip of the lemon-infused water he set in front of her. Why was she so nervous? She shut her eyes for a moment, less in appreciation of the food and more because she knew the answer to the question. She was nervous because she hadn't been on a date in years. Two years. She groaned, then raised her brows so Logan would think it was inspired by his sushi. "Mmm. Wonderful."

The awful fact was, the last date Claire could remember was with one of Kevin's buddies—a gangly, sad-eyed engine company volunteer. He'd taken Claire to her brother's favorite burger dive about a month after the funeral, then drove her home early after he broke down over his order of onion rings. Grief date. And—sad but true—way more than she'd even wanted. Then and since. It felt like everything inside her that believed in love and happy endings had died along with her brother that awful day in the trauma room. A happy ending was what Kevin and Gayle were supposed to have.

"So," Logan said, lowering his drink, "why nursing education?"

"Oh, I . . ." Claire hesitated, guarding her words so casual picnic conversation wouldn't turn into painful revelation. She took a sip of water before continuing. "I guess I saw enough of how the nursing shortage is compromising patient care that I wanted to help do something about the quality. To help improve what we have left. A smaller but mightier nursing force?"

Logan laughed softly. "No-brainer. Just clone Erin and Sarah." He shook his head. "I wouldn't mind having a dozen of them; nothing I throw at those women rattles them. Not too many nurses like that."

She stiffened, words tumbling out before she could stop them. "Why? Because most of us are weak links?"

"What?" He blinked, obviously stunned by the sharpness of her tone. "No, I wasn't saying—"

"Yes, you did," Claire insisted. "Or at least that's what you implied the first day I met you in ER." Her brows furrowed, remembering their prickly conversation at little Jamie's bedside. "You said if your staff was forced to go through the CISM debriefing—" she narrowed her eyes, mimicking his words—"and 'explore their feelings,' they would become weak links." *Like I was after Kevin's death?*

She pushed the thought down and continued, fueled by a confusing new anger that prodded her mercilessly. "Why are you fighting against your staff instead of for them? You're blessed with incredible nurses like Erin and Sarah and with good-hearted people like Inez Vega, and you don't value them enough to care about their well-being and to . . ." She trailed off as she recalled what Erin said about the nurses in Reno and the complaints against him there. Maybe he didn't care.

"Of course I do." Logan set his plate down and wiped his mouth with a napkin. "It's just that I don't put much stock in counseling." He raised his palm before she could respond, his eyes holding hers for a moment as if he was deciding what he wanted to say. "Because I did that once. With my wife. Back when our marriage was in trouble a few years ago. Didn't work. She left me."

"I . . ." Claire's throat constricted, and she was instantly sorry. She'd seen a flicker of pain in his eyes. What could she say?

"Hey, long time ago," he said, dredging up a smile. "Everybody's fine now. No condolences required." The rascal gleam came back into his eyes. "Nor applause for the good sense of my ex."

Claire smiled, feeling more comfortable again.

"Look," Logan explained, "I care about my staff. I'm willing to do whatever I can to keep my team functioning on all cylinders. But counseling . . . count me out." He raised his water bottle like he was making a toast. "So, here's to agreeing to disagree?"

Claire lifted her bottle toward his. "Done." She pulled her bottle back a few inches before he could clink it. "However, 'functioning on all cylinders'—though it has a certain automotive sense of poetry—doesn't quite do it for me. I was going more for happy team."

He laughed and reached forward until their bottles were a hairbreadth apart again. "I thought I was doing pretty well today," he said, glancing back toward the masses of blooms. "Even *you* looked happy for a minute there, Educator."

Even me?

Logan leaned nearer, his gaze holding hers for a breath-catching moment, and Claire saw that there were flecks of gold in his eyes like the sparkle of treasure in some clear California stream. She could feel the warmth of his skin, smell the soapy clean scent of it, and see the soft texture of his lips. She wondered what it might be like to . . .

"Cheers, then!" she said much too loudly, clinking her water sharply against Logan's, then scooted backward so fast that she crashed into the chicken pecking at her abandoned sushi. It squawked furiously and scurried off . . . almost as fast as Claire wanted to.

Logan was silent and she didn't dare look back at him. She busied herself with retrieving the sushi, hoping to hide her blushing face. She was a fool to have come here today. She hadn't had enough sleep to make rational decisions. Obviously. Or why else would she go off into the woods with a man she barely knew, probably didn't even actually like, and then start imagining what it would be like to . . .

"I wasn't trying to kiss you," he said, breaking the silence.

Oh, Lord, help me. "What? Oh . . . I wasn't thinking that." Claire forced herself to look at him, to stop panicking. He was a doctor, not a mind reader.

"You were . . . You sat on a chicken."

"I . . . well . . ." Claire sputtered helplessly for a moment and then struggled futilely against a surge of laughter.

"Frankly," Logan said, watching her laugh, "I'm insulted by that. Traumatized maybe. Yes." His voice faltered, slowly dissolving into deep laughter that blended with hers. "I might . . . need . . . counseling."

She threw the sushi. He ducked.

They laughed together for a few more moments. When the

silence came back, it was still awkward to Claire but different somehow. She stood and hugged her poncho around herself as the afternoon breeze rustled the pines around them. Somewhere in the distance, there was the tinkling laughter of children. A dog barked.

"Not that I didn't want to kiss you," Logan said barely above a whisper. His eyes were serious, but he made no attempt to move toward her. "Just wanted that on the record." He glanced down at his watch. "And now it looks like I should get you back to the fairgrounds."

Thank heaven.

He sighed like he was about to ask something to which he already knew the answer. "And maybe convince you to stick around for the band. A little country two-stepping? I'm not very good, but . . ."

"No, I'd better not," Claire said in a rush. "I've got some things to do before work tomorrow."

"I thought so," he said, finally crossing the short distance to stand in front of her. "You'll be in the education department, and I'll be way over in the ER."

"Right," she said, telling herself it was so much better that way. That it was the only way it could be. "But I want to thank you for my daffodils. Seeing them today meant more than you can know." *Ever, ever know.* A lump rose in her throat without warning, and this time Claire was helpless to resist hugging him.

Logan's arms closed around her tentatively as if he knew there was a line he couldn't cross. His chest was warm and solid against her cheek, and Claire could hear the muffled thudding of his heart. For one crazy moment the world felt right again. "No problem," he whispered, his chin brushing the top of her head. "And I want to thank you for . . . the afternoon."

Claire closed her eyes, feeling the comfort of his warmth against her. Then she moved away.

+++

Smokey dragged a piece of reheated chicken enchilada from his bowl and ate it under the kitchen table, growling low in his throat. He watched Claire warily.

"Great manners," she told him. "See if I bring you any leftover sushi next time." She sighed. Except there wasn't going to be a next time. Couldn't be.

She'd wrestled with the idea all the way home tonight after Logan drove her back to the fairgrounds and dropped her off in the parking lot. She'd driven Kevin's SUV to Kevin's house and then took a long run before the sun set on her brother's beloved foothills. She let the endorphins replace whatever she'd felt in Logan's arms.

Ever since she'd been called back to the ER, her plan for a peaceful new life had begun to erode into confusion and chaos. There were flashbacks the first time she walked into the Sierra Mercy trauma room, followed by that awful sense of suffocation at the CISM debriefing. She'd battled sleeplessness and nightmares almost nightly since.

Now there was Logan Caldwell, the source of the worst confusion of all. When Claire was around him, her usually well-controlled emotions got the best of her. There was that strange, prickly anger that seemed to go deeper than mere advocacy for the nursing staff, a raw new awareness of her loneliness, and—worst of all—an unbearably painful need for . . . hope. Hope that it might be possible to feel good again. That happiness could be as real as those glorious hills of daffodils.

The trouble was, she couldn't seem to have one without the other. It was like one emotion set the others spinning; a sliver of hope—that wonderful hug—started a painful rush of memories. Claire wouldn't risk that. She couldn't come undone again, because she might not survive it this time. Even if Logan's arms around her and the brief silly laughter had made her feel more alive than she had in a long, long time.

She wasn't going back to the ER. She was sticking to the plan she'd made. She'd pray harder, that's all.

Claire tossed the dusty silk daffodils into the wastebasket. They didn't fit in Kevin's house, and she couldn't look at them anymore. She rinsed Smokey's dish and headed for the shower.

The blinking light on the bedroom answering machine caught her eye. Claire shook her head. Mom again, she'd bet, with information on Phoenix hospitals. She'd told her mother that she'd consider moving only as a backup plan; she was going to get that clinical educator position. She'd been interviewed, and she'd hear within a couple of weeks. *Sorry, Mom.* Claire sat on the bed and pressed the button.

"Claire, Merlene Hibbert. I'm sending you to the urgent care clinic tomorrow. One of the ER nurses quit, and I can't find a replacement."

Claire held her breath as the nursing director continued.

"I know how you feel, but this is temporary. Erin's pulling the clinic nurse into the ER. She'll do the acute care, and you'll take her place in the clinic. Should be a snap for you." Merlene sighed. "I know you want all your hours assigned to the education department, but your hiring status allows us to float you to other departments when need arises. And right now I'm in a bind. If Dr. Caldwell is short-staffed tomorrow, there'll be the devil to pay."

CHAPTER SIX

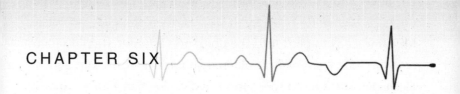

Sarah Burke checked her watch and picked up her pace, her lavender clogs squeaking double-time against Sierra Mercy's flooring.

She popped the pull tab on the morning's second Diet Coke and held the can safely out of splash range as she hustled. It wasn't that she was late, but she wasn't as early as she'd wanted to be today. Six thirty, and she'd planned to be in the ER by six fifteen, which would have given her plenty of time to make sure things were organized and ready to go by the start of day shift. She didn't give a flying fig that the night crew hated her second-guessing their ability to stock the department. Or that she didn't trust them to check the resuscitation equipment: cardiac defibrillator, bulbs in the laryngoscopes, the suction machines, oxygen tanks . . .

The only time Sarah could be assured everything was done right was when she did it herself—lives depended on that. And Logan *counted* on Sarah's extra diligence. Respected her competence. She wasn't about to let that end; it had become as important as breathing. Sarah swallowed against a lump in her throat. The truth was, Logan's respect made Sarah feel better about herself than anything had in years.

She rounded the corner at the radiology suite, snapped a salute as she passed Merlene Hibbert riding herd on a group of nursing students, and strode along the last corridor leading to the ER. She frowned as she spotted overfilled linen carts, several abandoned wheelchairs, and an unloaded supply cart.

Then she continued past the doors to the chapel. Open doors . . . *Oh, that's right.* Sarah slowed, then stopped and backed up a few steps to peek into the drab, nondenominational sanctuary. She took a sip of her cola and shook her head. Erin and her Faith QD. She'd never met a more dedicated charge nurse, and she had to give her an *E* for effort on this undertaking, but was Erin ever going to find any more recruits? Only two people had ordered those logo T-shirts.

Sarah peered cautiously into the room used most often by families of very sick patients, a place to pray for the strength needed to wait, to cope, and sometimes to let go. It was where the hospital chaplain offered informal services for staff pulling shifts on Easter and Christmas, and once the site of a wedding between two wheelchair-bound oldsters who'd fallen in love in the skilled nursing wing. Someone said they'd had accordion music and bread pudding with pink candles instead of wedding cake.

But now it was just Erin, Inez, and a ruddy-cheeked woman with a hairnet whom Sarah vaguely recognized as a new cafeteria employee. Bowing their heads and voicing concerns, asking God to be present during their workday. Or at least that was the plan Erin described when she invited Sarah. An invitation she'd quickly declined.

Sarah stepped backward as Erin raised her head; then she hurried toward the ER before the charge nurse could spot her.

Erin didn't need to know that Sarah left God on the outskirts of Pollock Pines a few years ago. That awful Sunday morning her mother confronted her in the church parking lot. "You don't belong with these good people," she'd hissed. "Sin's written all over you, and I can't bear it—be packed and gone by the time your father and I get home. You're a disappointment, Sarah Lynne."

Faith QD: faith every day. Nice thought. She hoped it worked for Erin and the rest of her staff. But Sarah wouldn't be ordering a T-shirt. You could count on that.

Sarah emptied the cola can and took aim at the trash container outside the emergency department doors. Then noticed the tremble in her fingers. Too little sleep, too much caffeine. She was so tired, but she had to soldier on. There was work to do.

+++

Logan bit back a curse and forced himself to concentrate on the task at hand, stitching up a writhing, tattooed drunk. So far it was the highlight of the day, which explained his mood. Not that Merlene Hibbert hadn't just come right out and asked, "Now then, what's got our knickers in a twist today, Dr. Caldwell?"

Logan chuckled to himself; the woman was one of a kind, for sure. Maybe he was irritable but not without reason. Two very good reasons. One of them was the fact that the hospital's chief of staff was suddenly nosing around, his crisp khakis, blue blazer, and dotted Brooks Brothers tie standing out like a foreign costume in the ER's sea of scrubs. What was up? Was it about the nurse who had walked out after her public tirade about Logan? All he needed was another barrage of complaints like he'd had in Reno.

The other reason for his mood, the one that was making him even edgier, was the fact that Claire had shown up this morning. The educator, but without her usual workday suit and briefcase, too-tight smile, and armload of pamphlets. Dressed instead in soft pink scrubs and white clogs, a purple stethoscope around her neck, and all that dark hair piled on top of her head like she was headed for a garden party instead of a clinic shift. In truth, she'd taken his breath away.

She'd parked her SUV beside Logan's bike and stridden in with her shoulders squared and pretty chin lifted with determination, but he caught the look in those gray eyes. Easy to diagnose: out of her element and a little vulnerable. He already knew her enough to know she'd hate feeling that way. It had taken all his strength to resist putting his arms around her.

And now Claire was working in the urgent care just a few steps away. A clinic he was responsible for, but it was under the direct supervision of a very competent nurse-practitioner. So competent, unfortunately, that there was little likelihood Logan would need to go over there. Unless . . . No, he wasn't going over there. Just like he wasn't going to lose any more sleep thinking about what it might have been like to kiss Claire yesterday. Ah, man, he'd wanted that. But she hadn't wanted to be kissed. She'd probably rather slug him. Hadn't she tried to take his head off when she accused him of not caring about his staff? Yes. But then there was that look on her face when she'd thanked him for the daffodils, followed by an out-of-the-blue hug.

"Hey, buddy, hold still, okay?" Logan tapped a gloved finger against the green towel covering his patient's head. He skillfully pierced each edge of the scalp wound with a semicircular cutting needle, grasping its end with a needle holder and pulling the nylon suture taut before tying triple knots. He snipped the suture and inspected his work. It would likely take a total of eighteen stitches to repair the damage caused by the business end of a broken bottle. This guy wasn't having much of a morning either. After a night that had continued long after the bars closed.

Logan set the scissors down and sighed with frustration as the man thrashed on the gurney, sending a stack of iodine-soaked gauze squares hurtling to the floor. The sterile drape slid away from the tidy line of sutures to expose the man's bullish, blood-speckled neck and a partially visible *Born to be Wild* tattoo.

"Easy, Wild Man," Logan said, trying to protect his sterile field. He nodded with gratitude as Sarah arrived from out of nowhere to assist. "I'm not a rodeo vet," he advised his patient. "Hold still for me, okay? Almost done here."

The man mumbled, gave a beery belch, and Logan grimaced. Not that he wasn't used to moving targets, or drunks, for that matter. He'd learned way too much about alcoholics firsthand. It was the reason he never took a drink himself.

The painful lessons started early. When at age eight Logan learned to hide his mother's car keys, snuff her discarded cigarettes, cajole her during raging hangovers, and make excuses to friends and teachers. More than once Logan had to talk his father out of punching the daylights out of a neighbor man he'd caught her kissing. By twelve, Logan had taken charge of his two little brothers and struggled to hold his father together after she wadded her clothes into grocery sacks, drained their Christmas account, and caught a Greyhound bus.

"You'll be out of here soon, pal," Logan told the drunk.

Sarah reached a gloved hand over the sterile field to snip the last of the sutures for Logan, leaving the nylon exactly long enough for easy removal later on. Too long and the sutures would mat in the hair and increase the chance of infection. Too short and they'd be a beast to find later for removal.

Logan pulled the last suture through. "You spoil me for anyone else. How'd you learn to read my mind? I could understand if you were a battle-scarred nurse with fifty years in the OR, but . . ."

"My dad," Sarah said, snipping the last suture. She smiled, and there was something in her eyes that Logan had never seen before. Wistfulness, maybe even happiness.

"Your father's a doctor?"

"Nope. A mechanic," Sarah said with a chuckle. "The best. He owns a body shop in Pollock Pines. I used to help him work on our cars at home and at the shop sometimes too when he stayed late and everyone else was gone. We'd have the Stones jammin' on the speakers, and we'd drink bottles of Coke and eat spicy pepperoni sticks. I would do this impression of Jagger, holding a huge Crescent wrench like a microphone: 'I can't get no satis-fac-shun,' and he'd laugh so hard. . . ."

Her voice got thick and she cleared her throat. "I knew all the tools, exactly what he'd need next. He used to say I could read his mind. Same way you did just now. Anyway, that was a long time ago. And lucky for you I went to nursing school instead of working at the speedway." She grinned. "They begged me, you know."

"I'll bet." Logan smiled back, having no problem imagining Sarah in grease-smudged overalls and a backward ball cap. It struck him this was the first time they'd talked about anything personal. "So you're Daddy's girl?"

Sarah hesitated before answering. "I don't get to see him much."

"But Pollock Pines is only like twenty minutes away."

"My mother and I . . . have some issues." Sarah looked away. "You want me to finish up here?"

"Yeah, sure." Logan said, sorry he'd pushed it. He was the last one to judge the dynamics of family relationships. "I suppose I'd better go see why the chief's nosing around our department."

"He's gone." Sarah pointed toward the door. "Out of the war zone and back to the safety of administration, no doubt." She squeezed antibiotic ointment onto the flat end of a tissue forceps and smoothed it across the suture line. Her hand trembled slightly as she reached for bandaging material.

Logan noticed the shadows under her eyes and how her fair lashes seemed to flutter in fragile hollows. Had she always been that thin? Maybe he'd get her some pizza for lunch. Double cheese and make sure she ate it.

Sarah looked up, her pale eyes lit with sudden amusement. "Our Claire, on the other hand, has been drawn to the dark side."

"Hmm." Logan busied himself with prying the patient's eyes open to check pupil responses. The man's eyes were reddened and jerked slightly side to side—nystagmus, from the effects of alcohol intoxication. But his pupil sizes were normal and equal on both sides, constricting in reaction to the penlight. Wild Man would have a CT scan to check for brain injury, then a gurney to sleep on until his blood alcohol level legalized. Logan set the light down and glanced at Sarah, keeping his voice casual. He was not going over to that clinic. "So, how's Claire doing over there? Using brochures as compresses?"

Sarah smiled and shook her head. "Hey, careful. Code of honor—can't let you disrespect a fellow ER nurse."

"Education nurse," Logan corrected as he began to strip off his bloody gloves inside out. "There's a mile of floor between those offices and ER." *And I've been tempted to walk it a dozen times this past week.*

"But she worked ER first until a couple of years ago." Sarah rolled a soft Kerlix gauze bandage around the patient's head to cover the wound and reduce swelling. "I talked to one of the nurses at UCD in Sacramento, and she heard of her."

Logan let the glove dangle and stepped back toward the gurney. "Really? The trauma center?" He shook his head, remembering asking Claire about her career yesterday. It was odd she didn't mention ER. Most nurses considered that experience a badge of honor. He'd seen some with a few measly shifts in ER label themselves trauma nurses forever after.

"This nurse said Claire left after the big warehouse disaster a couple of years back." Sarah's brows drew together. "It sounded like she had a family member injured in that fire."

"Whoa, that's rough. I've talked with docs who worked that disaster. Weren't there like seven firefighters—?"

"Dr. Logan!"

They both turned as Inez shouted outside the patient cubicle.

Sarah pulled the curtain aside to reveal the breathless and flustered clerk.

Inez clasped her chest, her dark eyes wide and blinking. "*Lo siento*—I'm sorry . . . ," she said, gulping for air, "but Erin said grab you quick. They've got *mijo* Jamie in urgent care. And something's going very, very bad!"

+++

Claire fought a dizzying mix of emotions as Logan entered the clinic exam room, but bone-deep relief surpassed all else. Jamie had been sent down from pediatrics for a routine bandage change and a look-see at some breathing trouble, but now his asthma was full-blown and he was deteriorating fast.

No. Claire's heart began hammering in her ears. This boy

was the hospital darling, the sweet face of life after tragedy. *Please, God, don't let me crumble like that other time. Don't let me fail this child.*

"Second treatment's nearly finished," she explained as Logan bent down for a moment to make eye contact with the sick boy. She watched as he began to speak, eyes gentle but concerned, patting the boy's shoulder. He called Jamie "buddy" and reassured him that Doc Logan was going to make him well. Claire's heart squeezed. *He does care.* Overhead, the PA buzzed with a stat page for respiratory therapy.

Claire adjusted the misting treatment mask, alarmed that Jamie's blue eyes now swam listlessly and his breathing rate was more than twice what it should be. His dark pupils drifted side to side and then partially disappeared beneath his drooping upper lids.

She stroked his head gently, trying to comfort him, then looked at Logan. "He's far more fatigued now. Respirations are 56 per minute, and—" she glanced at the red digital display on the monitor, and her stomach sank—"oxygen saturation is still too low—only 86 percent, even with the supplemental." *Oh, please.*

Claire brushed the child's flaxen hair from his forehead, and her hand came away sickly damp. Jamie leaned forward to support himself on both little arms, the flesh around his ribs and over his breastbone retracting with each fish-out-of-water breath. His nostrils flared wide with the effort, and his lips were ashen.

"His heart rate's dropped from 160 to 90 . . . 86 now," she reported. Slowing pulse—bradycardia—from impending respiratory failure. *We could lose him. I can't do this again.*

Logan frowned and glanced at Glenda, the nurse-practitioner, and then back at Claire. "You've given steroids?"

"Prednisone syrup. But he vomited, so I'm not sure he got the full dose." Claire turned toward the door at the sound of Erin's voice. Behind her were a trio of respiratory therapists and Sarah.

Logan's brows furrowed for a split second before he nodded. "Let's get him to the ER. I need to be ready to tube this kid. He's tiring."

Claire's throat tightened, imagining Jamie on a ventilator with an endotracheal tube down his throat and the terror that would bring his mother. Carly was in a room upstairs. Had they told her there were problems yet?

Logan pressed a fingertip gently into Jamie's forearm and watched the skin color blanch white and return sluggishly to normal, another indication his condition was worsening. "I'd like to get an IV in, though. We'll need it for steroids." His eyes met Claire's. "You want to pop one in before we move? He's looking dry, and if his veins collapse . . ."

Collapse. Logan's voice and the familiar order yanked Claire across the span of two years and back to the Sacramento trauma room. The words from her nightmares filled her ears, her own voice, that horrible day. *"His veins are collapsed, Doctor. I can't get the line in. Oh, please get someone else. . . . I can't do this! My brother's dying—don't let my brother die!"* Claire's legs weakened and the walls closed in, suffocating her like she was trapped in a smoke-filled room. She saw it all clearly again: her brother's eyes, lashes singed, staring helplessly up at her from the gurney as she reknotted the tourniquet around his blackened and blistered arm and tried and tried. *No, stop this.*

Claire nodded at Logan. "I've . . . got it," she whispered, reaching for a tourniquet as Jamie's head began to wobble and nod behind his nebulizer mask. The wheezing continued but his respiratory effort grew weaker, his reddening eyes trying to focus as drowsiness overpowered his anxiety. Ominous signs. *Don't panic. Help him.* She forced her hand to steady and reached for the tray with iodine swabs, tape, and needle sets. She'd been very good at this once. She could do it again; she had to.

"No. Wait, Claire." Erin hurried forward and released the brake on the gurney. "Let's move him, Logan," she said, gesturing for the respiratory therapist to switch the oxygen to a portable tank. "I've got everything set up in the ER; IV therapy's there too. It'll just take a minute to get him there. And we can let the clinic staff get back to their other patients."

"Good point," he agreed. "Let's roll."

Claire released a sigh and helped prepare for Jamie's quick transport down the short corridor to ER. She met Logan's eyes for an instant before he marched away but could read nothing in them. His team followed, closing in like soldiers in formation; then they all disappeared out the door.

She stood alone in the littered exam room, wondering at her sudden jumble of emotions. Strangely, part of her wanted to follow Logan and be part of the team working to save Jamie, and yet . . . She picked up the discarded tourniquet and frowned. She'd nearly panicked over the thought of starting an IV, a skill that had been second nature before. Had Logan noticed her moment of hesitation? Had the others? Was that why Erin interrupted?

Claire stretched the tourniquet tight and let one end go, feeling the latex strip snap sharply against her wrist. It stung far less than a disturbing new suspicion: *Am I a weak link?* Tears filled her eyes, and she wiped them away before returning to the clinic's nursing station. Two more hours and she'd be out of here.

Claire waited an hour before peeking into the ER's code room, listening first from the doorway and expecting to hear the mechanical whoosh of a ventilator. But when she parted the curtain, she was amazed to see Jamie smiling. With his mom in a wheelchair beside him and flanked by two pediatric nurses, he was holding a lime green Popsicle and sitting cross-legged on the gurney like a prince holding court. If it weren't for the tethers of the oxygen tubing and an IV, Claire was certain he'd be toddling out the door to visit with the ER staff. His cheeks were pink, his breathing nearly normal, and—*thank you, God*—his eyes bright and animated. He waved at Claire just as Erin appeared by her side.

"The third treatment turned him around," Erin explained, "along with the IV steroid. We're going to send him back upstairs to pediatrics in about an hour."

Claire blinked quickly before tears could well. Goose bumps rose. How could she have forgotten how good this kind of moment felt? So amazingly good.

Erin raised her hand in a high five and kept nodding until Claire joined palms with her.

"And we're thinking this team's more than ready for a little celebration," Erin said with a smile.

"Celebration?"

Erin nodded. "Tonight's Denim and Diamonds Night at the fair. It's that family event, the benefit for Sierra Children's Services. They've got it all fixed up with a root beer bar, fake cowboy shoot-outs, and someone said the chaplain and his wife are teaching country-western dance lessons. I bought a few extra tickets, so now we've decided to go as a group. Come with us, okay? My treat. We'll dress up like cowgirls, make fools of ourselves on the dance floor, and eat way too many nachos. Maybe even ride the mechanical bull." She winked. "After today, I'd say it's just what the doctor ordered."

Doctor. Claire glanced around the department. Where was Logan?

"So, how about I stop by and get you around six thirty? C'mon. I think Sarah's coming and Glenda. Maybe even Inez." Erin rolled her eyes. "Logan never comes to these social things, but who needs him anyway?"

But he came to the rodeo. To see me. Claire's face warmed, and she laughed to cover it. She started to make some excuse about going for a run, getting home to feed Smokey, then turned as she heard a boyish squeal in the code room followed by cough-peppered giggles. Jamie was batting a SpongeBob balloon and laughing. A boy who an hour earlier could have been taking his last breaths was now embracing life. Just for tonight, Claire needed to feel that way too. For the first time in a long time, being alone felt . . . lonely.

"Count me in," she said, giving Erin a thumbs-up. She shook her head, remembering the chaplain's advice: dancing and laughing. Looked like she was going to do it after all. Without Logan. But then he'd never been part of her plan, anyway. Erin was right. Who needed him?

+++

Logan hesitated outside the door of the 4-H pavilion housing the Denim and Diamonds fund-raiser event. He smiled; hopefully they'd relocated the livestock. He glanced down at his watch. Seven thirty and he'd just seen Erin standing in the gravel parking lot beside her boyfriend's Corvette. They seemed deep in conversation. Though he didn't really know Brad well, Logan was glad to see Erin having a little fun. From what he'd observed, most of

Erin's activities revolved around the hospital. That wasn't much of a life. Of course, he was a fine one to point fingers—or give dating advice.

At any rate, it wasn't the best time to ask her if Claire was here. Not even a smart idea in the first place, considering the hospital's eager gossip mill. Logan grimaced, remembering how the painful stories of his divorce made the rounds in Reno, details morphing with each repetition like that grade school telephone game. Then he thought of Beckah's wedding invitation lying still unanswered on his dresser at the condo. What did a guy give his ex-wife for a wedding gift? A gold medal for finding a better man?

But for tonight he'd simply be careful, or everyone at Sierra Mercy would think he had a thing for the educator, and—*whoa there!* Logan moved back quickly as the door opened from the inside and Claire stepped out to stand in front of him. His breath caught and warmth flooded through him. She was gorgeous.

"Oh, sorry!" She looked into his face. "Logan?" Her eyes widened with recognition, long lashes blinking quickly.

"You're leaving?" he asked, not caring if she could hear the regret in his voice. He didn't want her to go, not unless it was with him.

Claire smiled, brushing her fingers through her hair, and he caught a whiff of her perfume. Kind of spicy and sweet. He suddenly wanted, more than he'd wanted anything in a very long time, to be close enough to smell it on her skin.

"Just a little cowboyed out, I guess." Her gaze dropped and she chuckled, and Logan knew she was teasing him about his denim jacket, big-buckle Western belt, and tooled cowhide boots. In the distance, behind the doors, the band was playing Willie Nelson's "Blue Eyes Crying in the Rain."

"Cowboy-doctor," he corrected, resisting the urge to take hold of her hand. All at once he needed to know how it would feel in his. "Big difference. Honest."

She opened her mouth to speak, then hurried to move as the door opened and a trio of preteens barreled out, pelting each other with popcorn. They giggled apologies as Claire sidestepped to avoid them and stumbled in the process.

Logan reached out to take Claire's arm, steadying her. He couldn't let her go home. *Stay with me.* "Come back inside," he said, hearing the plea in his voice.

Claire hesitated, and Logan remembered how she'd leaped away when he got too close at Daffodil Hill. She'd come within millimeters of squashing a chicken. He needed to be careful with this woman.

"Just for a little while. Let me buy you a root beer. Yeah." He nodded, pleased that at least she'd begun to seem amused. "Consider it a mercy thing. For a man who wrestled a drunk and got called on the carpet by administration all in the same day."

"Hmmm." Claire peered at him out of the corner of her eye.

Logan could tell she still wasn't convinced. He'd give it another shot. "Okay, a celebration then. For two people who saved Jamie's life today."

Her brows drew together for a moment, almost as if his words were troubling somehow, but then she smiled and he knew he'd finally said the right thing.

Behind them, through a crack in the door, he heard the band begin a rendition of Patsy Cline's "Crazy." Very appropriate, considering his current state of mind. Logan grinned at Claire and waited.

"Okay," she said slowly, taking a step toward the door. "I think

I can deal with one more mug of root beer, Doctor. For that kind of celebration."

Logan opened the door, and Claire led the way inside and walked toward the tables. He smiled with appreciation. She couldn't know it, but the privilege of following her was something to be celebrated in itself. She wore a lace-trimmed T-shirt above trim black jeans, a silver concho belt, and soft leather boots. Her glossy dark hair brushed her shoulders with each subtle sway of her stride.

He shook his head. Rumor mill or not, the truth was he did have a thing for this educator. *Now what?*

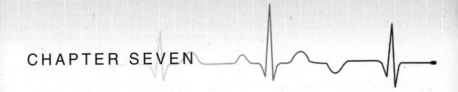

CHAPTER SEVEN

Erin sighed. She should've taken her chances on the mechanical bull; that situation ended in eight seconds or less. You either vaulted off the top with a big "Yahoo!" or fell flat on your behind. A blessing compared to endlessly second-guessing relationships.

She crossed her arms and rubbed the sleeves of her rhinestone-studded Western shirt, fighting shivers that had nothing to do with the night air. Things were so new with Brad. How could she make him understand her responsibility to the ER crew? Hospital teams were a lot like a family; not everyone understood that kind of closeness. But it was vital. Especially after the shifts they'd had lately.

Brad leaned against his car, a festive swag of overhead bulbs splashing color like pirates' jewels over his close-cropped blond hair and undeniably handsome features. A boyish smile teased his lips. "So, are you coming with me or going back in there for more root beer?"

"I reminded you about this fund-raiser. You didn't want to come, but if you've changed your mind, I think they're still selling tickets at the door."

"No thanks," Brad said. "And I don't get why you need to be here." He counted, bending his fingers back one by one: "Five work shifts this week, an extra hour every day to put that hospital prayer group together, half your day off in a disaster meeting, and . . ."

Bible study class? Erin's jaw tensed, wondering if he'd include something so important to her in his list. She'd heard it often enough from previous boyfriends, hadn't she? Still, she'd met Brad at church. Surely he could understand. But they'd been dating barely three months now, hardly time to know each other. Could she really expect him to honor what was important to her?

Before she could find words, Brad stepped forward and drew Erin to him. His arms closed around her until her cheek lay against his shirtfront. She breathed in scents of shampoo and soap. "Look," he said, nestling his chin against her hair, "I'm only trying to figure out where I fit in, you know?"

He stepped back, holding her away so he could look into her eyes. "I understand work pressures. I may not be saving lives at the dealership, but I put in plenty of long hours. Especially on the days my uncle's hanging around, trust me. Because it's a family business doesn't mean they make it easy for me." He touched a fingertip to Erin's chin. "But I also know how to play. And what I'm saying is, I want you to come play with me. That's all." Dimples appeared as his smile widened into the grin that would set hearts aflutter in a hefty percentage of the nurses at Sierra Mercy. "Come on. What's the point of living an hour from Tahoe if you don't go enjoy it?"

"The lake? Tonight?" Erin considered the ER group. How many of them had come? Brad was asking her to take off when it was her idea to get everyone together in the first place? She'd given Claire a ride.

"Yes!" Brad's eyes glittered. "We could make it there by ten, catch a late show at South Shore, and maybe hit the seafood buffet." He stroked his thumb gently along her jaw. "I know you don't gamble, but you could browse the gift shop for a few minutes while I duck into the casino and roll the dice. Maybe I'll win some cash for that charity of yours. Wouldn't you like that?"

Cash. Erin's stomach lurched and she looked down, scraping the toe of her boot in the gravel. She still hadn't found the Little Nugget Victim Fund envelope. The donations for Jamie and his mother. She hadn't admitted it to anyone at the ER yet, let alone Brad. It was probably not a great idea to tell a guy you're just getting to know that you can't be trusted with money. She'd have to use part of her paycheck to reimburse the cash.

Brad took hold of her hand. "In case you're worrying, I'm not making moves to get you to stay overnight. I'll drive you back home. Scout's honor." He raised two fingers and grinned. "So that's the plan. What do you say?"

"I don't know. It was my idea to put this evening together. My crew's been having a tough time lately. . . ."

"So am I." Brad's smile vanished. "Ever since I started dating a woman who can't make time for me. Where do I fit in? Tell me that."

What was that, an ultimatum? Erin's teeth clenched as she fought a familiar urge to turn and walk away. The same way she had in so many other relationships. But then she'd promised herself she wouldn't do that this time. That she'd try harder to make it work and not be so judgmental. She took a slow breath, telling herself that plenty of women would find this dilemma flattering and wouldn't think Brad's spontaneous—if ill-timed—offer of fun was . . . what? A red flag that he shouldn't be trusted? A sign he was too slick, too smooth, insincere—destined to hurt her, just like . . . ? *Am I ever going to trust any man?*

"Brad, it's just that . . ." Erin glanced toward the doorway to the Denim and Diamonds event in time to see Claire step inside. Followed by . . . Her eyes widened. *That's Logan.*

+++

Claire walked under strings of colored lights and across sawdust-strewn planking, passing the foolhardy volunteers for the mechanical bull and entire families thumping their boots to the chaplain's finale of the Boot Scootin' Boogie lesson. She had absolutely no idea where she was going or, for that matter, even why she'd accepted this invitation. The only thing she felt certain of was that Logan Caldwell's eyes were glued to her back. Which gave a whole new meaning to Merlene Hibbert's cryptic warning, "I'd watch my back if I were you." Claire chuckled, then grew thoughtful. Logan said tonight was a celebration. *"For two people who saved Jamie's life."*

She tensed, remembering her anxiety during the toddler's emergency, how nearly impossible it was to keep her hands from trembling. And the way the flashback about Kevin caused her to hesitate over starting Jamie's IV. When, in a critical moment, she could have stalled out. Claire's stomach sank. Was that why she'd agreed to come inside with Logan, to find out for sure if he'd noticed her moment of hesitancy?

"How about over there?" Logan asked, stepping up beside her and pointing at a couple of empty chairs.

Squeals of delight and laughter rose from children gathered at the air rifle shooting gallery and whirling cotton candy machine just beyond.

"Um . . . sure," she said, fighting a new wave of ridiculous paranoia. If Logan had a problem with a nurse's work, everyone knew it—stat. He wouldn't be offering a critique tonight. Just a silly root beer. And nothing more. She reached the table and pulled out a chair when Logan stopped her.

"Whoa, cowgirl." He nodded toward the dance floor. "They're starting a two-step. C'mon."

"What . . . you mean, dance?" Claire scanned the square of wooden planking crowded with dancers of all ages—a father with a daughter in his arms, her tiny pink boots dangling; two elderly women in cowboy hats, laughing as one gingerly twirled the other; a young couple wearing matching Western shirts. The band—in hospital scrubs and cowboy hats and made up of three OR techs, an anesthesiologist, and the chief of pediatrics—belted out a familiar and lively Alan Jackson tune. Claire looked helplessly at Logan. "I don't know. . . ."

"One dance." He motioned to a volunteer passing a hat among the people gathered around the dance floor. "Remember, this is for charity."

Before she could protest, Logan draped his jacket across a chair and reached for her hand. He threaded his way through the tables, leading Claire, then stopped in front of the dance floor. He smiled at her. "And now," he said, taking her into his arms, "watch your toes. They don't teach this in med school."

Claire reminded herself to breathe. When was the last time she'd danced?

Logan took hold of one of her hands and slipped his other hand around her waist as they merged into the one-way stream of dancers, following the still-giggling senior cowgirls. His dark brows furrowed, and Claire saw Logan's lips move silently. She remembered with a quick tug of her heart how Kevin counted the cadence aloud when he'd taught her the two-step before her first dance at middle school. *"Quick-quick, slow, slow. Quick-quick, slow,*

slow. You're doing fine, Sis. And try to smile, would ya? You don't want to scare the guy."

She summoned a smile. Logan returned it, looking anything but scared, and Claire was suddenly very aware that these weren't her brother's arms. Surprisingly, for the first time in a long time, she wanted to leave those old memories behind—even the good ones—and exist in the moment without worry or sadness. Just be. An unplanned detour. If only for tonight. One root beer. One dance. Nothing more.

Though he made no move to close the distance between them, Claire felt the heat from Logan's palm against her back as she followed the line of dance. She inhaled softly, and the scent of him—shampoo, trace of woodsy cologne, and warm masculine skin—made her feel unexpectedly woozy. She began to wish he weren't holding her quite so far away, that he'd lean down enough that she might feel his cheek against hers. Then she began to imagine the brush of his beard growth, the touch of his skin. . . .

"So am I making you crazy yet?" Logan asked.

"What?" Claire startled in his arms, blinking at him. Her face warmed as if he'd read her mind.

"With my dancing. I did warn you." He grinned at her, his fingers tightening a little over hers.

"No, perfectly sane here." She nodded and began moving away from him. "But thirsty. You promised me a soft drink."

"Oh no you don't," Logan said, reaching for her hand again as the band started a slower tune.

"You said one dance," Claire reminded him as other couples drew close.

"One slow dance," he qualified, slipping his arm around her. Onstage, the bass strings thrummed as the chief of pediatrics crooned something sappy about the stars over Texas. "That first one was practice."

She began to protest but found herself laughing instead when she saw the look on his face—boyish and charming, with his eyes plainly pleading. "Fine," she said, chuckling again. "But this is it, cowboy-doctor. End of this nurse's shift."

+++

Logan drew Claire closer this time, knowing since the moment of that unexpected hug at Daffodil Hill how perfectly she fit in his arms. He led her slowly, moving to the rhythm of the music, and she followed as naturally as breathing in and out.

Minutes passed, and it was as if she belonged in his arms, almost like she was something he'd been missing and hadn't even known it. Much the way he'd felt when he first escaped into the profound silence of the Sierra Mountains and realized his everyday life had too much noise. A revelation, a truth. Holding Claire Avery felt like that. He didn't want the dance to end. Logan stooped down so his cheek rested against the softness of hers. She smelled as sweet as he'd imagined . . . sweeter. He closed his eyes, then snapped them open as she called his name.

"Yeah?" he said, blinking and feeling like an adolescent fool when he noticed the music had stopped.

Claire nodded toward a neon cactus. "Erin's over there."

Blast. "Great," he said as the charge nurse spotted them and began to wave. Why did she have to interrupt?

"It *is* you," Erin said, arriving beside them and prodding Logan with a finger. "I thought I was seeing things." She shook her head at Claire, and her silver earrings shaped like boots swayed with the movement. "We've been trying to get him to join us in some R & R forever."

Go home. Logan smiled at Erin and shrugged. "Guess you finally did." He glanced around the room. "Where's Brad?" *He could take you home.*

"Out in the parking lot, and that's exactly my problem." She turned to Claire. "Did Sarah ever call? I wasn't surprised that Glenda and Inez bailed on us, but I was sure Sarah would show."

Logan frowned. Who was coming next? Merlene Hibbert? Maybe the chief of staff in a bolo tie and Stetson?

"She called my cell maybe twenty-five minutes ago. She accidentally dialed me instead of you, but she wanted to say she couldn't come." Claire's eyes clouded with concern. "She sounded kind of upset or maybe just tired. Not sure. My wireless connection was bad and it's noisy in here, but it sounded like . . . something about her baby?"

"Baby?" Erin shook her head. "Nope, no baby. Not Sarah."

"Well, then I'm not sure," Claire said. "But she isn't coming."

Erin touched Claire's arm. "I'm sorry about this, but I need to leave. Brad's feeling . . . Well, it's complicated, but I need to do some damage control there, meet him at my apartment and talk things over. I wouldn't have offered to drive tonight if I'd known that he'd show up like this."

"I'll drive Claire home," Logan offered hastily, causing Claire's eyes to widen. She glanced down at her boots, and Logan knew she was squirming. "I mean, I could if she wants to stay longer. No problem."

"Great!" Erin nodded at Claire. "I'd feel so guilty for inviting you out and then dragging you away. Is that okay? Or should I call Brad and tell him I need to drop you off first?"

No. Say no. Logan held his breath for what felt like forever, filled with the memory of Claire in his arms.

"No," Claire said, shifting in place. "You go on, Erin. I understand. I'll get a ride with Logan. If it's not out of his way."

Logan exhaled and waited a few casual seconds before answering. "Going right by your place," he said with the linen-cool nonchalance of Cary Grant. "No problem."

Claire raised her brows, and Logan's smile faltered as he realized—and then hoped Erin hadn't—that, of course, he would have no idea where Claire lived.

+++

Logan stopped the Jeep in front of a modest A-frame cabin and told himself, though it was barely 9 p.m., there was no way Claire was going to invite him in. She'd gotten quieter during the hour after Erin left, and he was fairly sure she'd been embarrassed the charge nurse had seen them dancing.

They'd finally had the root beers, but the only further dancing Claire had agreed to was a line dance. Some idiot thing called the Watermelon Crawl that made him look like a stumbling Neanderthal. At least she'd laughed, laughed hard enough to double over, and that was worth the embarrassment. She had such a great laugh. There were so many great things about her. But it was frustrating to have no clue what she was thinking about him, and there was every reason to believe she'd bought into all the ugly complaints she'd heard. The nurse who quit probably spray-painted them on the wall of the nurses' lounge.

"I'll walk you to your door," he said, breaking the silence after he'd switched off the engine and headlights. He peered up the dark, pine-studded driveway and then turned to her. "Although

I forgot my grizzly rifle. I'll have to wrestle 'em bare fisted, like Daniel Boone."

Claire laughed and her beautiful eyes lit up. Logan told himself to settle for that and to stop thinking about holding her again. It wasn't going to happen. She stopped laughing, and he prepared himself for the fact she was going to say she could walk to the door by herself, thank you very much.

"You'd better come inside, then." Claire's lips curved into a smile. "The three bears could already be tasting my coffee."

+++

Sarah pushed the cell phone's End button and watched its screen until the familiar Pollock Pines number eclipsed into darkness. It was the phone's first assigned speed dial slot: Dad. Her shoulders sagged beneath the old flannel robe as the irony struck her. The only "speed" in this call had been a rush to disconnect when her mother answered. And before she could hang up on Sarah.

She reached for the near-empty bottle of merlot and refilled her plastic juice glass, spilling some of the liquid onto the apartment's tidy breakfast bar. It welled up for a moment, dark as blood on the white tile, and then seeped slowly into intersecting grout lines. She frowned. Sloppy, careless. She'd retrieve that old toothbrush from under the sink, grab a bottle of bleach, and get the stain out. It would wipe away pure and clean like it never happened and . . .

Sarah's throat squeezed. Did her mother guess how desperately she'd needed to hear her father's voice? Was that why she answered the phone herself? Had the call been purposefully intercepted, the way it had been this same time last year? Could her mother know how completely unbearable the next few days would be for Sarah? *Oh, Mama, please. Please.* She bit her lower lip, unable to stop the mournful groan. Did she remember that next week was Emily's birthday?

Two. She'd have been two years old.

Sarah slid from the kitchen stool, letting a brief rush of dizziness pass. She stretched, pressing her knuckles into her lower back, then glanced down at the cell phone on the breakfast bar. She'd called Erin to say she wasn't coming to that Denim and Diamonds fund-raiser tonight, hadn't she? The memory was fuzzy, but . . . oh yeah, she'd accidentally punched Claire's number. But at least Erin would get the message. No problem, then. She imagined Erin and Claire and the others who'd planned to go tonight, and the thought struck her. What had the social worker advised at the critical incident debriefing? *"Do the things that feel good to you"?* Yes. And that's exactly what they were doing. Good for them.

She walked across the short stretch of carpeting to the painted wooden rocking chair and eased into it. She pushed off with her bare toes and set the chair into gentle motion, hearing its familiar creak. Her body began to relax, and she sighed. This was what felt good to Sarah. Rocking. Imagining her baby in her arms, her daughter's downy head brushing against her lips. Remembering the sweet scent of her skin. She closed her eyes, seeing a chubby blonde birthday girl laughing and riding on the shoulders of her adoring grandpa. *Emily* . . .

After opening her eyes, she patted the pocket of her robe, making certain the pill bottle was there. The sleeping pills prescribed by a doctor she'd worked with in Sacramento. She'd had them for a year and never taken one. But if the wine didn't do the trick, she'd break a pill in half and take it. This one time. She needed to sleep, and it had been so hard this past week. She shook her head. Wine. Pills. She hated them both, but she couldn't work if she didn't sleep, and it was critical to stay on top of things at the ER. People's lives were at stake. Children's lives. And Dr. Caldwell was counting on her.

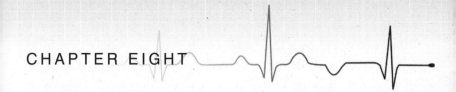

CHAPTER EIGHT

Logan watched the one-eared animal glare at him from a perch on the back of the suede couch, its tail twitching. He wasn't sure, but the thing might have growled. "Hey, should I be worried about this cat?" he called out.

The clatter of dishes in the kitchen beyond was replaced by laughter. "Well, I'd watch my back if I were you," Claire answered. Then laughed again, like she'd remembered some private joke. "But we're taking our coffee out to the deck, so no need for panic."

Panic. Logan smiled to himself. She was a fine one to talk. Which was exactly why he'd left the kitchen instead of continuing to watch Claire do things like measure the coffee, find the cups, and retrieve some coconut cookies from a tin on top of the refrigerator. Though he'd liked watching all that. Especially after she'd pulled her hair up into a big clip and swapped her leather boots for pink flip-flops. But he'd also noticed that Claire chattered too quickly as she tried to avoid his eyes. Logan's presence made her nervous. Which was the last thing he wanted. But then, what exactly *did* he want? Good question.

Normally a Friday night would find Logan taking off on his bike, maybe meeting one of the Placerville docs for some basketball. Then going back to his condo to finish off a pizza and call his dad. Or he'd spend a few hours wrestling with that oak stump rooted deep in the middle of his planned home site. Anything but making small talk in the confines of a woman's living space.

Logan looked around. Not that there were any frilly pillows, fashion magazines, or scented candles anywhere in sight. It struck him once again how the rustic cabin was completely devoid of feminine touches. Or anything that seemed personal, except a pair of women's running shoes sitting by the front door. Otherwise there were simply paneled walls, a woven rug, a neat stack of logs by the woodstove, a rock wall. . . . Logan's gaze moved to the collection of framed photos on the mantel. He glanced toward the kitchen before crossing to look at them more closely.

In the first, a young man wearing a Superman T-shirt under firefighter gear clowned for the camera. He was muscular, dark-haired, and good-looking. A twinge of jealously surprised Logan. Was this firefighter someone Claire had dated . . . maybe still dated? Because there he was in the next photo with Claire and an older couple who looked like they could be her parents. So this guy knew her parents? A serious relationship.

His attention moved to the adjacent photo, a tin frame wedged between the parent photo and what appeared to be a hand-stitched line of Scripture. The photo was a black-and-white enlargement, draped with a metal cross: the same young firefighter, but this time he had one arm around a Hispanic child and the other across the shoulders of a different young woman—holding her close— obviously his girlfriend. *Not Claire.*

Logan exhaled, realizing he'd been holding his breath without knowing it. And recognizing too that this unconscious act may have answered his question about why he was here tonight. For the first time in a long time, he was letting himself become interested in a woman. Hard to deny. *Am I ready for something like that?* Logan stepped away from the mantel at the sound of Claire's voice.

"We're ready in here," she said, beckoning from the doorway.

+++

Claire watched as Logan, standing beside her, lifted the dainty shell-pattern cup carefully to his lips. She smiled in the darkness. If he risked putting his index finger through that delicate handle, he'd be wearing the porcelain cup to work tomorrow. She should have offered him one of those big mugs from the set of hand-painted Mexican pottery that Gayle and Kevin—no, Claire wasn't going to think about her brother tonight. She'd promised herself that. One root beer, one dance. Now one cup of coffee? Her unplanned detour was lasting longer than she'd imagined.

"So what's with your cat?" Logan asked, leaning back against the weathered railing that surrounded the hilltop deck. Behind them, the seasonal creek burbled in the darkness, already filling with melted Sierra snowpack. Stingy illumination from a string of solar lights lit the surrounding landscape in hit-or-miss fashion, outlining pine branches, the cabin's shingled eaves, a long-abandoned copper fire pit, a small redwood table . . . and Logan's handsome profile set against a backdrop of sparkling stars. He raised his coffee cup toward where Smokey, his single ear flattened, pressed his black nose against the sliding door to the kitchen. There was a thumb-size spot of fog on the glass from the cat's breath. "He's not allowed outside?"

Claire rolled her eyes. "More like, won't come out. He's got that little pet door, and sometimes he pokes his head out during the daytime. But he won't risk even that after dark." She tapped her finger against her temple. "Poor Smokey's not quite right after the raccoon ate his ear."

Logan's eyes widened. "What?"

"We . . . I mean, *I* . . ." Claire paused, telling herself she wasn't being disloyal to her brother. It was only that she couldn't talk about Kevin. To anyone. "I think it was a raccoon, anyway. There are so many of them up here. Smokey's a rescue cat. He's only lived here with . . . me for a couple of years now. He's never purred. Not even once. I suppose he won't come outside because he's afraid he'll have to face another raccoon."

Logan set his cup down on the table next to the plate of coconut cookies. "Poor guy." He shook his head, his eyes on hers. "I guess we're all afraid of something."

Claire's breath caught at Logan's words and she looked away, helpless to stop the memory of Jamie's desperate struggle for air. And her own crippling doubts as she'd tried to help him—the way the incident forced the memories of Kevin's death to surface again. Had Logan noticed all that? Was that what he'd just implied?

She fought a jaw-trembling shiver and then decided it was smartest to take the offensive. Turn the tables on this thread of conversation pronto. She took a sip of her coffee and faced Logan, lifting her chin and forcing a smile. "So what are you afraid of, Dr. Cald-w-well?" Despite her bravado, Claire's chin quivered, goose bumps rising as her words dissolved into another full-blown shiver.

Logan pulled off his jacket and held it out, insisting until Claire set her coffee cup down and slipped her arms inside. The jacket was huge, and the denim, warmed by Logan's body, smelled so much like him that Claire shivered again.

He stepped closer and turned up the collar. "Right now, I'm mostly afraid I'll have to treat you for hypothermia." He clucked his tongue, chiding her like a protective parent. "Flip-flops and no coat. Should we go inside?"

"No. I'm fine now," Claire said, finding her voice somehow.

He was silent for several seconds as his fingers lingered on the jacket's collar, and she held her breath, very aware of how close his face was to hers. When he finally broke the silence, Logan's whisper warmed her skin. "What about you? What are you afraid of, Educator?"

Claire's heart leaped to her throat. *I'm afraid I want to kiss you.*

+++

Logan watched Claire's eyes and realized what she was most afraid of right now was him. And since he didn't want that, he let his hands fall to his side. By the time he'd taken a step away, she managed a laugh and a glib answer to his question.

"Afraid of? Only that I've let your coffee get cold. Would you like some more?"

"Sure, thanks," he said, knowing he'd drink fifty of those awkwardly small cups of coffee and even pet the one-eared psycho cat if it meant he could stay here longer. Learn more about this woman.

"Coming up." She smiled and then walked—the foolish sandals making slapping noises against the soles of her feet—to where she'd set the coffee carafe on a table near the door.

He watched, staggered by how beautiful she looked dwarfed in his faded jean jacket, the loose strands of hair escaping the clip to trail down over her shoulders. And how those amazing eyes still looked a little anxious. It took everything Logan had in him not to rush forward and take her in his arms. But instead he took the coffee and was grateful she was back beside him at the railing.

He'd have to be careful, watch what he said, and move slowly with this woman. She was different. Logan shook his head. When had he ever worried about these kinds of things before? When hadn't he simply rushed ahead full throttle right on down the road? A deep chuckle escaped his lips as he set his cup down on the redwood table.

"What?" Claire asked. "What's so funny?"

"Uh . . ." *Careful, slow. Safe subjects.* "Nothing really." Logan swept his arm wide, glancing around the deck. "I was only thinking that I wouldn't expect you to have a cabin way out here in the woods. I don't meet too many pioneer women." He lifted his brows. "So, how'd you and crazy Smokey end up with this place?"

He waited, and when the silence stretched longer and longer, his smile faltered. *What did I say? What's wrong?*

Claire's pupils widened and she opened her mouth but said nothing, studying Logan's face for a moment as if trying to make some important decision. He had a gut-level feeling that somehow he'd made a giant mistake.

Claire's voice finally emerged in a raw whisper, confirming Logan's fear. "It's my brother's house," she explained, pain flooding into her eyes. "He died and left it to me."

Logan's throat constricted. Her brother? The photos of the young firefighter on the mantel rushed to his mind. Then, with sickening clarity, he remembered what Sarah told him. How Claire had worked at the Sacramento trauma center. That she'd quit after a family member was injured.

"Kevin was a firefighter," Claire continued, her voice sounding hollow and faraway. "He was killed in that big warehouse fire two years ago. In Sacramento." She looked down at her hands, then back into his eyes, holding his gaze without blinking.

What could he say? He wanted to wrap his arms around Claire, but would she be okay with that? He settled for taking hold of her hand. She didn't pull away.

Logan brushed his thumb across the top of her hand and cleared his throat. "I'm sorry, Claire. I heard how bad that fire was. And getting a call saying someone in your family—"

"I didn't get a call. I was there." She swallowed and her eyes filled with tears. She stared hard at Logan, nodding to make her point. "I was working in the ER when Kevin came in." Her breath shuddered and a tear slid down her cheek.

In an instant, Logan's arms were around her.

+++

Erin reread Brad's scrawl on the square of paper:

> *Decided not to pressure you. Went to the lake by myself. Call you tomorrow.*
> Love,
> *B.*
>
> *P.S. Wish me luck. You'll get a donation for that charity.*

She frowned, not sure which she felt more, anger or relief. After all, she hadn't wanted to go. She couldn't stand anything to do with gambling; Brad knew that. Just the way he knew she'd promised to attend tonight's fund-raiser. But he'd seemed so upset, as if he expected her to drop everything and leave her friends in the lurch. And she'd done it, agreeing to meet him here at her apartment. She'd rehearsed it all during the drive back from the fairgrounds, practicing out loud how she'd say that relationships needed compromise. That while she couldn't ignore work responsibilities, she understood it was important to spend time together. Then she'd found his note. From a dealership-logo memo pad and stuck to her front door with a piece of duct tape. Leaving her confused, more than a bit bugged . . . and lonely. *Am I ever going to get this right?*

Erin sighed. She'd glove up and go a few rounds with the vinyl speed bag hanging from the ceiling—get her heart rate up, sweat a little. That would help.

As Erin crumpled Brad's note and pitched it into the plaid wastebasket beside her computer desk, she tried to forget his mollifying offer to donate his Tahoe winnings. To the Little Nugget Victim Fund. Jamie and his mother. She reached for her checkbook, ran her finger down its balance column, and gritted her teeth. She could do it. Barely. The cash donations had been $407.46. If she waited until next month to buy new tires for the Subaru, canceled her next two hair appointments, and stayed well beyond sniffing distance from Starbucks . . . yes, doable. She'd already swallowed her pride and called the people who'd written checks. She'd reimburse their stop payment fees, put her own check into the Victim Fund account at the bank, and then everything would be square again for the money that had been lost.

Or stolen? The question hissed in her head. How could she have lost that envelope? She didn't lose things; she hadn't even lost her front teeth until she was eight years old, for goodness' sake. But then, the only other explanation was making her completely crazy. Causing her to look at the hospital staff differently and wonder about that newly hired janitor; did he get paid enough to afford the sports shoes she'd seen him wearing yesterday? Hadn't that elderly volunteer with the batwing eyebrows been watching soap operas in the nurses' lounge last week?

But worst of all—so unforgivably bad—was when suspicion reared its ugly head this morning, presenting those very same words of doubt. At Faith QD. She'd joined hands with Inez to pray, then suddenly began trying to remember who had been there the day she'd had the envelope in her purse. *Lost or stolen?*

No. Erin closed her checkbook. She was putting the money back where it belonged. Any further questions regarding the how-who-why were in God's hands. Besides, Erin had plenty of other things on her plate. Like scheduling interviews to replace the latest nurse Logan managed to drive off. She doubted Claire would agree to work in urgent care much longer, especially after that episode with Jamie's asthma.

Erin tugged at her lower lip, remembering the look in Claire's eyes. She'd done everything fine, skillwise. But that look . . . Merlene Hibbert said Claire had plenty of ER experience. Why had she seemed so anxious?

+++

Logan managed to get a fire burning in the old copper fire pit after scouting around and producing paper, kindling, and matches like a lumberjack magician. He'd pulled a bench near so Claire could warm herself.

She was grateful because, though the unexpected tears were gone, going back inside the cabin—her brother's house—felt too raw. Too exposed. She couldn't believe she'd told Logan about Kevin's death. She hadn't talked about it to anyone in two years. Not family, not friends, not even her pastor. But then it could have been far worse; she could have confessed her panic during that horrible day and every shift afterward. Proving she was exactly what Logan hated most. A weak link. Then suddenly she'd felt his arms around her. Only for a few seconds, but it was so comforting.

"Warm enough now?" he asked, poking at the fire one last time before sitting beside her.

"I'm good," she said, meaning it. She inhaled slowly, taking in the crisp night air scented with woodsmoke and pine. She was good as long as they didn't have to talk about—

"So," Logan said, turning toward her, "after your brother . . . you decided to go into nursing education?"

"Yes," Claire answered, reminding herself that this subject, like her checklists marked with red ink, were familiar and safe. She met Logan's eyes. "I've already interviewed for the full-time clinical educator position. Cross fingers, I'll hear something soon." She chuckled. "Beware of a woman with a spreadsheet and a master plan."

"You sound like Erin. She's always coming up with these new ideas for rallying the staff, like an ER softball team and sponsoring that therapy dog." He shook his head. "And now this prayer thing in the chapel."

This prayer thing?

"You mean the God huddle?" Claire asked, hearing a hint of accusation in her voice. *Same cynical guy. Don't forget that.*

Logan laughed. "Oh, you heard. Okay, I'll confess; I teased her. Hey, I can understand how trotting a Labrador retriever through the nursing home might be viewed as therapy. And I'll tell anyone that Erin is the best charge nurse I've worked with. But asking the staff to come in early, just to hold hands in the chapel—"

"You don't believe in God?" Claire interrupted. She watched him react to the bluntness of her question and felt a quiver of anxiety, not sure if it was because she'd made Logan uncomfortable . . . or because his answer was so incredibly important to her.

+++

Logan felt sucker punched. Where did that question come from? He should've stayed home and hacked at the oak stump. He opened his mouth to speak, and his mind went blank. But for only a merciful second, only until Beckah's face intruded in memory. Along with her tearful voice: *"Logan, where's your faith?"*

"Yes. I mean, no. I believe in God, sure. It's just that . . ." Logan hesitated, recalling the photos on Claire's mantel, the metal cross draped over the picture of her brother. And the Scripture neatly stitched on fabric inside that other frame. She was religious. Another reason to be careful. Land mines everywhere. He shrugged. "It's just that I don't hold much stock in prayers. I'll be honest; I'm not convinced God even hears them, let alone answers them."

Claire glanced toward the fire and was silent, and Logan sensed that though they sat side by side, the gap between them had stretched miles beyond that too-brief moment he'd held her close. He knew the answer he'd just given Claire—gave Beckah, too—was generic, pat, and evasive.

Logan picked up the fireplace poker, listened to the flames crackle for a few seconds, and cleared his throat. Even so, his voice emerged husky and halting. "I . . . used to pray." He leaned forward to prod a log with the poker. The motion released sparks that glittered in the darkness and then quickly disappeared. "When I was a kid, I was always praying. You know, 'Bless Daddy, my two little brothers, and that old lady on the next block who gives out Hershey bars for trick or treat.' But mostly I prayed about my mother. That she'd stop drinking so much, wouldn't fight with my dad, that she'd come to parents' night at school . . . and stop sitting outside in the dark in men's cars."

He tried to swallow an age-old lump. Out of the corner of his eye, he saw Claire watching him. "After she left us—when I was twelve—I prayed every day she'd come back. When she didn't, I prayed every weekend that she'd call. I moved on to praying before I checked the mailbox on everybody's birthday." He swallowed again. "I tore this picture of Jesus holding a lamb out of a library book at school, smuggled it home in my lunch box, and hid it under my pillow. Kept it there until the lamb wore away from holding on to it. I asked Jesus to help my dad stop crying, to help me make my brothers believe she was coming back . . ." He turned to Claire. "Finally I stopped praying."

It occurred to Logan to shut up, but for some reason he couldn't. He saw Claire's brows draw together and felt her lean closer as she listened. His voice lowered to a near whisper. "A week before my fifteenth birthday, my dad and I drove to Las Vegas to identify a Jane Doe at the coroner's office. At the last minute, my father couldn't look. So I did." Logan's jaw tensed, and he closed his eyes for a second to buffer the memory. "They estimated my mother was doing ninety miles an hour when she hit a highway abutment."

When his gaze met Claire's, he saw that her eyes were glistening with tears. He struggled against a rush of guilt. *Why didn't I stop?* After all she'd been through, the last thing she needed was to hear him recite a list of childhood miseries. Then Logan's breath caught as Claire flung her arms around his neck, burrowing her head against his chest. She was warm and smelled faintly of coffee and coconut cookies.

"Logan." Her soft lips moved against the hollow of his neck as she whispered, "I'm so, so sorry."

"Hey, hey. It's okay." He nestled his face against her hair, breathing in the sweet scent of it, aware once more of that incredible sense of rightness and peace that came with having her in his arms. "And I'm the one who's sorry. I shouldn't have brought all that up. It was a long time ago, and—" He stopped as she leaned away, letting her arms slip from his neck. She looked at him, the firelight reflecting gold against the gray of her eyes. Her expression made his heart ache.

"I'm saying I understand. That I care." She leaned forward and brushed her lips against his cheek.

Before Claire could move away again, Logan tipped his head and gently kissed her.

+++

Sarah set the alarm beside her bed, synchronizing it with the one on her watch. Four thirty would give her plenty of time. She could wash her hair, iron her angel scrubs, grab a PowerBar, and be on the road to the hospital by five fifteen. She frowned. Five thirty if she decided she needed to scrub that wine stain on the kitchen tile one more time. It still seemed kind of pink; she'd be able to tell for sure in the daylight. But the point was, Sarah would be at the ER ahead of Erin—that wasn't easy. The charge nurse put in plenty of hours beyond the time clock herself. But she knew Sarah liked to get there in plenty of time to make sure the department was properly stocked and the resuscitation equipment ready to go. Bad things happened in the blink of an eye. Little Jamie came to urgent care for a simple bandage change and ended up fighting for his life. What if they hadn't been prepared? A mother could have lost her child.

No. There was no room for error, no excuse for mistakes. Logan would be the first to agree with that. And since they were still relying on temporary nurses, he would be depending on Sarah more than ever. She wasn't going to disappoint him. Sarah shut her eyes, willing the painful, intruding memory to pass. *"You're a disappointment, Sarah Lynne."*

If she took the other half of that pill, maybe she'd sleep. After Emily's birthday, she wouldn't need them anymore. She would find a measure of peace again.

Meanwhile, there was her work.

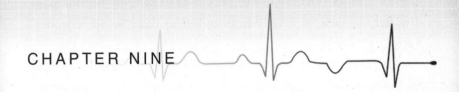

CHAPTER NINE

Smokey poked his head into the brisk dawn air and then yanked it back through the pet door like a turtle escaping into its shell. He turned toward Claire, black tail twitching and yellow eyes wide.

"Not quite there yet, are you?" Claire set her coffee cup on the kitchen table next to her cream cheese bagel. She tapped the pages of a printed outline and sighed. "Trust me, big guy. I completely understand." She grabbed her red pen and made a check mark alongside the words *Interview for clinical educator position March 15.* Then drew an asterisk beside the next entry: *New educator to be announced at the April board meeting.* It was the job Claire needed. Not quite there yet.

She gazed through the glass door toward the deck, now rosy gold with early sun. So different from last night's stars and firelight. One root beer, one dance, one coffee . . . one kiss. Completely unplanned. Claire's face warmed. Logan Caldwell had kissed her. *And I kissed him back.* She still wasn't certain how it all happened. She only knew that despite the fact that the kiss fit nowhere in her plans, the moment itself had seemed a natural progression. Had felt warm and wonderful and right. A moment shared with the man who'd given her a sea of daffodils, laughter and dancing after such a painful stretch of wilderness, and who somehow made her feel safe enough to talk about Kevin's death. The man who'd shared a remnant of his painful past. Claire cringed at the image of Logan as a boy holding that secret picture of Jesus and praying for his mother to come home. He'd had to face the horrific pain, the helplessness, of finally finding her in that Nevada coroner's office.

Claire rubbed at her forehead, attempting to banish memories of Kevin lying in the Sacramento trauma room, his blistered lips and singed lashes, her own helplessness at being unable to ease his pain, save his life. Then her heartbeat filling her ears, beating her senseless as she panicked, screaming—

She felt a brush of warm fur against her ankle. Smokey, curving his body against her. She reached down and stroked above the tuft of his missing ear. He leaned his head into her touch, butting against her outstretched palm. Claire shook her head, thinking again about the strangeness of a cat without a purr. And then it struck her. Of course it made sense. The raccoon had taken it, along with the ear.

"I get it, Smokester," Claire whispered, picking a bit from her bagel and offering it to him. She sipped her coffee and lifted the red pen. She added a handwritten line to the neatly printed column. *Talk to Erin about staffing for the ER and urgent care. Offer to make calls to agencies for temporary nurses.*

She nodded decisively. *Because working there myself is nowhere in my plan.*

Claire tightened the laces on her running shoes, took her dishes to the sink, and glanced at Kevin's chrome-framed NFL wall clock. There was more than enough time for a three-mile run, her favorite opportunity to talk with God. Afterward she'd shower, change, and get to the education office early.

As she picked up her jacket and reached for the door to the deck, she saw the fire pit and paused. She needed to stop by the ER to talk with Erin today, and Logan would be there working. How awkward would that be? Could she stand in the emergency department and act casual after . . . Claire's breath snagged. *I kissed the medical director of the emergency department.* A newly hired nurse who was being considered for a key administrative position. Doing what—fraternizing? Was there a policy? If Merlene found out . . .

Claire swung the door wide and hit the deck running. *Pace yourself, Lord. You're getting an earful today.*

+++

Logan scraped the blade across the last of the shaving cream and then splashed water against his face. *Colder than socks on an Eskimo clothesline.* He smiled at his father's old saying. But that's what Logan got for showering and shaving in Sierra Mercy's surgeons' lounge. Although the alternative was to show up in the ER smelling like he'd been wielding an ax against an oak stump since dawn. Which he had.

He gazed into the mirror, imagining the complaint crossing the chief of staff's desk on that one. *"Dr. Caldwell is an insufferable beast and smells like one too."* Probably not worth it. Even if the ax time had taken Logan a few millimeters closer to pouring his house foundation, it hadn't helped him answer the question that kept him awake half the night. What was he going to do about Claire Avery?

He tugged a scrub top over his head, stowed the shaving gear in his backpack, and headed out of the lounge toward the cafeteria. Coffee. Black. And out of a decent, fist-size mug, not a torturously small china cup. He shook his head. Claire had surprised him by returning that kiss but had been shy afterward, filling the awkward silence with a steady stream of disconnected chatter. About today's predicted weather, the chest tube demonstration she'd be giving to the student nurses, and her speculation on when she'd hear something regarding her upcoming promotion. Logan chuckled, recalling her similar nervousness at Daffodil Hill. If there had been a chicken on her deck last night, Claire would have flattened it.

Still, he couldn't shake the feeling of holding her in his arms. How right it seemed and how unbelievably at ease she made him feel. For the first time in so long. Why else would he have told her about his mother? He'd given Beckah, his wife of nearly three years, far fewer details. And he'd never told anyone about stealing that page from the Bible storybook. Why Claire? Logan squinted, remembering her face in the firelight, her words. *"I understand. . . . I care."* Was it possible there was something different about this woman? Maybe so, but . . .

He winced. She was also a Christian, same as Beckah. What on earth was he supposed to do with that? She'd practically dared him with the question, *"You don't believe in God?"* Who actually said things like that? He needed to face it: beautiful or not, this woman spelled nothing but trouble. Logan strode through the cafeteria to the coffee station.

He depressed the spigot on the coffee urn, filled his cup, and then nodded to convince himself. He ought to be glad Claire's mind was set on taking the job in the education department way across the hospital campus. Otherwise she'd be joining the God huddle with Erin, and before you knew it, his entire staff would be praying instead of working.

Frankly he didn't need that kind of aggravation. He had

enough on his mind with building the house and convincing the chief of staff he could play nice with the employees. Plus Beckah's wedding at the end of the week. A familiar wave of confusion washed over him. He took a gulp of coffee hot enough to blister his lips, frowned, and checked his watch. Still early. Enough time to visit Jamie.

Logan headed out the door and down the hallway, passing Merlene Hibbert as she gave animated directions to a volunteer balancing a huge vase of red roses. He finished his coffee in the elevator and arrived on the pediatric floor within a few minutes. Jamie grinned as he walked in, and Logan's chest squeezed unexpectedly. This kid was exactly what he needed right now.

"Doc Logan!" The three-year-old waved from his bed and then turned to his mother to share the excitement. Though his facial bandages were gone, Jamie's blond hair, clipped away in spots to accommodate burn care, still stuck up in tufts like fledgling feathers. "Mommy, it's Doc Logan. He rides the motorcycle, 'member?"

"Hey, little buddy." Logan winked at Carly, noticing that the young mother was no longer in a wheelchair. Her lower leg, injured in the explosion, was encased in a bulky orthopedic walking boot. Only a few dabs of burn ointment dotted the side of her freckled face, and her eyes were bright and far more hopeful than when he'd last seen her. Some of that due to Erin's Little Nugget Victim Fund, he assumed. He made a mental note to make another donation today.

"They're saying I might be able to take Jamie home tomorrow," Carly said. "He's healing faster than we thought."

Logan laughed as Jamie raised his little palm in a high five. He smacked his hand gently against the boy's before facing Carly. "And his asthma?"

"Not a peep."

Logan smiled at Jamie and lifted his stethoscope from around his neck. "Okay if I take a listen, pal?"

"Yep." Jamie stretched tall as Logan pressed the plastic disc to his chest.

Lungs clear, heart strong and regular. Logan watched the child's curious blue eyes. "Want to hear something cool?" He took the rubber earpieces from his ears and eased them into Jamie's, then replaced the stethoscope over the child's heart. "Do you hear that? that soft thumping inside there?"

Jamie's eyes widened and a sweet smile lit his face.

"Know what that is?" Logan asked.

"Uh-huh." Jamie beamed with confidence. "It's Jesus."

Carly chuckled as he lifted the stethoscope away from her son. "It's part of our bedtime routine," she explained. "Jamie has this favorite Bible story picture book. Since he first began to talk, he's pointed at it and said, 'Jesus is in there.' So I started touching my finger first to his chest and then to mine, saying, 'Jesus is in here too. He lives in our hearts.'"

"'Cause he loves us and would never—*ever*—leave us." Jamie reached out and pressed his small, warm palm against Logan's chest. "Right in there, Doc Logan."

+++

Sarah glanced across the ER toward Logan's still-closed office door, then checked the clock on the wall above it. Logan, Erin, and Merlene had been in there more than twenty-five minutes. Not a good sign, but Sarah could have predicted Logan's reaction to the male nurse the agency sent them this morning. Erin asked Sarah to show the man around the department, and she had—after he finally arrived twenty minutes late with no apology and a mouth full of fast-food breakfast.

She guessed that this nurse, no doubt doomed to be called McMuffin from this day forward, would be sent packing within the hour. Dr. Caldwell had been surly and silent since the minute he hit the doors this morning. Though Sarah had done her best to get the new nurse oriented, the man had already made several serious errors in judgment and seemed unfamiliar with even basic ER procedures. Logan was beyond irate.

Sarah chewed at a fingernail. She was prepared to stay as long as needed; if Merlene filled in on the clinic side, they could pull the clinic RN over here. Sarah could skip lunch, no problem. That would cover things decently until the evening shift came. But what about tomorrow? What would they do about that? Sarah wished she could think of something to help Erin with staffing, but . . . She pressed her fingers to her forehead, hating that her brain still felt fuzzy and haphazard. One and a half of the prescription pills and she still hadn't slept longer than three hours. But she'd manage.

"Sarah?" Claire peeked through the doors to the ER wearing one of her crisp suits and carrying the briefcase she'd had stuffed with pamphlets that first day. The day they'd lost the little girl, Amy Hester.

No, stop. Sarah forced a smile and waved, watching Claire glance warily around the room, empty now except for an elderly woman awaiting a CT scan and one of the hospital engineers replacing a wall oxygen valve.

"I'm looking for Erin," Claire said. "Is she here yet?"

Sarah nodded, and Claire walked toward her. She stopped, as everyone had this last hour, to stare at the enormous bouquet of red roses sitting at the nurses' station desk. "Wow. Who . . . ?"

"Erin's. From Brad the cad." Sarah smiled at the look on Claire's face. "He apparently stood Erin up last night. But he's also promised to toss in a hundred bucks for Jamie's fund, so between that and the flowers, our car salesman might be forgiven. The jury's still out." She sighed and swept a hand over her hair, trying to remember if she'd put on makeup this morning. Claire looked so fresh and pretty in that soft gray suit. *Did I even take a shower?*

"You mean he didn't meet her after she left the fund-raiser? I know how fast she was trying to get home. We rode together and then—" Claire stopped, and her face flushed. "Anyway," she said after glancing toward Logan's office, "I was sorry you couldn't be there. I gave Erin your message, but my cell was acting up so badly I could hardly hear. In fact, you're going to laugh at this one: I told Erin you'd said something about your baby."

Sarah gasped against a rush of dizziness and her stomach lurched. "I . . ."

Claire moved closer. "Hey, are you okay?"

Smile. Stop this. Oh no. Did I? Sarah coughed, reaching for her Diet Coke. "Sure. I'm fine. . . . I'm great. Just fighting a cold. No big deal." She turned and pointed toward Logan's office, desperate to change the subject and get away. "Erin's in there with Merlene and Logan. Raising her fists for our staff—you know how she is. But she should be finished pretty soon. I need to go check vital signs, but you could hang out at the desk if you want to wait." She stood, avoiding Claire's eyes.

"Sure, okay. I—" Claire stopped midsentence at the sound of voices.

Then it was only one voice—Logan's, deep and final. "Let's make this happen, ladies."

Merlene, Erin, and Logan exited the office. Merlene's lips

pinched together in a tight line. Erin yanked her hair up into a topknot as she walked. Sarah's heart tugged. Logan looked frustrated and bone tired. Like her father at the end of a long day at the shop, a day when nothing went right.

She watched as Logan rubbed the back of his neck, then rolled his head side to side. Stretching his muscles as if he'd been doing manual labor since dawn. Even though he did his usual diligent scan of the ER, there was something different about the look in his eyes. Almost as if he were troubled.

Claire stirred and Logan spotted her. He took a slow breath before giving her a smile that seemed to ease the trouble in his eyes.

+++

"What? Oh, I haven't even checked my calls yet," Claire told Logan, dismissing his apology with a wave of her hand. And a half-truth. She hadn't checked them again in the last fifteen minutes.

She tipped her head to peer back through the glass doors and down the emergency department corridor. Claire still needed to catch Erin and make it clear she wasn't available to work anywhere within a thousand yards of the ER. Standing outside its doors right now within inches of Logan was unnerving enough. Because after last night it felt like she was seeing him with new eyes—the way the sunlight played across his hair, the striking contrast of dark lashes and blue eyes, the shape of his mouth . . . *Stop it.*

"Well, I'd intended to call." Logan lounged against the metal railing outside the ambulance bay doors and squinted into the afternoon sunshine. "But I've been doing battle all day. First with an oak stump, now with—" he grimaced and his voice lowered— "McMuffin."

"Mc . . . ?"

He laughed. "New nurse Merlene tried to force down my throat. That's why I was holed up with Erin and her for so long. This is going to stop if I have anything to say about it." He scanned the perimeter of the ambulance bay and beyond like a king surveying his realm. He turned to Claire and smiled. "Fortunately I have *everything* to say about it."

"I'm not sure what you mean. Why did you meet with Erin and Merlene?"

Logan's smile disappeared. "About the same thing I've been arguing for since I agreed to head up this department. Permanent staff. Moreover, competent staff. Honest-to-goodness ER nurses." He shook his head and his tone hardened. "ER nurses staffing an ER—what a concept. But you know what I'm saying. You've worked ER. You know what it takes."

Claire stiffened. *Everything I don't have anymore.*

"You can't throw just anyone in here and make it work. I need more nurses like Erin and Sarah. It takes the brightest and the best, staff who can fly by the seat of their pants, make decisions faster than that." He snapped his fingers. "You and I both know that at any given moment, anything can come through those doors."

She nodded, fighting the image of those stretchers hurtling through the doors in Sacramento. Firefighter after firefighter, until . . .

Logan's shoulders sagged as he sighed, and then his gaze fixed on Claire's. "Nobody gets that I'm not trying to be a tyrant. I don't wake up every day planning to be some insensitive, controlling jerk that pushes the nurses too hard. Expects too much."

Sarah's exhausted face flashed before Claire's eyes.

Logan rubbed his brow. "It's true; I do push hard. Because I'm responsible for those patients' lives in there. The buck stops with me. If someone doesn't do her job, I'm the one who has to answer. I can't afford to have any . . ."

Weak links? Claire's stomach sank.

Logan continued without completing his last thought. "Maybe I just learned very young that I need to scramble to hold things together. Maybe I try too hard to fix things."

She winced, thinking of the twelve-year-old Logan trying to ease the grief of his father and younger brothers.

"I don't know why I'm the way I am, but I can't take the time to figure it out. Because right now what I need is a team. And in a matter of minutes, I'll be losing another nurse." He nodded in response to Claire's raised brows. "That's right—McMuffin. Bottom line, I've seen enough and I'm not willing to take the risk with him. I'm not saying he's a bad nurse, only that he hasn't got what it takes for the ER. What if he'd been the one over there in urgent care when Jamie started going downhill? What if he didn't make the connection that a kid's slowing heart rate means he's headed into respiratory failure? What if he hadn't alerted the nurse-practitioner?"

Claire swallowed, her mouth going dry as she remembered Jamie's struggle.

Logan's thumb brushed against his stethoscope, and he was quiet for a moment. "What if he'd left Jamie alone in that exam room for ten minutes longer? It might have been too late." His gaze connected with Claire's, and it was all she could do not to look away. "But it was you over there in the clinic that day, and—"

Before he could finish speaking, the glass doors opened behind him and Erin shouted, "Code 3 ambulance coming, Logan. Six minutes out. Unresponsive teenager. Looks like a drug overdose. We're getting things ready."

Call respiratory therapy; get the cardiac monitor ready, intubation tray, IV supplies, overdose reversal drugs; prepare to pump the stomach, insert a Foley catheter . . . Claire's pulse quickened and her legs tensed for action as her mind ticked off the list, responses that came automatically despite the fact that she had no need for them. Logan's team would pull together to save this patient, not Claire. He'd have Erin and Sarah. They'd save this teenager. Claire breathed a silent prayer. Then her thoughts scattered as she heard the distinct wail of distant sirens.

She touched Logan's arm. "I came down here to tell Erin I'll do everything I can to help your team. I'm going to put out the word, make phone calls to qualified nurses, start an aggressive recruiting campaign—"

"Whoa, Educator," Logan said. "Put down the phone and pamphlets. You won't need them. I arranged it with Merlene. You're handling urgent care tomorrow."

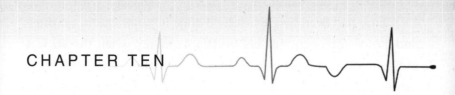

CHAPTER TEN

Not my plan, not my plan, not my plan. Claire's shoes struck the damp red-clay trail in perfect cadence with her thoughts.

She raised her arms overhead, rotated her wrists, and gulped a deep breath of oak-scented morning air, realizing that the usual balm of running wasn't happening. She'd covered more than three miles of the Gold Bug Park loop and hadn't left any of her worries behind. She may as well have zipped them into her backpack along with the bottle of spring water. God wasn't cooperating either. He was stubbornly allowing Logan and Merlene to send her to urgent care. Backward, not forward according to her carefully crafted plans. Why? He knew it was the last thing she wanted, knew that every minute near the ER was like ripping the scab off a wound.

Claire's stride shortened, her footfalls slowing and scrunching into the gravel as she caught sight of the familiar gnarled oak. Kevin's tree. She stopped and brushed her arm across her forehead, letting the sleeve of his firehouse sweatshirt wick her sweat. The oak, easily sixty feet tall, stood out in dark relief, its spreading branches already lush with spring leaves.

She circled the trunk slowly, her gaze traveling over the gray-brown ridges and deep crevices in the bark . . . *there.* She pressed her fingers to her mouth, blinking against a welling of tears. The letters carved just above her eye level had weathered since she'd last seen them but were still easily visible. *K. A.* and *G. S.* Kevin Avery, Gayle Satterfield. She traced the smooth hollows made by her brother's pocketknife.

Claire had been here when he'd done it. A fall afternoon three and a half years ago, just before Thanksgiving, when the air was pungent with woodsmoke, and crimson, orange, and gold fallen leaves crunched under their feet on the trail. They'd raced to this clearing, and she'd beaten him to the tree with a last lung-bursting sprint. Not that Kevin had cared. He was in love. He'd been giddy with it, boyishly vulnerable and invincible at the same time. Exuberant and hopeful. Loving Gayle had deepened Kevin's faith, and they'd thrown themselves heartfirst into Bible study, church volunteer work, and Mexico mission trips.

Her fingers moved to the carving below the initials. *Jer. 29:11.* Kevin's favorite Scripture. The one Gayle had stitched and framed as an engagement gift to him. For a wedding that never happened.

Claire shut her eyes against a burst of pain. *Heal my heart. Move me forward. Please, please . . .*

She pulled her hand away from the tree, feeling the shivers that often heralded the onset of an endorphin rush. Balm at last. But this time there was no runner's high, no respite. Just trembling followed by an empty, lonely ache. And a new whispering doubt: Was it possible that Logan was right? that God didn't listen to prayers? How else did she end up in urgent care?

By 9 a.m. Claire had showered and dressed, pulling her pink scrubs from the corner of her closet, where she'd banished them after her last stint in urgent care. She stuffed her purple stethoscope into her purse and headed to the kitchen to check Smokey's water bowl. It was full. And strangely so was his food dish. Untouched? She glanced around the room and spotted the black cat curled up on the back of the couch, sleeping in the same spot as when she'd left for her run.

"Hey, boy," she called out, reaching for his dish.

He lifted his head at the sound of her voice.

"What's the deal? You don't like Mom's cook—" Claire halted as muddy animal tracks on the deck just outside the glass door caught her eye.

She stepped closer, peering down at them through the glass. A series of dried paw prints that looked more like slender palm prints. Five toes. A raccoon. Right outside Smokey's pet door. He'd smelled it.

Claire glanced back at the one-eared cat, feeling a stab of guilt. She'd moved the dishes gradually closer to the little plastic door on purpose. With a grand plan of moving them outside in the next few weeks so Smokey would be lured into venturing into the world again.

After snatching up the dishes, Claire trundled them over to the couch and set them down. She walked back and slid the stiff resin cover over the pet door, blocking it. Then she went to the fireplace, lifted Kevin's pewter cross from the edge of the picture frame, and fastened it around her neck. The cool metal nestled into the hollow of her throat.

Long-term plans would have to wait. Today was about survival.

+++

Logan turned the bike in one last circle, beeped the horn, and then braked to a stop in a puddle, waving as the old Toyota pulled away from the hospital parking lot. Inside it, Jamie grinned from his car seat and waved back with both hands. Logan smiled. The little guy was barely visible in a backseat crowded with flower arrangements, balloons, and stuffed animals. He'd be missed at Sierra Mercy.

I'll miss him. Logan was once again aware of how this child affected him. Drew him far beyond doctor-patient responsibility. Not something Logan was used to and most likely a result of all the rallying by the hospital staff or because Logan had also treated Jamie's mother after the day care tragedy. *Or because he makes me wonder what it would be like if I had a . . .*

Logan shoved the thought away. He'd promised to say good-bye to Jamie, and he'd done that. He glanced at his watch. And now it was going on ten o'clock. The rain had cleared, and he had the whole day off. He could zip up to Tahoe, hike along the river, eat a steak on the deck at Sunnyside resort, and enjoy the quiet solitude. He scanned the parking lot, and his gaze came to rest on Claire's SUV. Her urgent care shift started in fifteen minutes. Since he was the one who'd put her there, he might as well see how she was doing.

He parked the bike, slipped in the door beside the gift shop, and was heading for the clinic when he passed the partially closed chapel doors. He spotted Claire standing in a circle along with Erin, Glenda, and some of the part-time ER registration staff. All with eyes closed, praying.

He started to chuckle about Erin escalating her God huddles to twice daily when instead he found himself watching Claire. Her beautiful face seemed paler than usual, and a length of dark hair escaped a clip to hang alongside her jaw. Dark lashes nestled against her cheeks, and there was a tiny line of tension between her brows as her lips moved earnestly. A knotted leather string with a metal cross hung around her neck. The one he'd seen at her house on the photo of her brother.

Erin began to speak, and they joined hands. "Father, you've called us to be caregivers. Give us the skills to aid and comfort those in our care so they might know your healing presence. Make our spirits tender, our words compassionate, and our touch gentle. . . ."

Logan exhaled softly, realizing that he'd been holding his breath. He inhaled again to ease an ache in his chest. To the left of center and way down deep. If a patient described the sensation, Logan would order a stat electrocardiogram and a five-grain dose of aspirin. But this had nothing to do with his health. And everything to do with his long, awkward struggle with faith. It was the reason he'd lain awake last night thinking of Jamie. About how the child pressed his small palm over that same spot on Logan's chest and said, "Right in there." A little boy with Jesus in his heart counseling a man who'd stopped praying long ago.

+++

The stump won out over Tahoe, and after three solid hours hefting the ax, Logan felt like a new man. His arms and shoulders ached like he'd wrestled a wildebeest, but the moment he finally let go of the ax, he had a much better grip on his priorities. If he was going to have any peace of mind, he needed to make a couple of important decisions. First, Beckah's wedding. It was in Carmel only a few days from now. She'd invited him months ago and left at least two messages on his machine. *"Are you coming?"* Logan wiped his face on the sleeve of his thermal shirt and groaned. Could he? That was the question.

He shook his head, picked up the sheet of house plans, and walked to the outcropping of granite boulders that would one day be part of his backyard. Thirty yards beyond, the earth dropped steeply away, affording a breathtaking view of the American River gorge and the tree-studded western slope of the Sierra Mountains. Dotted squares of apple orchards gave way to sprawling oaks, then to stands of cedar and, as the altitude climbed, to lofty and majestic pines. His house would be contemporary, utilizing redwood beams and stainless steel cable and slabs of local stone, with an entire wall of energy-efficient glass looking out over a deck to the view beyond. He'd let the acreage remain rustic and natural, a refuge for deer and California quail, with no lawn to mow or formal plantings.

Logan smiled, remembering Beckah's very different idea of a dream house—a midtown Sacramento Victorian fixer-upper with shutters and gables, window boxes full of flowers, old family furniture, hand-stitched pillows . . . and babies. Logan swallowed. He hoped she'd have that now. All of it. That she'd start fresh, remembering only the good parts of the years she'd shared with Logan. What they'd had. *Not what we lost.* How was he supposed to watch Beckah marry another man when he still didn't understand why she left him?

Frustrated, Logan strode back to the oak stump and picked up the ax; he'd chop until dark if he had to. Hack it down to the roots and start quarrying the bedrock beneath. But by the time he lifted the tool to his aching shoulder, he remembered that there were two questions he'd come out here to answer. What he'd do about Beckah's wedding and what he should do about Claire.

Beautiful Claire, the intelligent and determined educator intent on protecting his own staff from him. The ambitious professional with an unwavering career plan and the sensitive woman who fit in his arms—and spoke to his heart—in a way he hadn't believed possible. *"I understand. . . . I care."* Logan raised the ax a few inches from his shoulder, his brows drawing together. There was still the issue of their conflicting views on faith. But maybe he could work around that. Maybe they could find an answer.

He gazed out across his home site, imagining, like so many times before, how it would be one day. But this time he saw scattered clumps of flowers rising among the rocks and grasses, yellow daffodils swaying in the breeze. And Claire's beautiful smile. He set the ax down. Some things didn't take a bushel of wood chips to figure out. Sometimes you had to trust your gut and take a risk.

+++

Just like riding a bike . . . I can do this.

Claire unwrapped the needle set, an 18 gauge—a large enough bore to infuse IV fluids rapidly. This patient was more than a little dehydrated. She glanced at Jada Williams, a twenty-three-year-old who'd been sent to urgent care by her obstetrician because of persistent vomiting. *Beautiful face, sweet smile—and almost as nervous as I am.*

"I'm going to do this as gently as I can," Claire reassured her. "I'll explain everything. So don't worry." Her heart tugged as she watched the mother-to-be bravely extend her right arm while keeping the other hand spread protectively over her barely rounded tummy.

Jada's eyes, dark as a fawn's, lifted to Claire's face, and she sighed. "I've had IVs before. I'm not really afraid. Only for my baby. Over five months along and I'm still sick. It doesn't seem right. My doctor says not to worry, that some women have this problem, but . . ."

"But mothers worry." Claire tore strips of paper tape. "That's a perfectly normal feeling." She wrapped a tourniquet around her patient's arm, just above the elbow, stretching it taut and tucking an edge under to secure it. Then pressed her gloved index finger against Jada's skin, hoping—*oh, please*—to find a decent vein. *Here it comes, thank heaven.* She reached for an iodine prep swab and began wiping concentric circles across Jada's molasses-dark skin. "You've had a recent ultrasound?"

Jada smiled, her eyes lighting up. "Yes. It's a boy. You should have seen his daddy's face when they told us! He's so proud. He was trying to get here today, but he's working three jobs right now." Her smile widened. "Because there's this little house, and we're hoping to buy it. It needs a lot of work, but it's got a backyard and a bedroom perfect for a nursery—my husband's got all these big plans."

"That's so great." Claire nodded, glad to see the smile replacing Jada's earlier anxiety. "Trust me, I know all about making plans." *Plans that are supposed to keep me from being here right now.* She picked up the needle set and removed the cap. "Are you ready to get this done? Your vein looks good, and I'm going to be as gentle as I can. I promise you."

"I'm fine. I just want my baby to be okay."

Claire pressed her finger one last time against the vein, feeling its spongy bounce under her glove, then carefully slid the needle, bevel side up, through the skin and toward the vein. *Please, let there be . . .* She grinned, resisting the urge to shout with relief as blood flashed back into the short length of transparent tubing attached to the needle set. Proof it was in the vein. *Like riding a bike . . .*

"Looks good," Claire said, securing the needle set with a strip of tape and connecting the IV tubing. "I'm just going to finish taping this; then we'll get these fluids flowing. So you and your baby boy will be—" She looked up to give her patient a reassuring smile but stopped short when she saw Jada's eyes filling with tears. "What's wrong? Did I hurt you?" Claire stood and moved close.

"No, I just . . ." She raised her other hand and pointed. "That cross . . . you're a Christian?"

"Yes." Claire's fingers moved to Kevin's pewter cross at the neckline of her scrub top. "Is something wrong?" She raised her brows, sensing that Jada's emotion came from far more than worry over morning sickness.

Jada swallowed. "This will be my first baby, but . . . it's not my first pregnancy. I did something . . ."

Claire's stomach sank and she nodded, understanding all at once the source of her patient's pain. She exhaled softly, then rested her hand on Jada's shoulder.

"I was young and scared, and I made an awful mistake . . . a choice I've regretted every day since. Now with this new child—" her fingers spread across her abdomen—"I know what a precious gift God's given me." Jada's tears spilled over, her eyes searching Claire's. "Would you pray with me? It's not against hospital rules, is it?"

"No," Claire whispered as best she could around the lump in her throat. "Not against any rules at all." She smiled and patted Jada's shoulder. "And better than any medicine we have." She glanced at the drip chamber of the IV, feeling completely humbled; this moment had nothing to do with clinical skills. Yet it had every-thing—*everything*—to do with care and healing. *Thank you, Lord.*

Claire joined hands with Jada and bowed her head.

Ninety minutes later, Claire scanned the clinic's exam rooms from her desk at the nursing station: child with a fever in room one, migraine patient in two, woman with urinary symptoms in three, four was empty, and a teen with mild asthma in five. Everyone in a holding pattern after initial treatment.

She exhaled slowly. So far so good. She was on top of things, and thankfully there had been no Code 3 sirens arriving at the ambulance entrance to rattle her nerves. Glenda, the nurse-practitioner, was confident and efficient, and the nurse's aide more than helpful. Another hour, and Claire could go back to her office in the education department. And call every single agency she could find. Stay until midnight if she had to. She'd find a new nurse for the ER, and Merlene wouldn't make her come back here. Claire was pressing her luck. Even her most challenging task—starting Jada's IV—had been without the pressure of emergency conditions. But what if she were faced with another critical situation like Jamie's?

She looked up as Erin approached the desk.

"Thought I'd better do a welfare check over here," Erin said, sinking onto a rolling stool beside Claire. "Make sure you're not fainting or anything."

Claire froze, her eyes widening. "Why would I . . . ?"

Erin continued, oblivious to Claire's discomfort. "Like Sarah."

"Sarah fainted?" Claire asked, concern mixing with a rush of guilty relief that Erin hadn't been questioning her competence.

"Almost. About half an hour ago. Said she was woozy because she'd skipped lunch. So I had the cafeteria bring her a sandwich, along with a huge slab of banana cream pie." Erin rested her elbows on the desk. "I stood over her while she ate it." She glanced around. "How're you doing over here after being shanghaied by Logan?"

Claire's stomach did a ridiculous dip at the mention of his name. Which gave way to continuing irritation at his insensitive arrogance. *"Put down the phone and pamphlets. . . . You're handling urgent care."* She'd been awake for hours last night, wrestling with anger at him for sending her here. And fear that he'd find out what a mistake he'd made.

Erin watched Claire's face for a moment. "I told him I wasn't sure you'd be willing to do it. I thought you might be uncomfortable doing bedside care."

It was a statement, but Claire could hear the question beneath it, and her throat tightened. Erin knew. Of course she did. She'd been there during Jamie's crisis; she must have noticed Claire's apprehension.

"How long has it been since you worked ER?" Erin asked gently.

Claire's pulse quickened. "Two years." She cleared her throat. "I'd been working on my bachelor's degree in education. And did some part-time work with the Loaves and Fishes clinic in Sacramento. But now I've been getting good experience in the education department, and I've interviewed for the clinical educator position. That's my plan. It's not that I'm unwilling to help you, but . . ." Claire's words faltered. There was no way to explain without dredging up the past. *I can't do that again.*

"No problem. I understand. I really do." Erin smiled warmly. "And I appreciate your being here. But if you need help—need anything—just holler for me, okay?" She reached over and touched Claire's arm. "Besides, I loved having you show up for Faith QD."

Claire smiled, remembering the sense of comfort and the infusion of much-needed confidence she'd felt when gathering with the clinic team in the chapel. "I loved it too. I've missed that kind of fellowship," she said, surprised by her revelation. *It's true. I miss it.*

"Good, then," Erin said, patting Claire's arm. "I only wish Dr. McSnarly could hear you say that. He thinks I'm bribing people with donuts to get them there. The day I lure Logan into that chapel is the day this humble mission goes on the map. Trust me, I've tried." She shook her head. "He said Beckah had wanted them to start going to church together, but . . ."

"Beckah?" Claire adjusted her stethoscope and feigned casual interest despite the fact that her stomach had plummeted. A girlfriend?

"His ex-wife," Erin answered. "I never met her, but I can sure understand what she was trying to do. I see so many solid couples at my church that I have to believe there's a real connection between faith and successful relationships. Maybe it would have made a difference for Logan's marriage."

Except that he doesn't believe in prayer. Since his mother left. And he doesn't trust counseling, either.

Claire blinked, realizing that knowing those things—such intimate things—meant that she already knew Logan Caldwell far better than Erin or likely any of the Sierra Mercy staff. He'd shared those personal insights with her, taken that risk. She knew how vulnerable it felt to do that. Had Logan regretted talking with her? And kissing her? *Is that why he hasn't called?* Claire forced the thoughts aside.

"But then—" Erin pulled at a long strand of her hair and sighed—"what do I really know about relationships?"

"You?" Claire tossed her a teasing smile. "So I imagined those roses in the ER?"

Erin groaned. "You can't know how much I wish Brad hadn't done that. I look at them and it's like a neon sign blinking, 'fool, fool, fool' in flaming red a dozen times over."

Wow. Claire raised her brows, clueless of how to respond. "You mean . . ."

"I only mean those roses came with an apology typed on a florist card by some anonymous person he dictated to over the phone. Long-distance from across the state line no doubt. I met Brad at church. But lately his idea of Sunday morning gatherings is the all-you-can-eat brunch and playing slots at Harrah's. Although I guess I have that to thank for his donation to Jamie's fund—hope it's not all in quarters." Erin frowned and doubled her hand into a fist. "I should install a punching bag in the nurses' lounge; I always feel better after a couple of good jabs." She lowered her hand and smiled. "Sorry. I didn't mean to dump all this on you."

"No, you're not. I guess I assumed when I saw those flowers . . ." Claire spread her hands and shrugged.

"Maybe I'm jaded. I won't bore you with the details, but let's just say that my father isn't going to win any awards for sincerity and honesty. Trust doesn't come easy for me. But just once, I'd like to meet a man who gets it, you know? Gets that it's not about the big show, that simple is fine—no, that simple is *way* better." Erin tapped her finger against her scrub top, in the vicinity of her heart. "A guy who understands that it's what's *right in here* that counts." She pressed her hands together and threw her head back, gazing toward the clinic ceiling. "Show me that guy!" Then she chuckled and turned back to Claire, her eyes playful and warm. "Amen?"

Claire laughed. "Amen," she agreed, feeling a rush of affection for the passionate and gutsy redhead. Erin deserved all that and more.

The sun was setting, tinting the sky purple and orange and pink, by the time Claire set out across the parking lot to where she'd parked Kevin's SUV. She took a deep breath of cool air and exhaled slowly, feeling her shoulders relax for the first time in hours. God must have been listening to her prayers at Faith QD; it felt so good to be there for Jada Williams.

In truth, the worst case she'd faced today was helping Glenda pluck a blue LEGO from the nostril of a two-year-old bucking harder than a rodeo bronc. Claire shook her head, remembering how the mother had insisted the little girl say thank you for their help. Yeah, right. The wary and sniffling child had compromised by waving bye-bye furiously in a blatant attempt to get away as fast as possible.

Claire couldn't help but empathize. She felt the same way. *I'm outta here.* And since Merlene had convinced an on-call nurse to pick up some shifts starting next week, Claire wouldn't be needed in urgent care for more than a couple of days in the interim. Tomorrow was her day off. She'd get up early, take a long run, maybe go to the pet store and find a consolation toy for Smokey after his raccoon scare. Claire stopped as she arrived at the SUV. *What on earth?*

She walked around to the front and lifted a cellophane-wrapped bouquet from the hood. Her breath caught. *Daffodils?* Before she could move, she heard Logan's voice.

"Hi, Educator."

She turned and saw him smile, the fading sunlight casting rosy warmth to his features much the same way the fire embers had that night on her deck.

Logan looked at the bouquet and then at her face, shrugging. "I was at the Jeep store. It's next door to this flower shop. And when I saw those, they made me think of you, so . . ." His brows scrunched. "That's not true."

He took a step closer, and once more Claire was aware of his height, the effect he had on her breathing, and . . .

Logan sighed. His expression seemed vulnerable, his eyes sincere. "The truth is I went looking for those daffodils because I've been thinking about you all day. I have another day off tomorrow, and I want to spend it with you. Would that be okay?"

Claire looked down at the blooms tied with a ribbon and wrapped in paper and thought of Erin's words, the way she'd tapped her fingers over her heart. Simple, heartfelt.

"Yes." She smiled. "I think that would be very okay."

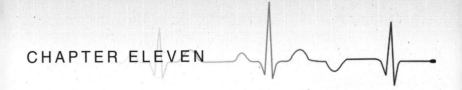

CHAPTER ELEVEN

Oh, man. Logan bit his lip, willing himself not to laugh as the rainbow trout escaped Claire's fingers for a third time. Spotted and silvery pink, it arched and flopped in tall grass along the narrow stretch of the Truckee River. He was too smart to risk laughing, but it took everything he had not to, watching that determined look on her face and her nose wrinkling as she planned her next move. Her cat-like stealth turned into Three Stooges clumsiness by the borrowed rubber wading boots as she grabbed, missed, and grabbed again.

"Need some help . . . there?" Logan asked, his voice rising an octave, then choking on the last word despite his efforts.

"Nope, I'm fine." Claire turned, her eyes narrowing below the brim of her ball cap. "Hey, you're not laughing at me, are you?"

"Me? Do I look that crazy?" Logan leaned back on his elbows on the bank, blinking into the sun and watching as Claire finally got a grip on the slippery fish. He smiled as she released the ten-inch trout into the clear and ice-cold water. "I wouldn't risk laughing at a woman who's beaten me at everything all day. I'm just hoping you don't want to arm wrestle. Frankly my masculinity couldn't take it."

She whirled around, dark ponytail whipping across her shoulders, then planted her hands on her hips and grinned.

This time he did laugh. And warmth flooded through him. *She's so incredible.*

Logan stretched his legs out in front of him, feeling the early afternoon sun seep through the denim, and watched Claire gather her fishing gear. He'd offer to help, but he knew she'd shrug it off. Her independence and spunk were in high gear, and for some reason she seemed far more confident in this environment than at the hospital.

He shook his head. He hadn't been kidding about her besting him all day. She'd climbed like a gazelle up the rocky trail ahead of him, not breaking a sweat, while he'd worked hard to catch up— and struggled to cover the fact that the heart-pounding effects of altitude were limiting his conversation to basic grunts and nods. She'd shinnied agilely down the steep slope to this fishing spot like she'd done it a thousand times before, while he lumbered behind determined not to sit down and slide. She expertly tied the knots on her fishing line—and his—then caught the biggest fish of the day. Even if she couldn't hold on to it.

Logan took a deep breath of pungent alpine air and let his gaze drift, taking in the height of the pines, the speckled granite boulders rising through clumps of red-branched manzanita, and knee-high grasses dotted with wildflowers below blue, blue sky. And the soul-soothing sound of water tumbling over river rocks. He loved it here, and it had always been exactly what he needed when the pressures and turmoil of the ER squeezed in on him. Quiet and solitude.

No, not solitude today. But then this was so much better. Because Claire was so easy to be around. He hadn't expected that. Although cold pizza for breakfast and the hassle-free ease of sharing tube socks four ways, straight out of the dryer, definitely had its benefits, spending much of his life in an all-male household hadn't prepared Logan for dealing with the delicate intricacies of relationships with women. Their sensitivity and exasperating attention to details eluded him, and there was always that white-knuckled need to be careful that things he said and did wouldn't be misinterpreted. Like with Beckah. It had been both mysterious and frustrating, and maybe that's why being with Claire seemed so great. He blinked up into the sun as she appeared.

"So I've intimidated you?" she asked with a smirk. She leaned her pole against a boulder and tossed a pinecone out of the way before sitting beside him.

"Yes, brutally," Logan said, wishing she'd move a few inches closer but completely happy that she was . . . here. It felt better than anything had in a long time, and he wasn't about to mess it up. "Who knew that a nurse with pink scrubs could . . . ?"

"Could what? What exactly am I doing?" Claire asked, her eyes widening in the shadow of the ball cap. "Tell me. Now I'm curious."

And so very beautiful. Her eyes, Logan noticed, were the same soft gray of a dove's wing. Almost a lavender gray, with flecks of white, and lined with those long dark lashes. He blinked, remembering that she'd asked him a question. "I only meant that who knew you had all these outdoor skills? I haven't met many women who can climb rocks and scramble down a cliff without worrying about her clothes or breaking a fingernail. Or who knows how to lock in a Jeep's hubs for four-wheeling, tie a fisherman's knot, and handle salmon eggs and red worms." He raked his fingers through his hair and smiled. "I mean, it's great. You're easy to be around, almost like you're—"

"A guy?" Claire interrupted, her eyes narrowing. "You're saying I'm almost like a guy?"

"No, I didn't mean that at all. I . . ." *Couldn't have said anything more stupid.* "I'm saying I'm having a great time. And that it's cool that you're . . ." Logan groaned, flailing to dig himself out of the hole. "Hey, I'm sorry. I didn't mean to imply—" He stopped, realizing she was laughing.

"I'm kidding." She laughed again as she pulled off her cap and tugged her hair free from the elastic band. It spilled down around her shoulders, shiny as mink in the sunlight. "I know what you meant, and—" her eyes rose to his—"I'm having a great time too. Don't worry."

"Good." He exhaled, not sure how much of his breathlessness was due to mountain altitude and how much was relief. At any rate, he was back on track. "So, where'd you learn to be such a pioneer woman?"

Claire's gaze dropped to the ball cap in her hands. When she looked up again, her beautiful eyes looked achingly sad. "Don't forget that I have . . . *had* . . . a brother."

I'm a fool, Logan thought, using all the restraint he had not to wrap his arms around her.

She was quiet for a moment, and then she reached for her fishing pole. "Didn't you promise me lunch?"

"I did. Pack up your worms, mountain girl. Then give me a decent head start to the Jeep. I know where to find the best burgers in Tahoe."

+++

Erin set her sandwich on the dashboard as Brad handed her a cashier's check, not the rolls of casino quarters she'd half expected to see. It was made out for two hundred and fifty dollars to the Little Nugget Victim Fund.

She looked sideways to where he sat at the wheel of the parked Corvette convertible, afternoon sun glinting off the surface of his sunglasses. It hadn't gone unnoticed, either, that he'd dialed the radio to her favorite station. The rhythm of contemporary Christian music blended in harmony with the distant laughter of children playing in Gold Bug Park. A lunchtime escape, perfect breeze, impromptu picnic in a fabulous car, music that spoke to her soul, and now a generous donation to her favorite charity? All on the heels of that extravagant bouquet of roses. How could she still doubt him?

"Happy now?" Brad asked.

Erin sighed, willing the uncertainty to vanish. "Well, it's really generous. Jamie's mother can definitely use this." *Along with the money that wiped out my checking account.* She smiled with sincere appreciation. "Thank you." She tapped the paper wrapping on her prime rib sandwich. "For all of this. The surprise lunch and the car ride. It's nice."

"Just nice?"

What was she supposed to say? That all this stuff made up for the fact he'd shown up at the children's charity to pressure her into leaving, then taken off to South Tahoe without her? That duct-taping a note to her door was consideration enough? She exhaled slowly to dispel a wave of anger. *Lord, keep one hand on my shoulder and the other one clamped tight over my mouth. Please.* Erin tossed Brad a weak smile, deciding silence was her best option.

"Hmm. Okay, then." Brad pulled off his glasses and pointed toward the glove compartment. "But do something for me, would you? Open that and take out what's inside."

Now what? Erin glanced covertly at her watch before following Brad's instructions. She needed him to drive her back to the

ER. So . . . she opened the glove compartment and lifted out a square, flat box embellished with a shiny gold Angel Store sticker. "Brad . . ."

"Go on. Open it. You'll like it. I promise."

She lifted the lid warily and then murmured with genuine delight. It was beautiful—beads of gold filigree interspersed with crystal on a stretchy band. She lifted it out, letting the charm, a tiny box, dangle and glint in the sunlight. "It's the prayer bracelet! It's wonderful. Exactly the one I'd been wanting. Oh, thank you so much!" She leaned over in the leather seat and brushed her lips against his cheek. Then felt his arms close around her.

"I'm glad I finally got something right," Brad whispered against her ear. "I want to make you happy, Erin." He nuzzled her cheek, then took her face in his hands and lightly kissed her.

"I . . . well, thank you." Erin leaned away. "But I've got to get back to work. Really. I have to relieve Sarah for her break, finish writing my agenda for the staff meeting, and put up flyers in the nurses' lounges about Faith QD. . . ." She let her words trail away when she saw him frown.

"You've got to cut back. I keep telling you that. You need to learn to have some fun." He slipped on his glasses, started the Corvette's powerful engine, and raised his voice to be heard. "We'll start Sunday morning. Drive to Reno and catch the car races. Think about it." He retrieved her sandwich from the dashboard and steered away from the curb.

Sunday. Meaning church didn't figure into his plans—again. She nudged the tiny prayer box with her finger, her emotions tumbling faster than the Corvette took the corners. Guilt over her continuing doubts despite Brad's obvious attempts to please her, anger at his lack of consideration for her priorities, and a continued wistful longing for what she'd talked about with Claire yesterday. Men with sincere hearts. They'd agreed completely, almost like long-lost sisters, and she'd loved that feeling.

Erin grasped the door handle to keep from sliding as Brad took the last of the curves before the straightaway leading into the Sierra Mercy Hospital parking lot. She peered at him for a moment and smiled, picturing a teeny slip of paper tucked into the beautiful little prayer box. She tapped her finger over her heart, imagining words printed in the smallest of type: *Help Brad understand that what counts is right in* here. Yes. She'd give it to God.

She tapped her heart once more for good measure as they roared up to the doors of the ER.

+++

Claire stopped at the doorway leading onto the marina restaurant's deck, catching a glimpse of Logan in the distance. She shook her head. What she'd thought that first day she'd met him in the ER was true; his eyes were exactly the blue of Lake Tahoe. In fact, right now . . . She studied his face as he spoke with the waitress, dappled sunshine spilling across the shoulders of his rugby shirt and unruly curls, his rugged features silhouetted against the beautiful vista of the alpine lake. Claire's breath caught. She'd been wrong; his eyes were bluer than Tahoe.

What about the other things she'd thought about him that first day when they'd butted heads over her staff interviews? Had she been wrong about those too? She'd thought him insensitive, a bully, a callous, unbending Goliath. The enemy. And had been beyond angry when he'd mentioned weak links. Still was.

Claire stepped out of the way of a waitress and then saw Logan waving at her. She waved back and walked toward him, a thought making her smile. *Supping with the devil again.* But maybe it was the risk she'd have to take if she was going to learn more about this man. She had to admit that there were things she was curious about. His interests, his family . . . Beckah?

"See," she said, settling into the chair opposite Logan and raising palms still damp from washing. "Perfectly respectable. No one would know I—" she smirked—"caught the biggest trout of the day." She laughed and glanced around the umbrella-studded deck and at the other patrons, glad she'd been able to freshen her makeup and pick the pine needles out of her hair.

Sunnyside Mountain Grill, a favorite with both locals and tourists, was casually upscale with men and women sporting trendy resort wear and sunglasses no doubt worth half a nurse's biweekly paycheck. A jazz combo played at the edge of the deck, its bass-heavy music blending with soft laughter, tinkling glassware, and the crisp flutter of sails in the marina below. In the distance, the majestic Sierra Mountains, peaks white with snow, seemed to rise from the glassy blue surface of the lake itself.

Claire closed her eyes for a moment, letting the sun warm her face and inhaling the wonderful mix of scents: pine trees, oiled decking, coconut sunscreen . . . and sizzling orders of burgers and fries. Her stomach rumbled and she smiled. This was not her typical day, for sure. She opened her eyes as Logan spoke.

"So, what would you be doing right now if you weren't here, humbling me with your fishing skills?"

Claire laughed. "Huge, important things. Like buying Smokey a catnip toy. The one that looks like Jiminy Cricket. That might get him to purr." She frowned. "The poor cat had another raccoon scare."

"You mean—?"

"No, he's okay," Claire said quickly. "But there were footprints on the deck outside his little pet door, and he was clinging to the back of the couch like the whole house was surrounded." She sighed. "Sometimes I think I should have sent Smokey to Phoenix with my folks."

"You're from Arizona?" Logan leaned back as the waitress presented their plates.

"No." Claire smiled, realizing he'd already beaten her to the punch in the get-to-know-you inquisition. "I'm a local. Sacramento. My dad took a job transfer to Phoenix after . . . my brother died." She grabbed a fried zucchini stick, crispy and hot, and pointed it at Logan, determined to turn the conversation back to him. "And your family, Dr. Caldwell?"

Logan lowered his Angus burger. "Still in the San Jose area. My father has two small hardware franchises now and hasn't remarried. One of my brothers manages the businesses for him, and the younger one is pretending to go to Foothill College but spends most of his time playing bass guitar for a country band. Silicon Posse. They're not half bad. I go see them as often as I can. And . . ."

Claire leaned forward. *And Beckah Caldwell? Where is she? Do you see her too?*

"That's it for my immediate family." Logan raised his brows, gesturing at her rapidly disappearing halibut sandwich. "Aha, we see yet another impressive thing about Claire Avery: her hearty— and completely feminine—appetite."

"True." Claire chuckled. "I'm never going to be the woman who faints from skipping a meal. Like Sarah yesterday. In fact, people would accuse me of—"

"Whoa. Back up." Logan's eyes clouded with concern. "What happened to Sarah?"

Sarah glanced toward the doors of the nursery conference room and then continued checking the contents of the neonatal emergency crash cart. It was a perfect time to do it, with most of the nursing staff at their monthly meeting. This way she could be certain everything was in order and do it discreetly enough that the staff wouldn't think she doubted their competence. There was no room for even the smallest error when a baby's life was at stake. She could get this completed and buy a carton of yogurt from the cafeteria on her way back. So Erin wouldn't go all mother hen again about skipping meals. She sighed. Not that yesterday's near faint had been only about food. But she couldn't let Erin know about the insomnia, the wine, and the sleeping pills.

The pills—one at bedtime, then another half pill at 2 a.m.—were the reason she'd been late this morning. Late. For the first time since she'd started working at Sierra Mercy. Twenty-three minutes late because she'd slept through both of her alarms. It still made her sick to think about it. Erin had graciously brushed it off, but Sarah couldn't stop the painful rush of what-ifs. What if someone had come in under CPR and the defibrillator failed? What if a baby started choking and the suction machine wasn't connected properly? *What if it was my fault? All of it?*

Sarah snapped the guide blade into the laryngoscope handle and watched its tiny bulb light, proving its readiness to aid in the insertion of an infant breathing tube. She repeated the process for all the blades and all the bulbs, then took one more look at the gauges on the oxygen tanks and nodded with satisfaction.

After closing the last drawer of the crash cart, she stared at it for a moment, smiling. The rolling cart, red metal with half a dozen lockable drawers, was actually the same kind mechanics used, that

Sarah's father always used down at the body shop. She'd explained that to him once and he'd gotten a kick out of it, saying doctors could learn a thing or two from mechanics. He always joked that way, always had a ready smile and a hug and an encouraging word. *Does he remember it's almost his granddaughter's birthday?*

She turned to look through the window of the nursery at the neat rows of infant carts. Their bundled occupants were in various states of wakefulness: some red-faced and squalling, some peaceful with lips puckering in their sleep, and some squinting at the overhead lights. All achingly precious. Each requiring infinite care and protection.

Sarah checked her watch as she walked toward the elevators. She had time to get the yogurt and be back from her lunch break early. And then she'd stick around the ER another half hour or so after she clocked out tonight to make up for being late. She couldn't let it happen ever again. Erin didn't deserve that; she was too good of a charge nurse to be burdened with sloppy staff. Sarah would sleep better after Emily's birthday passed. Meanwhile, she'd be careful with those pills. She wouldn't be late again. She couldn't let Logan down.

+++

"It's been great," Logan said, steering the Jeep into the grocery store parking lot where they'd arranged to meet this morning. He pulled in next to Claire's SUV and left the engine running. "And I . . ." *Don't want to let you drive away.* So why was he? Why was he letting her gather her things, sort her fishing gear from his, fumble with those rubber boots? "No, Claire. Don't do that."

"What? Oh, are these your salmon eggs?" She looked up, lips parting and cheeks pink from a day in the sun.

Logan's heart thudded in his ears. *Don't go.*

Claire held up the jar of fluorescent orange bait. "Did I take yours by mistake?"

"No," Logan said, his voice sounding as breathless as it had when he'd clambered after her on that mountain trail early this morning. "I'm saying the only mistake is ending this day. I mean, hey, it's not late—it's barely six. We could . . ." He smiled foolishly, his mind a complete vacuum. "Let's go do something else, okay?"

Claire bit her lip, and Logan knew she was trying not to laugh at him. He waited, half expecting her to beg off and say she had to go buy Smokey's toy or run a marathon before dark, that she'd already spent way too much time with him. But he had to try. *Stay with me, Claire.*

She narrowed her eyes. "Where? Where would you take me?"

The idea came to Logan as naturally as breathing, though it had never occurred to him to take any woman there before. Hadn't wanted to. Until now.

"To my land . . . my building site," he said. "I want to show you the sunset."

CHAPTER TWELVE

Claire rested her palm on the sun-warmed granite boulder and gazed across the vista, awed by its beauty. Mountaintop after mountaintop brushed with late afternoon sunlight like molten gold, tree-dotted valleys of purple and indigo, scattered meadows of green, and the river slicing through the gorge below . . .

She spread her arms wide and turned back. "It's . . ." She shook her head helplessly, feeling a wave of dizziness. "I can't even find the words."

Logan's smile widened and spread to crinkle the edges of his eyes, and Claire sensed that her breathless attempt at words had been exactly what he'd hoped for.

"Wait until you see the sunset. But first, let me show you this." He held up a rolled sheet of paper. "My house plans."

They pulled camp chairs from the back of the Jeep, along with their jackets and the containers of coffee and oatmeal cookies they'd bought en route—treats Claire insisted on paying for this time. Then she followed Logan as he paced off the perimeters of his rooms and described in detail the solar heating system, the redwood and steel cable decks, a ceiling-high river rock fireplace, and even a future golden retriever—likely named Scout in honor of his first dog—who'd doze in front of it one day.

Logan stopped and pointed skyward. "You can't believe the stars I can see from here. I'm thinking of putting in a skylight, right up . . . there." He looked at Claire, tapping the house plans. "We're standing in the master bedroom."

"Oh." Claire glanced away, fighting a teen-worthy blush and realizing that her wish to know more about this man couldn't have come truer. Even if he hadn't broached the subject of his past marriage, Logan was sharing something just as intimate—his future plans, his hopes, his dream dog . . . and bedroom skylight. Claire cleared her throat. "And I see that you also have a sizable oak stump in the middle of your floor."

"Tell me about it." Logan groaned. "Are you as good with an ax as you are with a fishing pole?"

They laughed and set their chairs side by side on what would one day be a deck, then dug into the cookies and coffee while waiting for the sunset. Claire leaned her head back, closing her eyes and thinking that this time with Logan, which had been penciled nowhere on her long list of plans, had been perfect. From the daffodils on the hood of the SUV last night to that ridiculous tussle with the trout, lunch in Tahoe . . . all of it. And there was nothing more she needed to hear about Logan or his past. It was enough to be sitting here close enough that their shoulders brushed, ready to share a sunset. Claire glanced at Logan out of the corner of her eye and saw his eyes were closed too and that his lips had curved into a half smile. Maybe he was thinking the same thing about their day.

"Beckah would change everything about this house," he said, opening his eyes.

Huh? Claire's breath stuck in her chest. What on earth was she supposed to say to that?

Nothing apparently, since Logan continued without looking her way. "My ex-wife," he explained. "I can see it now. She'd have French doors, painted shutters, stained glass, and Victorian birdcages in the breakfast room."

"Your ex-wife . . . liked . . . birds?" Claire asked, knowing that the silly question would completely derail his train of thought. But she wanted to respond in a gentle way so as not to appear intrusive. No, that wasn't it. That wasn't it at all. Claire nearly groaned at the irony. For days she'd been dying to know more about Beckah Caldwell. *But now I don't want him to talk about her. I don't want to think of him ever having a wife.*

Logan laughed and turned toward Claire. "Ever step into a tub and find a pair of finches perched on the showerhead? It was bad enough we didn't have a real shower and the showerhead was so low I had to stoop down to wash my hair, but . . ." His voice faded into a chuckle and he shook his head. "Yeah, you might say she has a thing for birds."

Has. Present tense. *Because he still talks to her.* Claire glanced at the mountains. Suddenly she wanted the sunset over and done with. So she could go home to Smokey and go to work tomorrow, then go on doing anything else but listening to Logan talk about—

"Beckah and I are two different kinds of people," Logan said, his expression growing serious. "And we didn't want the same things out of life. I should have paid more attention to that." He shrugged slightly and his shoulder moved against Claire's. "If I had, we might not have gotten married."

"Um . . ." Claire reminded herself to breathe. Unfortunately she'd gotten exactly what she'd asked for in this awkward conversation. Logan wanted to talk about his ex-wife. So be it. "How long were you married?" she asked as casually as she could after taking a sip of her coffee.

"Almost three years. Seemed shorter. Probably because I was working an insane number of hours. Commuting between hospitals in three different cities to pay down my student loans, studying for the Emergency Medicine Boards, and . . ." He sighed. "You know how this business is."

"I do," she answered with complete sincerity.

"Well, she didn't . . . doesn't. That was part of it, I suppose. She's from a family with seven kids. With those Sunday suppers where you risk being stabbed with a fork if you try to reach for more than your share of meat loaf?" He smiled. "Nah, really, they're great people. Beckah's mother especially. They made me feel like part of the family from the very beginning. I'm sure that had a lot to do with it."

Claire's throat tightened, imagining Logan in that warm setting after a childhood filled with loneliness. It must have seemed like a second chance at having a complete family. *It had everything to do with that, Logan.* She nodded, watching him take a sip of his coffee. "What does Beckah do? I mean, does she work?" Claire realized with surprise that she was now feeling concern for a wife whose husband was never home.

"She's a preschool teacher." Logan broke an oatmeal cookie and handed Claire the larger half. "And she's really good at it. Finches in the shower and dozens of finger paintings taped to the wall of our kitchen." He gazed out toward the mountains, quiet for a few seconds. "She wants at least four children."

Like Gayle did. Claire swallowed, thinking of Kevin's fiancée and so many dreams that never came to be. The sun was lowering in the sky, and Claire watched as the gold deepened on the mountaintops.

Logan turned to look at Claire, the emotion on his face difficult to read. Was it concern, confusion . . . regret? "Maybe she'll have that chance now."

Claire raised her brows, not certain what he meant.

"She's getting married. On Saturday," he whispered.

"Ah." Claire nodded, not knowing what she could say after a statement like that or what Logan wanted her to say. The sunset couldn't come fast enough, because she did know one thing for sure now. *Logan still has deep feelings for his ex-wife.*

+++

Erin pressed her eyebrow tweezers into the tiny filigree box, tamping a last strip of paper down against the half-dozen others. *Stay there this time.* She held her breath and reached for the miniscule latch of the prayer bracelet charm. Before she could close it, the fan-folded strip of paper sprang upward like a child's jack-in-the-box. Erin moaned. *More like Brad-in-the-box.*

The paper, fortune cookie thin, was Erin's printed prayer that Brad was the kind of man she might have a future with one day. A man she could finally trust with her heart. It was the very same thing she'd prayed for with the last guy she dated, the guy before that, and every doomed relationship she'd had in the last ten years. All the frogs that flunked Prince 101. Was it possible she was destined to meet every bad egg in northern California? *Or is it . . . me?*

Erin stood and left the bracelet lying on the bed next to her red leather boxing gloves, sighing as she walked into the living room. She pushed aside her roommate's newest stack of bridal magazines and curled up on the couch, wondering if it was time to admit the ugly truth. Erin was nearly thirty-two, and if she was ever going to find someone to love, *she* was the one who had to change.

The froggy brotherhood hadn't been shy in offering plenty of advice along those lines. Usually in a last indignant croak when Erin broke things off. All she had to do was stop being so opinionated, independent, stubborn, judgmental, devoted to her family, loyal to her friends, obsessed with her career, quick to lead a cause, short-tempered, bossy, and religious. She glanced at her tabbed Bible lying on the coffee table next to her newest study workbook. *Too religious?* How on earth could she have a relationship with someone who didn't understand that she was far from being the Christian she wanted to be?

She thought of her starry-eyed and newly engaged roommate's gentle advice. "Don't be so picky. Don't get riled up about the small things—no one's perfect. Any counselor will tell you that successful relationships are all about compromise."

Compromise. Erin wove her fingers through her thick hair, lifting it from the shoulders of her hooded sweatshirt, and thought about Brad's plans for Sunday. Compromise would mean someone else would sit beside her recently widowed grandmother at church. It would mean missing her ten-year-old nephew's colorful account of the Scout troop pinewood derby and her pregnant sister's photo from her first ultrasound. It would mean trading all that for a smoky and crowded Reno breakfast buffet, followed by three hours of shouting to make conversation over the roar of stock car engines.

Erin let her hair fall back to her shoulders. Not that the Reno races weren't exciting and fun, but Brad knew how important Sundays were to Erin. Her schedule only allowed her to be off every other weekend, making that one family day all the more precious. Didn't that matter? Was it impossible to find someone who understood things like that?

Once again she reminded herself of Brad's kindness to her mother, his generous contribution to Jamie's fund, and his recent questions about church membership classes. Then she reminded herself that they'd been dating only a few months and that not all men were like Dad.

She pushed the thought aside and then nodded decisively. She was sticking to the promise she'd made herself. To have more patience and leave judgments where they belonged—in God's hands. Brad was trying, and so would she. She was going to risk trusting him. Even if she had to go three rounds with her punching bag every night to keep herself from a frustration meltdown. She'd give Brad the benefit of the doubt.

Meanwhile, Erin had other problems to solve. She needed to go over her grandmother's credit card statements. There was no way Nana authorized those ridiculous charges. And then she'd reread the RN résumés. She and Merlene finally had some qualified applicants for the ER position. Logan would find something wrong with every single one of them, though.

Erin groaned. At her cynical worst, she wasn't even close to being as picky as Logan. That poor man was never going to find someone to love.

+++

Logan watched the fading sun, sitting close enough to Claire that he could feel her shoulder stiffening against his, and wondered why in the world he'd spent the last ten minutes talking about his ex-wife. He'd heard somewhere that was a huge taboo in dating. So was he really that much of an idiot? To be sitting beside this beautiful and intelligent woman, after one of the best days he'd had in years, after sharing his house plans, minutes from a spectacular sunset . . . and end up talking about something as pointless as birds in a shower? And the wedding on Saturday. Why had he done that? More importantly, what could he do to make Claire comfortable again?

"The sun's finally starting to move down," Claire said with a second furtive glance at her watch. "Not much longer."

She's acting like she can't wait to go home. Say something. "I'm glad. I mean, I'm glad you're here to see it with me." He smiled, noticing that the fading sunlight was making Claire's gray eyes turn sort of smoky lavender. "You're the first person I've ever brought here to see it."

She smiled back, and Logan knew with a rush of relief that he'd finally said something right. *Telling her the truth feels right.* Maybe that was why he'd said those things about Beckah. Not that he was planning to do it again.

"Well, then I'm glad too." Claire's smile widened. "Although—" she lifted a brow, her voice taking on a teasing tone—"I'd half expected to find a path worn by the feet of single women."

Logan laughed. "Yeah, maybe by the feet of a dozen nurses waving picket signs and shouting curses. All led by our chief of staff."

"You mentioned being called on the carpet. What was it about?"

"Same old, same old. Another complaint from another nurse." Logan ticked the specifics off on his fingers. "I'm insensitive, critical, expect way too much, and am completely unappreciative. I'm the devil incarnate—" He stopped, hearing Claire's sudden laugh.

"Sorry," she said, pressing her cookie against her lips. "Really, go on."

Logan frowned, feigning insult. "That was it. You think there should be more?"

"No, not at all." Claire furrowed her brows like she was rethinking the quick dismissal. "Only that maybe . . ."

"Only what?" Logan prompted, realizing he cared what she thought. Very much.

Claire pursed her lips and then exhaled. "I was going to ask if you've ever considered easing up on your staff a little."

"Easing up?" He stared at her.

"Yes," Claire said, lifting her chin as she met his gaze. "Easing up, lightening up, throttling back. Whatever you want to call it. Put yourself in the nurses' shoes for once."

"In their . . ." Logan hesitated, telling himself to go slowly. Whatever he said here could be very dicey. There was more at stake than the doctor-nurse relationship.

"I haven't forgotten what you said about the buck stopping with you," she continued, spreading her hands. "It's obviously true. As a doctor, you're ultimately responsible for a patient's outcome. But have you considered that the nurses feel just as accountable? That we're as much under the gun in a critical situation as you are? Maybe more than you are?"

"More?" *Oh, boy, here we go.*

"You bet. Think about it. You have a critically ill patient, and as a doctor, you make an assessment and a treatment plan—granted, a brilliant plan—then you give orders and walk away. Who's left at that patient's bedside? Who's injecting complex drugs into his bloodstream, watching for dangerous side effects and all the while trying to say something, anything, to ease the fear in that poor soul's eyes? Trying to convince him that it will be all right, when you know that at any given moment something could go wrong." Claire sighed and looked into Logan's eyes. "Nurses. You'd be lost without them."

Logan raised his hands in surrender. "Hey, truce. I'm not about to argue with that. In fact, Erin and Sarah are among the best nurses I've ever worked with. I'm not kidding when I say I'd like to clone them. But . . ."

"But what?"

"It's competence I'm talking about. There's a huge difference between being there and being competent to be there." Logan scrunched his brows. Surely Claire could understand that; she'd worked ER herself. "Take that nurse who was working the day of the day care incident."

"The one who threatened to quit?"

"Yes. And you want to know why? Because she couldn't handle it. Because I told her to get a grip or get out of my department." He shook his head, feeling the anger return. "The paramedics are off-loading this little girl who's been trapped in a burning building, who's just stopped breathing. *Stopped breathing.* They're trying to control her airway; we're scrambling to get things going, and then this nurse starts panicking. Wailing like a civilian. And becomes completely and totally useless to me. I'm trying to save burn victims, and I've got a useless nurse! You understand what I'm saying, don't you?"

Claire didn't answer, and when Logan turned in his chair, he saw that her face had gone completely pale. Her eyes were wide, pupils dilated. What's wrong? What did he . . . ? *Oh no. Burn victims. Her brother.*

"Yes," she whispered. "I understand."

"Claire, wait." Logan twisted his chair so he could reach her and took hold of her hands. "I'm a fool," he said, rubbing her cold hands gently between his. He had to make this better. "I'm sorry. I should have thought about your brother before I said that."

"No, don't." Claire slid her hands away from his and shut her eyes for a few seconds. Then she took a deep breath. "Don't apologize, Logan. Please. Just listen. I need to explain something."

+++

Claire couldn't believe what she was doing, but she had no choice. Having this conversation without explaining felt like continuing a lie. She took another breath and let it out slowly, but her insides kept trembling. "I was that nurse. I panicked too. Back then."

Logan leaned forward again, started to reach for her hand but stopped himself. "It's not the same thing. You shouldn't have had to see your brother like that." He glanced away for a second, a muscle on his jaw tensing. "No one should have to see someone they love like that. You couldn't be expected to function as a nurse in that situation."

Claire wanted more than anything to stop there. To let it rest and move into Logan's arms for the comfort he so obviously wanted to give her. But she couldn't. There was more to say. *Confessions of incompetence to the doctor who hates that above all things.* Claire muttered under her breath, "It wasn't only that day."

Logan's forehead wrinkled with confusion. "Meaning?"

"I panicked over and over. Every ER shift I worked from then on. I couldn't keep my hands from shaking. I'd walk over to the medicine cupboard and completely forget what I was there for. I'd jump out of my skin every time I heard a siren. I was . . . *useless.* Exactly what you called that other nurse just now." Claire's lips tightened as she struggled against a surge of anger. Where had that come from?

Logan winced, and Claire was instantly sorry. *What am I doing?* What had she been about to do, compare Logan to the Sacramento doctor who'd shredded her confidence after Kevin's death? That was completely unfair. The only things Logan had done were . . . wonderful. He'd given her a day like she hadn't had in years, made her laugh, brought her up here to show her his house and the sunset. And now she was trying to spoil it?

Claire squeezed Logan's hand. "I'm sorry," she said, managing a smile. "All that was a long time ago, and none of it had anything to do with you. Really, I'm sorry, Logan."

He brushed his thumb across the top of her hand, and the tenderness in his expression made Claire's heart ache. "There's nothing to apologize for," he said simply. Then he turned and pointed toward the range of mountains turning pink, purple, and orange. "It looks like we're about to have that sunset I promised you."

Claire felt Logan's arm slide around her shoulders. Then the thought hit her: She'd just told him things she hadn't told any other person. Painful parts of her past she'd been afraid to tell anyone but God. It seemed so impossible, yet at the same time completely natural. And as comfortable as Logan's warmth beside her.

They watched silently as the sun slipped behind the mountains and dusk began closing in around them. In minutes, it would be dark and Logan would drive her back to her car. Claire didn't want the day to end. She turned at Logan's voice. He was standing.

"C'mon," he said, offering his hand. "Let me show you the lights on the river."

Claire took his hand and they walked over to stand beside the granite boulders, their surfaces now shadowy in the diminishing light. Below, the sunset's last colors glinted on the surface of the American River like metallic threads in a little girl's hair ribbon. Lights began to dot the banks above.

"It's beautiful," Claire said, very aware of her hand inside

Logan's. "The sunset, the river, your house—this whole day." She blinked against unexpected tears and looked at Logan. "Thank you so much."

Logan let go of her hand and brushed a strand of hair away from the side of her face, trailing his fingers gently along her jaw. "You," he said, tracing his thumb across her chin, "are the very best part of today." Logan leaned down and touched his lips first to the side of Claire's face and then lightly to the corner of her mouth, the warmth of the connection making her breath catch. Then he leaned away just far enough to look into her eyes, as if asking for permission.

Somehow Claire managed the barest nod, and when Logan kissed her again, she wound her arms around his neck, feeling his silky curls under her fingers. His arms slid around her waist, drawing her close as the kiss deepened. And she returned it measure for measure.

+++

Logan waited as Claire unlocked her car door, then took hold of her hand, thinking once again how perfectly this woman fit in his arms. *In my life?* He didn't want anything to ruin the chance it could be true. Blast, he didn't even want to let her go right now. "So," he said, squeezing her hand, "these big plans you have for your career—that's all local, right?"

"Local?"

"I meant you're not planning to climb the nursing education ladder in, say, Phoenix?"

"No," she said with a short laugh. "Not that my folks haven't been trying to finagle that, trust me. But it looks fairly certain I'll get the educator position at Sierra Mercy." She sighed. "At least that's my plan. I've been praying about it forever."

Praying. There was still that faith hurdle and . . . He looked at Claire, realizing that she'd said something. "I'm sorry. What was that?"

"I said it helps me."

"What?"

"Praying."

Oh, boy. Logan shrugged. "That's good. I'm . . . glad."

"And uncomfortable?"

Logan opted for the truth. "You mean about the subject of prayer?" He saw Claire nod. "No, prayer doesn't make me uncomfortable. I see it all the time with our patients. And there's Erin, of course. She's waving prayer around my ER like a personal battle flag. Not to mention advertising it on T-shirts. You haven't seen me trying to stop her, have you?"

"No." Claire smiled, watching him intently.

"But I'll be honest. I'm okay with God, but for me prayer doesn't work." Logan rubbed his brow. "Beckah started going to church after we broke up. She said things like 'Let go and let God.' You've heard that?"

"Sure."

"Well, I get the concept. But for me, letting go is giving up. I don't do that very well. It's like in the ER: a heart fibrillates, and I shock it with electricity; a severed artery cuts loose, I clamp it off before someone bleeds to death; a patient stops breathing, so I breathe for him. I do something always. I don't let go. I don't solve it with prayer. By blindly trusting that . . ." Logan let his words trail away, sure he'd said more than Claire wanted to hear. Aware too that he may have sealed the deal against her ever seeing him again.

Suddenly she stepped close and wrapped her arms around him, burrowing her face against his chest.

"Hey, what's that for?" He chuckled against her hair, relief washing over him.

"It's a good-night hug, Dr. Caldwell. We both have to work in the morning."

She stepped away, and Logan had a hard time reading her expression in the darkness. He needed to know what she was thinking. "Those plans that you've been praying about," he said, already missing the feel of her in his arms. "I was wondering if there's any room in there for me?" He tipped his head to get a better look at her face. "May I see you again, Claire?"

Her quick smile made his heart race. "Yes. But right now we'd both better get home. I have to do a final critical incident follow-up with the ER staff tomorrow. And I hear the doctor in charge is an impossible beast."

Logan frowned. "Hey. C'mon now. Am I really that bad?"

Claire's lips curved into a smirk. "Jury's still out."

+++

Sarah shivered inside the darkened phone booth and wished she'd thought to wear a sweater. She pressed the receiver to her ear and listened to the distant rings, knowing she wouldn't notice the cold—even if this gum-sticky and littered phone booth froze completely solid—once she heard her father's voice. *Daddy, please.*

She nodded, her chin quivering. The chances were better from a pay phone. No caller ID for her mother to screen. More chance that she'd think it was a telemarketer and continue to watch her TV show, yelling for her father to pick it up.

The rings continued . . . four, five, six . . . and then Sarah heard the message—her mother's voice—saying no one was home, have a nice day, and God bless you.

Sarah closed her eyes, holding the receiver against her chest as the line went dead. She needed her father more than she ever had before. It was almost Emily's birthday. And she wasn't sure she would make it this time.

CHAPTER THIRTEEN

Claire sank back against her pillow, smiling as the dawn brushed her windowsill melon pink, like paint on a fresh new canvas. She buried her fingers in her sleep-tangled hair and sighed, awed by two things. First, that she'd now spent a consecutive sunset and sunrise with Logan Caldwell filling her thoughts. Second—even more amazing—the fact that for the first time since she'd started whispering that prayer for healing, Claire had begun to feel it being answered.

Last night, when Logan kissed her and held her close, the emptiness in her chest had eased, its painful hollowness filled by something new. A warm and achy-good feeling. But . . . She glanced at the open Bible on her bedside table. How could someone live without the comfort and connection of prayer? She thought of Jada's heart-tugging need that day in the clinic. Could Logan be okay with God without ever praying to him? Could a lonely, motherless boy become a man . . . a husband without believing that God listens? *And could I love a man who—?*

Claire's eyes opened wide and her stomach fluttered. Love? Where did that come from? She shook her head. Love was nowhere in her plans. Brushing her teeth and getting to work? Absolutely. It was time to get moving.

Ten minutes later she pulled on navy yoga pants and a matching hooded sweatshirt, then slid into her flip-flops and padded toward the kitchen, stopping when she heard insistent tapping at the front door. She crossed to the door and swung it open, stunned.

"Good morning." Logan stood on the porch, wearing a University of California sweatshirt over faded jeans and looking like he was barely awake, with dark beard stubble, mussed hair, and his eyes half-lidded. He held a cardboard tray of coffee and a huge deli sack, and when he smiled, Claire's knees went so weak she had to steady herself on the doorframe.

She smiled back and managed to speak, her voice a breathless squeak. "Logan, this is so . . . early."

He nodded, grinning like a proud ten-year-old. "I know. I took a chance you'd be awake."

"And that I'd be hungry?" She eyed the bag in his hands, sniffing appreciatively at the aroma of steaming coffee.

Logan laughed. "Not much risk there." He raised his brows. "So, am I coming in?"

"Um, sure." Claire walked ahead of Logan into the kitchen, her mind a complete jumble—thinking her hair must look a mess, grateful she'd brushed her teeth, planning what she'd say, what she shouldn't say, and telling herself not to get her hopes up that Logan's coming here meant any more than—

She stopped and turned to him. "Why are you here?"

He blinked and pointed to the deli bag he'd set on the table. "Breakfast?"

"I mean, don't you have to be at the ER in . . ." Claire glanced at Kevin's football clock. "Twenty-five minutes?"

Logan repeated the proud smile. "I got the night doc to stay over for a couple of hours."

"But . . ." Claire stared at him, a man who was always early for his shifts, had been rumored to spend the night in his office, shower and shave in the surgeons' lounge, and didn't trust anyone to fill in for him.

"Because," Logan said, stepping closer to gently grasp Claire's shoulders, "I didn't want to wait hours to see you again." He took a breath, the look in his eyes warm and honest. "I couldn't wait. There's something about being with you that feels good, Claire. You make me feel kind of optimistic about things. I can't explain it. But I haven't felt that way in a long time. I like it." He shook his head, chuckling. "I'm not making any sense, am I?"

Perfectly wonderful sense. Claire nodded, afraid to speak over the lump in her throat. She moved into Logan's arms, sighing as he hugged her close. That amazing feeling was there again, warm, new, and tender. But fragile too, like a glistening spray of bubbles from a child's party wand. She didn't want to do or say anything that might end this feeling. Tears threatened as the truth hit her. *Lord, help me please. I think I'm falling in love.*

Then Logan stepped back, cradled her face in his palms, and kissed her thoroughly.

+++

Logan let the motorcycle idle at the edge of Gold Bug Park. He still had thirty minutes before he was expected to take over at the ER. Claire had shooed him out after breakfast, saying she needed to go for a run before work. Probably true. And had nothing to do with his bumbling attempt to express his feelings. *"You make me feel kind of optimistic about things."*

Logan's groan bounced off the inside of his helmet. Had he really said something that idiotic? Idiotic but true. Claire did make him feel hopeful, and she couldn't know how important and incredibly rare that was at this particular moment in his life. What he'd wanted to say to her was much more romantic and spontaneous. But way too corny. He'd wanted to tell her the moment she'd opened the door that she was the most beautiful woman he'd ever met. That he'd lain awake for hours remembering the way the sunset had seemed to change the color of her eyes, and . . . Logan shook his head. Never could have pulled that off. Better to hand a hungry woman a ham and cheese bagel.

Despite the fact that he was no poet, they'd had a great time this morning. Talking, laughing . . . he'd even managed to pet the one-eared cat without losing a finger. Best of all, being with Claire again convinced Logan that she was good for him.

In fact, she may have already helped him make a big decision. He wasn't going to Beckah's wedding. The confusing pull to be there didn't feel so strong now. Maybe it wasn't important to understand why she'd left him. Seeing Beckah walk down the aisle in a Carmel wedding chapel wouldn't accomplish that anyway. She'd left him because she didn't want to stay. Period. Anything beyond that would remain a mystery, the same as it had with his mother. And it was okay. At twelve years old, there hadn't been anything Logan could do about his mother. Except pray to a God who didn't listen. There hadn't been anything more he could have done to help Beckah after the miscarriage. Logan flinched at the memory of Beckah's pale face and tearful voice. *"Where's your faith, Logan?"*

How many times had he patiently explained that attending church together would have been as futile as the counseling? that it couldn't change anything? Some things just happened, that's all. The important thing was to get past it. Trust yourself to get tough and move on. Logan put the bike back in gear and twisted the throttle. He'd e-mail Beckah. That would be easier. He'd wish her happiness—he did, absolutely—and that would bring an end to it. It was good to finally make a decision.

Now all he had to worry about was the new nurse Merlene Hibbert was trying to force down his throat. Logan smiled. And how he was going to keep a professional distance when the beautiful educator walked into the ER later today.

+++

Claire paused outside the ER, thinking how much had changed in the scant two weeks since she'd first passed through these doors, when the day care explosion forced her into action as a peer counselor. The day she'd first met Jamie, Erin, Sarah . . . and Logan. She remembered how furious he'd made her with his sarcasm, the way he'd blown off Erin's concerns for her staff—"*Tough comes with the territory. . . . Do you see me crumbling here?*" And then his dismissal of Faith QD as a God huddle, along with his outspoken opposition to the stress counseling.

She glanced at her briefcase full of CISM pamphlets, feeling a wave of déjà vu and an unsettling doubt. She'd come full circle, and how much had really changed? She tamped the thought down and pushed open the door. Things were better and she could handle it.

The nurse at the desk was someone Claire hadn't seen before. She was petite and probably in her late forties, with curly dark hair, a pert nose, dark-framed glasses, and a warm, engaging expression.

"Hi," the woman said. "Can I help you?"

"I'm Claire Avery. Education department."

The nurse extended her hand. "Keeley Roberts. New kid on the block—even though I've been around that particular block more than a few times." She shrugged. "But then I always say, to get through it you've got to go through it." Her warm smile reappeared and spread to her hazel eyes, making her seem at the same time incredibly wise and a bit vulnerable.

Claire murmured agreement and grasped her hand, noticing Keeley's artsy silver bracelet, etched with calligraphy and inlaid with stones forming a pink-ribbon design. "Where's Erin?"

Keeley nodded toward Logan's door. "In with Dr. Caldwell." She fiddled with a pen in her plastic pocket protector, her expression showing a twinge of anxiety. "Staffing issues. It's been a little tense this morning, and—oh, here she comes."

"Hey, Claire." Erin closed Logan's door and strode toward them. She snapped a salute to Keeley and watched as the nurse went to check on one of the patients. Then Erin motioned to Claire to have a seat beside her at the desk.

"Argh." Erin tugged at her ponytail and rolled her eyes. "Just kill me now."

Claire glanced over the desktop toward the office door. "Logan?"

"Of course." Erin reached for her coffee cup. "Although to tell you the truth, the man walked in here this morning looking happier than I've ever seen him. He brought donuts for everyone and was singing—*singing*!" She laughed. "It was almost spooky. If I didn't know better, I'd have thought McSnarly had a splash of something extra to warm his coffee this morning."

"Uh . . ." Claire blushed and turned quickly, pretending to watch Keeley check a patient's vital signs. "Is that new nurse his problem, then? She seems so nice."

"Oh, she is. I almost did a backflip when I read her résumé—both

ICU and ER experience. And a great sense of humor, always a plus in my book. I liked her the second I met her." Erin took a sip of her coffee and glanced at Keeley. "She took almost a year off to care for her terminally ill sister—breast cancer—then wanted a change when she came back, a smaller hospital to sort of ease back in. A good thing for all of us, I hope. So far so good with Logan and Keeley. Not that we're out of the woods yet. But the reason Logan's pouting right now is that Sarah went home sick. Merlene's willing to give us a hand, but you know how he is."

"Sarah's sick?" Claire asked, thinking she'd have to catch her another day for the final CISM check off.

"It's not like her at all. That's what bugged Logan most; he thinks Sarah's invincible. Like he is. But . . ."

"But what?" Claire asked, feeling a vague sense of discomfort.

Erin looked around and then lowered her voice. "She fell asleep in the break room. Had her head resting on the table, almost on top of her breakfast burrito. You know Sarah. She was frantically apologizing, saying she'd had to take some cold medicine before work, then tried to make it up by offering to skip lunch." She sighed. "The fact is, she spent over four hours helping in the nursery last night—from midnight to four thirty—rocking babies. Not that she admitted it. I only know because I happened to run into the OB charge nurse as she was going off shift this morning."

"Yikes." Claire shook her head.

"And yesterday she was late. Not very late, but Sarah's always early."

"She went home willingly today?"

Erin grimaced. "I didn't give her much of a choice, I'm afraid. When she balked, I had to mention patient safety. I can't put my department at risk. I was gentle, I promise you, but I could tell she had a problem hearing that. I promised not to tell Logan she'd fallen asleep. That girl lives to please him."

"You're right." Claire reached into her briefcase, pulling out a bundle of pamphlets. "When I talk with her, I'm insisting she takes one of my health tip sheets. Will she be here tomorrow?"

"She'd better be, or Logan will have a fit. And—" Erin stopped, glancing over the top of the desk. "Heads up. Here he comes."

"Ladies." Logan approached the desk.

Claire struggled against another blush. This man made her senses swim. How on earth was she going to make it through her last urgent care shift tomorrow?

"Dr. Caldwell." Claire smiled, aware that she'd seen him at dawn, unshaven and sitting at her breakfast table, petting her cat . . . kissing her. And how great he looked now, his scrubs the same color as his eyes, a stethoscope draped casually across his broad shoulders. Those little crinkles starting to form as his smile broadened . . .

"I see you brought your pamphlets," Logan said, pointing at the bundle in Claire's hands.

"Yes." Claire lifted her chin, once again feeling an odd sense of déjà vu at having come full circle. So much had changed and yet so much remained stubbornly the same.

"She's doing a last follow-up with the staff," Erin explained, leaning toward Claire in an obviously protective gesture. "To make sure everyone's okay. It's required."

"Healing the healers?" Logan asked, his gaze moving back to Claire.

"That's right," she said, unblinking. *Counseling and prayer too.*

"Well," he said softly, his eyes holding hers, "can't hurt, I suppose." He picked up a reflex hammer and walked toward one of the patient gurneys.

Erin's breath escaped in a snort. "'Can't hurt'? I'm telling you, there was something in that man's coffee."

+++

Erin stopped at the red light and hit the speed dial on her cell phone one more time. Brad was working at the dealership, but he usually kept his phone on his belt. It rang once, twice . . . She glanced at herself in the rearview mirror and decided she liked the new shade of lipstick after all. It looked great with her hair. It was a delicate coral pink called New Dawn, pleasing, like her whole new attitude toward the relationship with Brad. Pleasant, agreeable, nonjudgmental, sweetly patient.

Why isn't he answering the stupid phone? She growled and jabbed the End button, then stepped on the accelerator when the light turned green. She'd drive over there, even if the traffic on Highway 50 was miserable this time of day. It would be worth it to surprise Brad.

Erin turned up the volume on the Subaru's radio and sang along with the music, feeling her spirits lift. Brad really was a nice guy, and he had a point that Erin should lighten up and have more fun; she did get too intense. But maybe that came with the territory from watching her mother pull herself out of the hole after so many painful disappointments with Dad, and . . . No point in dredging up the ugly past. Having more fun could be a good thing.

She laughed, thinking that it sounded like one of those tips in Claire's pamphlets: "Do things that feel good to you. Reach out. Eat right." Well, Erin was going to do all of them, starting tonight. She'd surprise Brad and invite him out to dinner. And she was going to be far subtler about church. If he wanted to take the membership classes, she'd be thrilled, but she wouldn't push it. Some things took time. Meanwhile, she'd knock Brad's socks off by showing up unexpectedly, with killer lipstick and a whole new gentle attitude of trust. *I have to trust him.* She'd pull into the dealership, packing a great big New Dawn smile.

Only, when she arrived twenty minutes later, he wasn't there. Erin crossed her arms and looked at the young salesman behind the desk. "But his car's here."

The man—Evan, according to his badge—nodded. "He borrowed the new Denali. Sweet vehicle. Heated leather seats, DVD entertainment system, rearview cameras—"

"Where'd he go?" Erin interrupted.

"Some meeting, I guess." Evan frowned. "You don't exactly ask the owner's nephew—"

"Can you reach him?" Erin blurted, ignoring her new promise of patience.

"No, and I've been trying," Evan explained, twirling a key ring on his finger. "I had a customer who wanted to see that Denali, but it looks like Brad left his cell phone locked in his office."

"Well, I'll leave a message with you then, and . . . Oh, never mind. Thanks."

She was halfway to her car when the idea came to her. *Why not?* Brad never locked his car, and he'd no doubt be back in plenty of time to go out to dinner. She'd leave him a note. A really sweet, agreeable, and fun note, telling him she'd like to see him tonight. She could already imagine his surprised expression.

Erin slid into the Corvette and found a sheet of paper in the glove compartment. But no pen or pencil. None in her purse, either.

She rooted around in the passenger-door pocket. Nothing. Then slid across to the driver's door, slipped her hand into its pocket and . . . bingo, a pencil. Along with a wad of torn papers. No, they looked more like . . . checks?

Erin flattened one of them out and read what she could. Her heart nearly stopped. *No. How can this be?* Heart pounding, she scooped everything out of the side pocket and spread the pieces of torn checks on the car seat. Four checks. Along with an envelope. Labeled in her own writing: *Little Nugget Victim Fund.*

+++

Claire, arms full of notebooks and binders, fumbled blindly with the key to the front door and nearly fell inside when it opened. She laughed, remembering Logan standing on that same porch early this morning, his arms full of breakfast. She set her pile of belongings on the table and shook her head. Less than twenty-four hours ago she'd been ending a day with Logan that began with fishing and concluded with a sunset and an amazing kiss. And this morning there had been so many more kisses—incredible, heart-melting tenderness. How was it possible so much had happened in a single day? It felt surreal, like a dream.

She glanced around the room, then whistled. "Smokey?" She rolled her eyes. He was probably on her bed, leaving black fur all over her white down comforter. Typical. But then, nothing really bothered her right now. She was too giddy to care.

Logan had called her office, and they'd arranged to meet out by the helipad for a few minutes. Just a short conversation, a covert but knee-weakening hug and a quick kiss, like two secret agents. Logan promised to call her later tonight when he got back to his condo. He was playing basketball with one of the Placerville ER doctors, part of his regular routine. She'd been touched when he apologized, but frankly Claire was relieved. Her mind was still jumbled, and she needed time to sort it all out. Time to accept the fact that . . .

She looked at the fireplace mantel and then walked over to Kevin's picture, a lump rising in her throat. "I've found someone, Kev." She took a breath and felt it escape without swirling through the old, painful hollow. "It's finally happened." She touched a fingertip to his smiling face. "And I think you'd like him. I know you won't believe this, but even your crazy cat likes him."

Claire turned around. How come Smokey hadn't found her? It was dinnertime, and she could set her clock by his demanding meows. She headed toward the bedroom. "Smokey?"

When she saw he wasn't there, she checked the bathroom, the shower, and the laundry room, telling herself not to worry. Then she checked under the bed, in the closets, and in the kitchen, feeling anxiety rise. She hardly ever blocked the pet door until nighttime, because that was normally when the raccoons and opossums came out. Smokey stayed inside during the day, so—

Claire's breath caught as she peered onto the deck. *Oh no.* She opened the door and knelt down, picking up the clumps of fur outside the pet door. Black fur, Smokey's fur. And a trail of dried footprints. Slender, like palm prints. With five toes.

+++

Sarah moaned, squinting into the light . . . too bright, too much. Her back was stiff and sore, and . . . oh, the rocking chair. She'd fallen asleep in the rocking chair; she'd get up and get into bed, get some z's before work. She moved and the prescription bottle rolled in her lap.

It had taken two pills last night, plus two glasses of wine. And still she'd slept precious little. She stroked the small quilted blanket on her lap. How could she sleep, with the pain of knowing that the stroke of midnight made it officially Emily's second birthday? But maybe now she could turn off the merciless blinding lamp and get into bed, and—*oh no!*

She rubbed her eyes and stared at the window. The sun. Not a lamp. Sunlight because it was—she jerked her head, looking frantically from the clock to her watch—quarter to seven? Fifteen minutes before her shift started? *No, no.* Her heart thudded in her ears. *I can't be late.* She shoved the pill bottle into her pocket and rose from the rocking chair, the baby blanket sliding onto the floor. Her sleep-deprived brain, fuzzy like it was wrapped in sterile cotton, scrambled to make a plan. She was still in her scrubs from yesterday, so . . .

Sarah took a step, and her knees buckled as a wave of dizziness swept over her. Her stomach roiled and perspiration prickled her forehead. It was hard to see. She shook her head, but it didn't help. Low blood sugar probably—she hadn't eaten last night, and there was no time now. She'd get something at the hospital. But if she was too woozy to drive, how would she get to work?

Think, think. She'd take a cab. Good. No. How would she explain that to Erin? What would Logan think? But then what would he think if she wasn't there? if she let him down again? if Erin had to explain that Sarah's behavior was unsafe to patients? Sarah squeezed her eyes shut, remembering the humiliation of being sent home.

If there was one way to honor Emily on her birthday it was to be where Sarah could make a difference, where her skills could save lives. In the ER. *The only place I count for anything.*

She was okay to drive. She was tough. She'd splash some water on her face, grab her purse, and take every shortcut she knew. Logan could count on her.

CHAPTER FOURTEEN

"Hey, Claire." Erin looked up as Claire walked into the hospital chapel, surprised and grateful to see her so early. A friendly face was exactly what she needed. Along with a plan for dealing with Brad that didn't result in eating prison food for the rest of her life. The angry snarl of disbelief twisted beneath Erin's ribs. *He's a thief. And I'm a fool. Again.*

"Hey yourself." Claire handed her a cup of coffee and then sat down beside her. "My turn—raspberry mocha."

"Thanks. It's exactly what I need right now." Erin fought against the sting of tears. *No.* No way was she going to cry. Or start any ugly venting. She wasn't about to dump all this on Claire and ruin her day. That's what punching bags were for. She cleared her throat. "Why are you here so early? Urgent care opens at ten; you could've stayed in bed another couple of hours, pal." She took a sip of her coffee, sweet and rich.

"I couldn't sleep."

Erin nodded sympathetically, though she doubted Claire's insomnia had anything to do with fantasies about lashing a certain car salesman to the hood of a luxury SUV, driving it to the edge of a Sierra cliff, and . . . Erin fought the image down.

"Actually I've been up since dawn looking for Smokey—you

know, the crazy cat. He's run off." Claire frowned. "But since I was up, I thought I'd get here early and catch the HR director about my application for the clinical educator position. They should be announcing the choice on Monday, and I want to do a little last-minute campaigning." Claire studied Erin's face. "Hey, are you okay?"

"Sure. Absolutely." She lifted the coffee cup. "Only not awake yet. This'll help. Hopefully I'll have some folks wandering in for Faith QD in a minute here. Who knows, maybe McSnarly will finally show. I'm not giving up on him yet."

"Well . . ." Claire's gaze moved toward the altar decorated by the women's auxiliary with a wicker basket of daffodils. "There's always hope." She turned back to Erin. "Anyway, I'm here. You're here." She patted Erin's hand and smiled, her eyes warm. "And I seem to recall this truly amazing book saying, 'For where two or three come together . . .'"

"Amen." Erin's eyes brimmed with tears despite her grin. "Good company, indeed." She held her coffee aside and wrapped one arm around Claire in a tight hug. "Thank you for being here. It means more than you can know."

"Ditto," Claire said as Erin leaned back in her chair again. "And I'm glad you'll be close by in case I need your help in the clinic today."

"Count on it," Erin said, suspecting once again that this former ER nurse was unsure of herself. "Just call me. I'll need a break. Logan will be watching Keeley Roberts like a vulture over a wounded jackrabbit, and I may end up as referee. Thank goodness Sarah will be here. She probably has Logan's coffee brewing already."

+++

Sarah slammed the Jetta into reverse, remembering at the last second to glance over her shoulder. It was garbage day, and her neighbor had a habit of pushing her can into Sarah's driveway. If she hit it, there would be precious seconds wasted getting out of the car to shove the can and disgusting mess aside. There was no time for any slipups. She hadn't even had time to brush her teeth, for goodness' sake.

She fumbled on the console for a stick of gum as she pulled out into the street, then groaned as the thought came to her. Garbage day. Perfect name for a day spoiled by those sleeping pills, wine, and oversleeping. In an instant, guilt jabbed without mercy and her eyes blurred with tears. No. Not garbage day. Emily's birthday. *The best day of my life.*

She had only herself to blame for the mess of today. And for all the sad yesterdays leading up to it. Her fault. *My sin.* No one else's. Now she had to do whatever she could to make up for it. To stop anything else bad from happening. Sarah glanced at the digital clock on the dash—7:04. Fortunately her fourplex was just minutes from the hospital. If she took the access road, she'd miss the stoplights. Then she'd hop onto the freeway for the last mile and cross the overpass. Sarah pressed the accelerator down hard and sped off.

By the time she'd passed the second corner, she managed to reassure herself a little. Though it was only Keeley Roberts's second shift, she was a skilled veteran and would be an acceptable backup in the fifteen minutes or so that Sarah would be gone. Erin was there, after all. Logan would still grumble undoubtedly, but Sarah could make him smile. He knew he could count on her. Sarah's stomach churned. That's a lie. She'd fouled it all up. Sent home yesterday, late again today. He'd never trust her again. *Never, ever forgive me.*

Sarah whipped her head side to side as she approached the four-way stop, then pressed the Jetta forward without braking. The freeway on-ramp was just ahead. *Almost there, almost there.* Her mouth was dry, and her pulse vibrated inside her sleep-fuzzy head as if her heart had torn loose from her chest somehow and drifted upward like a helium balloon.

Good, there it is. Sarah passed the freeway's hospital sign, spotted the exit, and flattened the accelerator. Light traffic, thank goodness. *Wait. Hold on.* Why was that yellow van going so slowly? Crawling along, for heaven's sake. A school van, with kids at the window, waving and laughing. Sarah's breath caught. *Oh no.* It was stalled, stopped. *No!*

She jammed her foot against the brake, but the distance kept closing like something out of a horrible dream; the faces of the kids getting clearer, their smiles fading, their mouths opening wide, screaming. *Oh, please don't let me hit them!* She gripped the wheel, nearly standing up as she crushed the Jetta's brake pedal to the floor and then made the only decision she could. *Don't hurt the kids. Don't hurt the kids. . . .* She cranked the wheel hard left, away from the van, using all her strength. Her shoulder strained in its socket as she struggled to prevent the wheel from straightening out.

She felt the impact at the rear as she clipped the van, her seat belt biting viciously into her collarbone as the car tipped sideways and slid across the intersection toward the overpass guardrail.

There was the acrid smell of smoking rubber, horrible sounds . . . honking, so much honking, shattering glass, ripping metal, and something hard slamming against her chest. Piercing and unbearable pain, her gargled scream . . . and finally merciful blackness.

+++

Logan glanced out his office window, thinking he could hear distant sirens. It didn't matter; if they were headed here, there was nothing he could do about it.

It was a completely different situation with the e-mail message on the computer in front of him. All he had to do with that was delete it without opening it. Right now. What point would there be in reading it? He'd already made his decision. He moved the computer mouse for the second time, letting the cursor hover over the line *From: Rebeckah Caldwell. Subject: Re: wedding regrets.*

Regrets. Logan frowned, thinking how ridiculous it had been to use that wording in his brief note to Beckah. The invitation had been worded something like "please respond with acceptance or regrets regarding your attendance," and he'd done it quickly without thinking. But now, seeing Beckah's name alongside the word *regrets* . . . He'd delete the message and be done with it. He didn't have regrets. Questions maybe. Once. But that was over now too. He was moving on. Tomorrow Beckah would walk down the aisle in Carmel and become someone else's wife. Good. She deserved every bit of happiness that came her way. And his being at her wedding wouldn't matter one way or the other.

Besides, he had plans for tomorrow. He'd take Claire out somewhere nice, somewhere that didn't involve hiking boots and fishing gear. He chuckled low in his throat. Or any risk of sitting on a chicken. Out to dinner maybe, at that great place on the Sacramento River next to where the Delta King paddle wheeler was docked. Rio City Café, the restaurant with all the windows and decks, the delta breezes, fresh-caught salmon, crab cakes, steaks, and those incredible St. Louis barbecued ribs. Claire might wear a dress, pull her hair up the way he liked it, showing off her beautiful, graceful neck. And she'd sit close to Logan, smelling so good and looking at him with those dove gray eyes. They'd talk and make plans.

Logan glared at the computer. Why couldn't he delete the

e-mail and get it over with? He needed to go back to the ER. Get to work. The new nurse was pacing like a caged animal; Erin had had her nose out of joint about something ever since she walked in. He moved the computer mouse over the message again. What did he think it was going to say? That Beckah knew he was a coward all along and wouldn't show up? That she was glad she'd found someone better than him? That she'd changed her mind and needed him to roar up on his motorcycle to rescue her? He clicked the mouse and opened the e-mail.

> *Logan,*
> *I understand.*
> *Blessings,*
> *B.*

He hit the Delete button, battling an exasperating mix of disappointment and anger. She understood? What kind of cryptic garbage was that? Understood what? What on earth did Rebeckah Caldwell understand? *That I don't?*

No. Didn't matter. It was done.

Logan turned at a knock on his door. "Come in."

Erin stepped inside. "Sarah's late. It's only ten minutes by the clock, but you know how early she always gets here. She usually beats me by a few minutes. Technically that makes her forty minutes late. And I can't get her on the phone."

"You tried her cell?"

"No answer there, either."

"How'd you leave things with her yesterday when she went home sick? Did she say she'd be here today?"

"I'm not sure I even asked. I only assumed." She crossed her arms, staring at him. "You know as well as I do that Sarah has never voluntarily missed a day of work. I think I told her to take as much time as she needed, but I never figured she would. If she did, I'd expect her to call me. I'm worried."

Logan hesitated, then nodded toward the ER. "What's going on out there?"

"Keeley and I are handling it. Just those same three night shift patients waiting for lab results and two more signing in for triage—a forehead laceration and a case of pinkeye. Nothing big. I think we're okay until urgent care opens, but . . ."

"But what?"

Erin took a deep breath. "I keep thinking about Sarah. About how she's been working too much. Everywhere. Not just ER. How she almost fainted the other day, how she was late for the first time ever last week and then fell asleep at work yesterday."

"Fell asleep?" Logan shook his head. "You said she was sick and had to go home."

"She didn't want you to know. I found her in the lounge with her head down on the table. She said she had a cold and took an antihistamine." Erin winced. "But I'm not sure now. What if it's something serious?"

"It's ten minutes. Some people think that's nothing—remember McMuffin?" He smiled, trying to reassure Erin, despite his own creeping doubts concerning how thin Sarah had become lately and those dark shadows under her eyes. That sadness when she talked about her family. "Some people think ten minutes late is on time."

"Not Sarah." Erin twisted her ponytail, her expression thoughtful. "My personal judgment hasn't been the best lately, and now I'm wondering if I missed something with her. Remember all those warnings Claire gave us about stress? And those symptoms that they mentioned at the debriefing. Do you think maybe—?"

Ah, brother. Not this. "No, I don't," Logan said, cutting her off. Sarah was a warrior, tough as he was. That was that. He stood and grabbed his stethoscope. "Sarah's running late. Period. We'll give her five more minutes, and we'll call her cell phone again. If she doesn't show, I'll get one of police units to drive by her place."

The ambulance radio squawked in the distance, fizzed into static, then started again as sirens began to wail from all directions.

+++

Claire walked out of the Human Resources office, frustrated. The director wasn't in. Something about an unplanned early meeting, and then she'd be attending a systemwide training session. Claire nearly jumped when Merlene Hibbert called her name.

The nursing director marched toward Claire, a no-nonsense look on her face. It was uncanny how the woman could sneak up so soundlessly; no wonder the nursing students toed the line. Claire squared her shoulders. If she'd had gum in her mouth, she would have spit it out. The woman was that intimidating. But when Merlene reached Claire, she smiled. For about two seconds.

"Busy morning, too many people out sick," she said in her sing-song cadence. "I've a mind to make a few house calls, take some temperatures, see how legitimate these illnesses are, you know?" She eyed Claire's scrubs. "Aren't you in urgent care today?"

"Yes, at ten," Claire answered, wondering if Merlene were about to take her by the scruff of her neck back to her assigned building. Except that only two weeks ago this building was her proper workplace. *And still my plan.* "I was hoping to catch the HR director to confirm the agenda for the meeting on Monday."

Merlene nodded knowingly. "You mean the decision about the new clinical educator. You're a bit anxious, are you?"

"Yes," Claire admitted. "I know there are only two applicants, but—"

"Three. Now that Renee is back."

Claire's stomach tensed at the mention of the nurse who'd held the position until three months ago. *She wants her job back?* "Renee Baxter? I thought she moved to Washington."

"Oregon. Except that she didn't. Her husband decided not to take that job." She shook her head. "Too rainy. And he didn't know this before?" Her expression warmed. "But I believe that Renee is only interested in half-time hours. Between you and me, administration's impressed with you. You're the only one of the three applicants with CISM training, and then there's your willingness to help out in the ER."

"The clinic," Claire corrected, her voice sounding as breathless as she suddenly felt. She struggled against a queasy rush of dread. "Only urgent care. Not the ER. And today's my last shift because they've found someone else." She took a breath and let it out slowly, willing herself to stay calm and focused. *Stick with the plan. Lord, you know my plan.*

"Nevertheless, you've made quite an impression," Merlene said confidently. "In fact, I put in a special word for you."

Claire's shoulders sagged with relief. "Oh, thank you. That means a lot." She turned her head for a moment toward sounds in the distance—sirens?

"Perhaps there would even be a possibility of a shared educator position. You could work part-time in education, part-time in the ER?"

"But . . ." Claire's stomach sank again. How on earth could this be happening? After all her hard work? all the planning and praying? She had to make Merlene understand. Stop her from suggesting this impossible—completely horrifying—idea to administration. *Back to the ER?*

"No, that isn't what I'd planned for. I don't work ER anymore. I can't—" Claire stopped and stared upward, certain she'd misunderstood the page. It repeated and her heart rose to her throat.

"Claire Avery to the emergency department stat. Claire Avery report to ER."

By the time Claire had jogged across the campus to the outside doors of the emergency department, the overhead announcement of Code Triage had been made, meaning they were working a multicasualty disaster. What type she had no idea, but another ambulance, its siren screaming, was rounding the curve into the parking lot as she hustled up the ramp to the doors. Metal scoop stretchers leaned against the brick entryway, and red biohazard bags—overflowing with bloodstained gauze pads, IV packaging, and cardboard splints—littered the entrance. Trauma. What origin? How many victims? *Why did they page me?* Claire hurried through the doors and into chaos.

Erin, holding an IV bag aloft, greeted her with a groan of relief. "I've never been so glad to see someone in my life." She stepped out of the way as a medic dragging a scoop stretcher—its buckles clattering against the floor—charged by them and headed back outside. "Motor vehicle accident on the overpass," she explained, raising her voice. "Sounds like four cars. A stalled school van with eight kids—minor injuries, thank heaven—and three other cars. So far a few fractures, a head injury who's conscious but needs a CT scan." She shook her head. "I guess the last car is still hanging over the guardrail. They're trying to stabilize it. There's supposed to be at least one victim pinned inside. No word on his condition."

Claire nodded, her hands clammy. She pushed down a wave of nausea, her mind whirling. "So, you need me to open urgent care early."

"No," Erin said, nudging Claire to the side as a firefighter rushed past carrying a crying child. "I need you in the ER with me. I need everybody I can get. Sarah didn't show, so it's just Keeley and me. Logan's shouting orders faster than an auctioneer." She glanced past Claire toward the ambulance bay. "Argh, there's the Channel 13 news van. C'mon, let's get in there."

"Erin, I . . ." Claire choked. *Please, God.* How could she do this? How could she refuse? *What if I panic?* Claire looked into Erin's eyes and nodded. "Just tell me what you need me to do."

Erin wedged the IV bag against her shoulder and reached out to squeeze Claire's arm. "Great. You're saving my life here. And I'm still praying that Sarah will show up any minute."

+++

"How 'bout that brain scan?" Logan asked, catching Keeley's gaze as she entered data into the computer.

"They said they could take him in five minutes," she answered, then amended it as she read Logan's expression. "I could call radiology again, and—"

"Do it." Logan sighed as he scanned the trauma room and checked the clock. Despite the fact the new nurse was far too slow, thirty minutes after the arrival of the first victims they had things relatively under control. He studied Erin's notes on the huge dry-erase board: fifty-year-old male with stable head injury and bruised ribs, thirty-four-year-old female with an uncomplicated leg fracture awaiting orthopedic consult, the teenager with multiple lacerations—he'd sew those later—and the kids, of course.

Logan thought of the eight grade-schoolers Merlene was watching in urgent care. The only injury was a five-year-old with a possible wrist fracture. A miracle.

His brows furrowed. No, not a miracle. The remaining victim, extricated from the car scant minutes ago and on her way in Code 3, had apparently swerved to avoid hitting that stalled school van. And ended up with her car dangling from a freeway overpass. A brave decision or a fatal one—he'd know which in a few minutes. So far, the woman's vital signs were relatively stable. If things changed, she'd win a helicopter ride to Sacramento. Meanwhile, security was watching the doors, the public information officer was handling reporters, chaplain services were on hand for the panicky parents, and Merlene Hibbert was making balloons out of exam gloves over in urgent care.

Logan glanced across the room to where Claire, wearing a plastic face shield, stood efficiently and quickly cleaning the teenager's wounds. He frowned at Keeley's careful and methodical pace. There was no comparison; Claire responded instantly to orders and worked with what appeared to be quiet confidence. Quiet, meaning she'd hardly said a word since she arrived. Except to answer his brief inquiry about Smokey—the cat was still missing, and he could see Claire was worried. Other than that, they'd barely talked. But that was okay; they were working. He only wished Keeley would do the wound cleaning and clinic-type tasks and Claire could be assigned to the more challenging patients. He'd need nurses with speed and efficiency when that Code 3 hit the door. Methodical, though safe, wasn't going to cut it.

But it wasn't the time to second-guess Erin's nursing assignments. She was more than a competent charge nurse. And right this minute he had no real complaints with the way things were going. If that changed, he'd—

The ambulance radio squawked and Logan turned.

"They're pulling in," Erin announced, striding away from the radio desk. "Our twenty-six-year-old female vehicle extrication. Semiconscious, facial wounds, bruised chest. BP 94 over 40, heart rate 100, respirations 28—here she is!" She signaled to the medics. "Put her in the code room, guys. Keeley, let's go."

+++

The ambulance crew swept past Claire and into the code room, two paramedics hustling the stretcher and a big firefighter in yellow turnouts trotting alongside, holding the IV bag shoulder-high.

The patient's face was covered in blood, her fair hair matted with it. A significant scalp wound likely. A stiff orange foam collar protected her neck, and much of her face was obscured by an oxygen mask attached to a high-flow bag. Her clothing cut away, she'd been partially covered by a silver foil survival blanket. A cardiac monitor lay wedged alongside her on the gurney. The woman's skin, beneath the dried blood, was pale—sickly pale. And her small hands motionless.

Claire's pulse quickened. She watched from the doorway as Logan talked with paramedics before starting his exam. Erin attached the ER's monitoring electrodes and switched the oxygen tubing from the portable tank to the wall source. Keeley took the IV bag from the firefighter and hooked it carefully onto a pole. Claire turned her attention back to the woman on the gurney, feeling irresistibly drawn and horrified at the same time. Her mouth went dry and leg muscles tensed as her heart rate accelerated—adrenaline, effective as an injection straight into her bloodstream.

Claire focused, seeing nothing but the trauma victim who remained completely still, without response to Erin's touch as she adjusted the oxygen mask. Claire leaned forward slightly, staring at the patient's chest to be sure it was still moving. It was, thank goodness. If her chest hadn't been moving, this poor, waxy-pale woman would look like she was already dead.

Claire grabbed the doorframe against a sudden and crippling wave of dizziness. *No, don't. Don't. I don't know this patient. It's not Kevin. It's a stranger.*

"Logan!" Erin cried out. "This is Sarah!"

CHAPTER FIFTEEN

"Sarah?"

Someone called her name, but Sarah didn't dare lose her concentration. The bicycle was wobbling and the pedals so hard to reach. She needed to sit up tall, hold on tighter, steer with everything she had or she'd crash again. And the pain was too awful to let that happen. If only she wasn't alone. *Are you there, Daddy? Are you holding on to me?*

"Open your eyes, Sarah." That voice again, deep, strong. And a touch, warm and gentle against her face.

Daddy?

"That's my girl. I need to check your eyes now—hang in here with me."

Sarah squinted into the pinpoint light, struggling to focus. So bright. Too bright. It hurt her head and made her eyes water. She blinked and tried to see beyond. Blurry faces, people gathering around. More lights, glowing like . . .

A sob rose in Sarah's chest, setting off a spasm of pain, but she smiled anyway. The joy was far stronger than the pain. She shut her eyes, warm tears sliding down her face. Lights. Of course. The glow from a hundred brilliant candles. Emily's birthday party.

You didn't forget us, Daddy.

Erin watched as Logan left the code room. It had been forty minutes since Sarah arrived. It seemed like forty years. And it was killing her not to be at that bedside, but she'd had to delegate Sarah's nursing care to Keeley Roberts. They were still on disaster status, and Erin was in charge. She was required to be free to oversee the department. As for Claire, Erin wasn't sure what was going on with her. Except that she'd turned white as a ghost when the Code 3 ambulance arrived and then kept her distance from the resuscitation room like it was full of rattlesnakes.

Erin looked up as Logan approached the desk. "Well? How's Sarah doing?" she asked. Logan's immediate frown nearly stopped her heart. "What? Has something changed?"

"No, Sarah's fairly stable. I don't like her heart rate yet, and those rib fractures could be a problem, but the brain CT report is back—it's normal." Logan shook his head. "The concussion made her so blasted squirrelly. She asked me if her little girl was okay. I was thinking, her little girl? She doesn't have a child. It really threw me until I realized she was probably asking about the five-year-old from the school van. The kid we treated for the wrist fracture. Sarah must've heard the medics talking about her." He was quiet for a moment, a muscle bunching along his jaw. "She nearly killed herself to avoid hitting that van. You know how Sarah is about kids."

"I do," Erin said, remembering Sarah coming in during that night shift to help with the babies. The same day she fell asleep at work and Erin sent her home—after she'd had a bout of near fainting and that strange late arrival for work. Erin's stomach twisted against another wave of guilt. Something had been going on with Sarah, and she hadn't paid attention. *Could I have prevented this?* Could her judgment be trusted at all these days? Look at the fiasco with Brad; didn't that prove it? Erin pushed the thought aside. If she started down that path, she'd be worthless, and today everyone had to be right on target. She sighed, thinking out loud. "I should go relieve Keeley."

Logan's frown returned. "Do better. Replace her. She's slow. And indecisive too. . . ."

Erin narrowed her eyes. "Give me one concrete complaint."

"I don't trust her."

"It's Keeley's second day. She's completely qualified. And she's doing great considering we've thrown her in on a critical trauma when she was supposed to spend several days in orientation, following Sarah around." The irony of the situation hit her like a punch in the gut.

Logan flattened his palm on the desk. "My point exactly. It's Sarah in that bed. One of the few nurses I'd trust completely with a critical patient *is* that critical patient. If things go south, I want a nurse assigned to Sarah I can count on. Make that happen."

"I don't have anyone to offer right now. Look, I'll be with Keeley as much as I can. I promise. You know how much I care about Sarah. But I'm also responsible for troubleshooting out here, answering the radio, and overseeing triage until our disaster status is cleared." She pressed her fingers to her forehead. "Merlene thinks she might be able to pull a nurse from ICU, but until then I'm afraid you'll have to deal with—"

"Give me Claire," Logan said abruptly. "Put her in with Sarah. Keeley comes out here with you. Problem solved."

Erin hesitated. How could she tell Logan that forcing Claire back into critical care nursing might be the worst solution of all? "I don't know if she'll agree to that. I could ask, but—" She halted midsentence, turning toward the nurses' station as the medic radio began to shrill.

"Sierra Mercy, this is Medic 5. We're coming in Code 3 with a bystander from the accident site. Seventy-year-old male in third-degree heart block. Hypotensive, diaphoretic, and complaining of chest pain."

Erin's mouth sagged open. "Unbelievable." She turned to Logan, a game plan already whirling in her brain. "Okay, it's like this: we set up cart two with the backup crash cart; I'll page respiratory therapy."

Logan nodded, the look on his face defying argument. "Assign Claire to Sarah. Right now."

+++

"Sarah? It's Claire. You're going to be all right. I'm here." Claire studied the overhead monitors, her heart leaping to her throat. Sarah's pulse rate was fast—114. Why was it climbing? How many liters of oxygen were running? Claire's gaze flicked to the oxygen gauge on the wall beside the bed, then back to Sarah's chest to count the rate of her breathing. Twenty-eight. Had it always been that labored? Was her skin paler than before? *You know I can't do this, Lord. It's so far outside the plan.*

Claire fought the image of Kevin's face, his suffering in that trauma room, and the unbearable memory of how helpless she'd been to save him. And now she was expected to . . .

Calm down. Claire breathed through her nose, willing her own pulse to slow and her shaky hands to steady, reminding herself that Sarah's condition had improved. That in fact she had been stabilizing. Logan would never leave her bedside if she were still in danger. *Wrong. Dead wrong.* Claire's stomach sank. Logan left because he had no choice, because he had another critical patient coming in. So he chose to trust Claire. With Sarah's life. *Trust this pathetically weak link.*

Claire's gaze darted toward where Erin, Logan, and Keeley were working on the cardiac patient some twenty yards away. Even from here, she could see the anxiety on the new nurse's face as she struggled to follow Logan's rapid-fire orders. It had to be a nightmare situation for a nurse who'd been out of commission for months, caring for a dying sister. Keeley was good, more than good, but she was recovering from a tragedy. Claire knew that feeling only too well. Even two years after Kevin's death, the Sacramento physician's overbearing criticism was branded into her memory. And today was a nightmare day for everyone. Especially Sarah. A dedicated nurse on her way to work in this very ER, waylaid by a tragedy she could never have imagined.

Claire checked the overhead monitor again, quickly noting Sarah's heart rhythm and oxygen saturation, and watched the drip rate of the IV solutions before glancing back down. Though Sarah's face had been cleaned, there was still dried blood in her nostrils beneath the prongs of the translucent green oxygen cannula. Her forehead and the bridge of her nose had swollen, and below the thick gauze bandage wrapped around her head, her left brow was already eggplant purple. She looked battered and fragile and achingly childlike. Claire's heart tugged, remembering the tough-cookie impression she'd had of this hardworking young nurse that first day they'd met at the CISM interviews. Sipping her Diet Coke and shrugging. Then dismissing the incredible pain of her day by saying, "I'm a nurse. I do what needs to be done. Then I come back the next day and I do it all again."

Claire moved forward as Sarah opened her eyes and attempted to speak.

Her weak voice was interrupted by shallow breaths. "Please . . . tell . . . him . . ." Sarah's eyes, startlingly blue against her too-pale skin, drifted upward, then focused again. Her lashes fluttered and she licked her lips, tongue touching the tidy sutures Logan placed at the corner of her mouth. "I'm so . . . sorry."

Claire leaned close. "Who? Tell who?"

"Logan." Tears welled in Sarah's eyes. "Tell him . . . I . . . tried . . ."

Claire's brows drew together with confusion. "What?"

Sarah moaned. "Couldn't . . . sleep. Bad nights." She gulped a breath and her eyes opened wide. "I tried . . . to get here. Can't be . . . late. Tried . . . so hard. The pills . . . shouldn't have . . ." Her tears spilled over as a ragged sob left her lips. "I'm . . . sorry. Tell him that . . . please. I let Logan down."

Let Logan down? Claire blinked with disbelief. She gently stroked Sarah's pale cheek. "Don't worry. Oh, sweetie, don't worry about anything like that. All that matters now is that you get well."

Claire drew back, acutely aware that Sarah's breathing had become labored. Far more labored. Like a fish flopping on a riverbank. Gulping, struggling. And not only because of the emotion and tears. Claire checked the pulse oximeter on Sarah's fingertip; then her gaze darted to the digital display on the monitor overhead—92 percent. Her blood oxygen saturation had dropped significantly, and her heart rate was rising to . . . 124. *Oh no.* Claire punched the button to start the blood pressure reading and lifted her stethoscope from around her neck. She squeezed Sarah's shoulder. "Sarah, talk to me. What's going on?"

"Pain . . . too . . . much . . . pain. My . . . chest." She stared at the ceiling, her pupils dilating, pale skin dotting with perspiration.

Claire swept Sarah's gown aside and pressed the stethoscope against her chest, noting with sickening dread the deepening bruises over her rib cage and how one side of her chest seemed out of symmetry somehow. Something was desperately wrong. Claire listened first to the right side of Sarah's chest: rapid air exchange, normal; and to the left side . . . nothing, no air moving. Claire shifted the stethoscope and listened again, pressing the circular plastic disc flat against Sarah's clammy skin. Her heart wedged into her throat. *No breath sounds. Lung collapse?*

Claire dropped the gown, her eyes riveted to her patient's face. Sarah's eyes were closed, nostrils flaring, respiratory rate rising, neck veins becoming more and more prominent, lips chalky gray. All symptoms, Claire suspected with mounting anxiety, of pressure from trapped air in the chest cavity around the collapsed lung. Pressure capable of pushing major vessels, even the heart, toward the opposite side of the chest and causing circulatory collapse. *Tension pneumothorax?*

Claire quickly replaced the oxygen cannula with a high-flow mask, fitting it over Sarah's face, cranking the oxygen to full flow, and watching the reservoir bag inflate and distend in response. "I'm making it easier for you to breathe. Sarah?"

Sarah opened her eyes, but they drifted upward, showing too much white as she fought to speak. "It's . . . Emily's . . . birthday," she whispered. "I'm . . . sorry, Logan. Daddy, please . . . help me."

Claire's breath stuck in her throat. *Please, God, don't let Sarah die.* She swallowed hard, her heart thudding inside her ears. *I can do this, Lord. I can do it . . . if you help me.* She jabbed her finger against the bedside alarm, then shouted through the doorway, "I need help in here. Hurry!"

She lifted the head of the bed to aid Sarah's breathing, all the while continuing to pray. *Help me, Father. Help me to help her.* Claire's heart pounded and she held her breath, and a comfort—almost like floating on still water—washed over her, steadying her hands and replacing the crippling anxiety with . . . peace. Unparalleled and amazing peace. Along with a feeling of being guided, almost like a parent's hand helps a child to write. Suddenly Claire knew that everything—every single thing—was going to turn out all right. No matter how ugly the numbers were on the monitors and how terrifying the sound of Sarah's lungs, Claire could do what needed to be done. All the help she needed to make this incredible miracle happen was right here with her. As close as her own heartbeat.

Claire leaned forward and looked into Sarah's eyes, nodding with calm assurance. "We've got you covered—hold on to that."

+++

Logan jogged through the door and saw in an instant why Claire had called him. Sarah's condition had deteriorated dramatically. She was barely conscious, eyes swimming and lips dusky. He met Claire's gaze as he lifted his stethoscope from around his neck. "Vital signs?"

"Pressure 92 over 40, heart rate 128—sinus tach—respirations 40, pulse ox—" Claire glanced at the display—"89 percent on the nonbreather mask." Her lips pressed together for an instant. "I can't hear any breath sounds on the left, Logan. And her neck veins—"

"Full," he agreed, lifting the stethoscope to his ears. "I'll take a listen, but I think it's tension pneumo. Let's be ready. Get me an 18-gauge needle; I'll need to decompress this before her heart's compromised. And go ahead and set up for a chest tube to follow." He looked at Sarah's face, deathly pale behind the translucent green mask. His gut wrenched. *I'll fix it, Sarah.*

Logan listened carefully to both lungs as Claire gathered the necessary equipment. Sarah moaned as he turned her to listen at the back of her chest . . . grating from the rib fractures, no air moving. "Sarah," he said after nodding at Claire, "I'm going to needle your chest to help you breathe. No time for anesthetic. I'm sorry. But hang tough for me, okay?"

She nodded almost imperceptibly.

In seconds he'd pulled on a pair of surgical gloves and, holding the needle in one hand, used his other fingertips to locate the intended puncture site on Sarah's hastily prepped chest. He counted ribs and felt the spaces between, easier than most patients because she was thin. *Harder than any patient before . . . because she's Sarah.* Logan pushed the emotion aside, found the site—second intercostal space at the midclavicular line—and without hesitation plunged the needle through her skin. He guided it over the second rib to avoid the vessels beneath, advanced it carefully deeper and toward the pleural space, holding his breath, until . . . there was a sudden hiss of escaping air accompanied by a fine spray of blood. *Yes!*

Sarah groaned, Logan breathed, and on the other side of the gurney Claire whispered over her efficiently organized chest tube tray, "Thank you, Lord."

+++

Erin closed her eyes, weak with gratitude. By the time she'd been able to leave Keeley and the cardiac patient, Logan had inserted a needle into Sarah's upper chest to relieve the dangerous pressure, then followed it with a sutured-in chest tube. A portable X-ray taken afterward confirmed her lung was re-expanding. And now, twenty-five minutes after the crisis, Sarah dozed with her heart rate and oxygen level markedly improved.

Erin looked down at Sarah, her mind still tumbling with a frightening list of what-ifs. What if the lung collapse had proceeded further? What if Sarah had stopped breathing and her heart rhythm deteriorated? What if . . . ? "Thank goodness you were in here," she said, turning to Claire. "You caught the tension pneumo just in time. I don't know what I'd have done if you . . ." She choked against a rush of tears.

"You know how hard I was praying. But—" Claire's expression grew troubled as she looked down to where Sarah dozed— "Sarah kept apologizing. She said something about having bad nights . . . not being able to sleep and that she couldn't be late and couldn't disappoint Logan. And something about . . . oh no." She pressed her hand to her chest, her eyes wide. "Where are Sarah's belongings?"

"Over there." Erin pointed toward a plastic bag in the corner of the room. "What's wrong?"

"Something else she said," Claire explained, grabbing the bag and dumping its contents onto a chair. "I just remembered." She poked through Sarah's purse, then began checking the pockets of the scrub top, snipped away by the paramedics and speckled with dried blood. "Sarah mentioned something about pills and . . . oh, boy."

"What?" Erin asked, stepping close to see what Claire found. "What is that?"

"A prescription bottle," Claire said, her voice dropping to a whisper as she glanced toward Sarah. "She's been taking sleeping pills."

+++

Logan rubbed his neck, then leaned back in his office chair with a long sigh, grateful there was a break in the day's chaos. He'd even had time to change into clean scrubs. Things were finally settling down. He checked the clock on the wall. Three thirty in the afternoon? No wonder he felt wiped out. But at least he had things under control. The cardiac patient went to the CCU with an external pacemaker, and the vehicle accident cleared hours ago, though the TV news kept running that footage of Sarah's car dangling from the freeway guardrail.

Logan refused to imagine any alternate outcome and tried not to dwell on the fact they'd found a bottle of sleeping pills in Sarah's belongings. Fortunately her blood toxicology screen showed only a trace of prescription medication and alcohol. Not enough to be harmful or legally compromising. The important thing now was that Sarah had stabilized and they'd sent her to the ICU. The surgeon would keep a cautious eye on her condition, and the pulmonary docs were monitoring her lung status. Tension pneumothorax—it could have been fatal.

Logan's instincts had been right about Claire. She'd been sharp to catch Sarah's symptoms and did everything right without wasting precious time. Without hesitating, like the new nurse might have. He frowned, remembering the uncomfortable conversation he'd had with Erin and Keeley thirty minutes ago. But then Logan had the right to insist that every member of his team be top-notch, didn't he?

The phone rang, interrupting his thoughts. "Yes?"

"It's Claire. I'm finished talking with the chaplain and I'm on my way out. Can you spare a few minutes? I need to talk with you."

Logan felt warmth spreading through his chest. "No problem. C'mon over."

He warned himself not to mention the stress interviews the chaplain was conducting. Ironic as that must seem to Claire, he didn't want to risk a confrontation over their stalemate regarding that subject. In fact, he wanted to forget all of this. He wanted to do something enjoyable. Which reminded him he needed to make that reservation. Tomorrow night, dinner along the river, Claire in the dress he'd been imagining . . . *Why wait for tomorrow?* Claire's urgent care shift had been covered by another nurse. He could make that date happen tonight, and after a day like today, nothing could be better. Yes, they'd celebrate their victories.

Logan smiled at the tap on the door and the sound of Claire's voice, but his smile disappeared when he saw the look on her face, her pinched brows, and the rigid set of her jaw.

"You told Keeley Roberts she should quit?" she asked, spitting the words out before he could speak. "How could you do that?"

Blast it. "Close the door."

Claire did as he asked, then turned back, crossing her arms over her scrub top. Twin splotches of color rose high on her cheeks as she trembled with emotion, eyes bright and long hair spilling around her shoulders. She'd look beautiful if she didn't have murder on her mind.

Logan took a breath and raised his palm.

But Claire wasn't about to stop. "I talked with Keeley. She was crying and angry, confused. Worst of all, she's doubting her skills, afraid she's lost her edge."

"She might be right," Logan stood behind his desk, hating that the conversation was headed down this slippery slope. He'd waited all day to talk with Claire, but this was nowhere near what he'd had in mind. "Look, I don't like being the bully here, but—"

"Yes. You do. I think you really do," Claire argued. "I think everything I've heard about you is true." She hesitated, her expression obviously pained. "I think you're insensitive, critical, and woefully uncaring."

Uncaring? He swallowed. "Claire, wait."

"Wait for what?" she asked, her voice deepening. "For the all-powerful and unbending Dr. Logan Caldwell to care? Or wait until you can understand that Keeley Roberts spent the last year watching her only sister die? Her. Sister. Died. Don't you get it? People are human and fallible. Not everyone can bounce right back after a tragedy. Sometimes . . . we . . . ." She covered her face with her hands and began to sob.

"Hey, it's okay. It's okay." Logan moved toward her, but Claire stiffened and stepped back.

"No, it's not okay." Tears spilled down her cheeks. "I wasn't okay either. In those first weeks after Kevin died. I told you I doubted myself, had trouble. Remember?"

How could he possibly forget Claire being on duty when her brother arrived critically burned and dying? Logan nodded, keeping his distance even though he ached to comfort her.

"What I didn't tell you was I quit that job in Sacramento. Because even after I'd begun to feel better, one of the ER doctors continued to question my competence—" Claire narrowed her eyes—"and made it his personal goal to have me fired. He applied more and more pressure until I began to hesitate, to second-guess every single decision I made. I started to believe I was incompetent, worse than useless—that I was the *weak link* in that trauma team." She leaned forward and stared unblinking into Logan's face, anger smoldering in her eyes. "A weak link. Your words. Remember?"

Logan winced, struggling for something to say. Anything to stop this. What could he say? "I'm sorry."

But that wasn't right either because she shook her head, wiped her tears away, and reached for the door.

"No," she said after clearing her throat. "Tell all those other nurses you're sorry." Then she shrugged and let out a soft groan. "Including Sarah."

"Sarah?"

"Yes." A look of inconsolable sadness replaced the anger on Claire's face. "She was hurrying to get here because of you. Because she didn't want to let you down. She said she hadn't been able to sleep, so she took sleeping pills. Then raced to get here after she overslept. So she wouldn't disappoint you, her boss. A man who doesn't understand that people have troubles and are sometimes . . . weak. A heart is more than an organ in your chest, Dr. Caldwell."

Logan stared at her, not trusting himself to speak. Not even sure he could.

"Keeley's already left," Claire said, almost whispering. "And I'm going right now. But you know where Sarah is."

CHAPTER SIXTEEN

Erin paused outside the doors to the ICU to shut off her cell phone, frowning at the display of unanswered messages—all from Brad. She hadn't talked to him since she found the checks in his car and still wasn't sure how she'd deal with that. All Erin could think of now was how near Sarah came to dying. *And it's partly my fault.*

She took a deep breath and walked into the ICU toward the nurses' station, squinting as her eyes adjusted. Erin never understood how the staff could stand working in semidarkness—or semi-silence for that matter, unless you counted the mechanical whoosh of ventilators and robotlike beeping of countless monitors. Or the crunching of popcorn. Erin waved to an evening shift nurse peeking out of the break room, a red-striped microwave bag in hand. Then crossed the last stretch of blue carpeting to Sarah's room. She was surprised to see her awake.

"How're you doing?" Erin asked, resisting the urge to check the monitor overhead and the fluid collection bags hanging near the foot of the bed. She wasn't going to be that obvious; besides, she'd already called Sarah's nurse for a full report. Roughly ten hours since the accident, Sarah's condition was remarkably stable.

"Okay." Sarah licked her dry lips. "Better, if you're packing a bag of M&M'S and a Diet Coke." She attempted a wan smile that did nothing to erase the discomfort in her eyes.

"Believe me, I asked about that." Erin's gaze moved over her teammate's battered face. Sarah's left eye was nearly closed by swelling, and the sutured side of her mouth was dark with bruising, like she'd been snacking on berry pie instead of eluding death. Erin's heart ached for her. "But you can't have anything to eat or drink until tomorrow. They want to be sure your abdomen's okay."

"Humph." Sarah snorted, then winced. "I'm no doctor, but I'd say this hose stuck in my chest says something about where the problem is."

Erin studied the length of transparent tubing extending from beneath Sarah's gown to its connection at a calibrated plastic collection container near the floor. A column of water, functioning as a seal to prevent further lung collapse, fluctuated each time Sarah breathed. Erin sighed. "It's the only way to keep you in bed, I suppose. Otherwise you'd be reporting for the evening shift down in the ER."

Sarah closed her eyes and the ICU's eerie brand of silence surrounded them: *whoosh-click-whir-beep*, interrupted only by the occasional distant moan from one of the other rooms and the soft, reassuring response of a nurse. Erin figured her friend had gone to sleep and was preparing to get up and leave when Sarah turned to her. "I probably can't do that anymore," she whispered.

"Can't do what?" Erin asked, seeing anxiety in Sarah's eyes.

"Come back to work in the ER."

"Hey." Erin reached out and took her hand. "Don't talk like that. You're going to be fine, and—"

"No," Sarah interrupted. "That's not what I meant." Her eyes searched Erin's. "I mean because I've screwed up so much lately.

And now this accident. If the investigation shows I'm at fault, I could be fired, right?"

"I don't know yet. It hasn't been discussed." Erin squeezed Sarah's fingers, exhaling softly. "How did all this happen, anyway?"

Sarah shook her head. "I haven't been able to sleep more than a few hours a night in a couple of weeks. I have trouble some-times . . . this time of year. A doctor prescribed sleeping pills about a year ago, but I'd never taken them before. Until now." She gri-maced. "I also tried . . ."

"Alcohol?" Erin asked, remembering that a trace had shown up in the blood screening.

Sarah's response was barely perceptible in the darkness, a mere dip of her bandaged head. "Wine. Another thing I usually don't touch."

"Why, Sarah? Why would you risk all that?" *What should I have known?*

"Sleep. I just can't sleep." She faced Erin, her expression guarded. "I only wanted to get enough sleep so I could work. Because I didn't want to let anyone down. We've been so short-staffed."

Erin gritted her teeth against a rush of guilt. Even if Sarah wasn't going to reveal the reasons behind it, it was clear that she'd been struggling with something and Erin missed it, completely missed it. How was that possible? She was in charge and yet apparently knew next to nothing about her staff. "Where's your family?"

A look of pain flickered across Sarah's face. "I . . . I don't have anyone."

"No one?" Erin asked gently. "Nobody we can call to come visit?"

Sarah smiled ruefully. "The chaplain's been here. Twice. Merlene and Inez too. And Claire. She said no one was seriously hurt in the accident. That the kids are all okay. I tried so hard not to hit them. But I guess my reaction time was too slow."

"They're fine. I promise. One little sling, not even a real cast. Otherwise, Logan gave them all a clean bill of health."

Sarah reached up to touch the stitches at the corner of her mouth. "He's still here at the hospital?"

"You mean Logan?"

"Yes."

"Actually, I think he left already." Erin frowned. "He hasn't been in to see you?"

Sarah glanced away, shaking her head. When she turned back, her eyes were filled with tears. "Logan knows . . . about the pills and the alcohol?"

Erin nodded, and then her own eyes brimmed with tears as Sarah's mournful sobs sliced through the silent ICU.

Father God, help her. Please help us all.

+++

Logan gunned the Harley's engine and leaned into the curve, relieved to see the live oaks and low-growing shrubs along the highway finally give way to tall stands of pine. Chill air whipped against him, snapping his scrub pants like a flag against his legs, and he was glad he'd taken the time to pull on the leather jacket. He'd almost forgotten it in his hurry to . . . *escape?* Logan snorted inside his helmet. Sure, he'd wanted to escape. Who wouldn't? He'd had a brutal day and deserved the comfort of some peace and quiet. Was that too much to ask?

He checked his rearview mirror and changed lanes, the obvious answer to his own question making him irritated all over again. It *had* been too much to ask, especially if he expected to find the comfort he needed in Claire's company. A quiet evening, the warmth of a woman who felt like she was made for his arms, the soothing sound of her laugh. He'd wanted that so much. It wasn't going to happen tonight. Maybe never. He squinted, remembering the look on Claire's face when she confronted him in his office, calling him insensitive, unbending . . . uncaring? She'd crossed her arms and spit those words at him as if his professional actions—his responsibility to keep things under control—somehow negated anything personal between them. Couldn't she see the difference?

Logan sucked in a breath, telling himself to let it go. But he couldn't. *Uncaring?* How could she say that? Of course he cared. He understood people had problems, knew full well it had to be rough for Keeley Roberts to care for a dying relative. But you had to leave that stuff at home. You had to buck up and get the job done. It wasn't like they were dishing up soft-serve ice cream. Lives were at stake every single day in the ER. As medical director, it was Logan's job to keep things together. He was good at it. He'd done that all his life, for his father and brothers when his mother left and for Beckah after she lost the baby. He'd been strong and logical; he'd had to. But to have Claire unjustly compare him to some jerk doctor in Sacramento who'd hassled her and—

He eased the bike to the shoulder, then pulled off into the gravel, braking to a stop. He slid his helmet off, recalling Claire's anger and how she'd parroted his words when he'd talked about weak links in his emergency team. Then she implied he didn't have a heart. She was wrong. It killed Logan to know Claire was there when her brother died, and it made him crazy to see her cry again today. It tore a hole in the heart she didn't give him credit for having.

But what was he supposed to do when everything around

him tumbled into chaos? Pray? Let God handle it? *Right*. The way God had handled the situation with Logan's alcoholic mother, the way God had kept Beckah from leaving? What if Logan had stood back and prayed for Sarah today instead of plunging that needle through her chest wall? She'd be dead now. Logan clenched his jaw and glared up at the blue Sierra sky. "I'm supposed to let go and let you handle it, God?"

He shook his head and groaned, his gaze dropping to the guardrail of the overpass ahead. Then winced at the memory of that TV footage, the car dangling. Claire said Sarah was racing to work because she didn't want to disappoint him. That she'd taken those pills because she needed to sleep so she could keep working all those long hours, all those extra shifts. Because Logan expected that from his staff. Claire was implying Sarah was stressed because of Logan, that the accident was somehow his fault. She was wrong. Sarah was just like him—tough, strong, responsible. The image of Sarah's face, bruised and beaten up and impossibly fragile, intruded.

Logan's throat constricted as he recalled Claire's final words today: *"You know where Sarah is."*

He put on his helmet, merged back into traffic, found the next exit . . . and turned around.

+++

"Smokey?"

Claire squatted down, lifting prickly branches aside and peeking into the underbrush. "Smokey . . . oh, please. Where are you?" She scrambled forward on her hands and knees, snagging her hair in the bushes, then dropped backward to sit in the red dirt, exhausted body and soul.

She'd rushed home after an awful day, posted flyers with Smokey's picture around the neighborhood, and searched for more than two hours. Not a black whisker in sight anywhere. Tears that had threatened all day slid down Claire's face. She wiped her nose on the hem of her T-shirt, then stared at the sky, realizing that absolutely everything was heading 180 degrees away from her master plan. Merlene Hibbert had dropped the bombshell about Renee Baxter's application for the job Claire needed, she'd ended up having to work in the ER, she saw one of her coworkers critically injured, and afterward she was handed one of her own stress pamphlets by the hospital chaplain. To top it off, she'd managed to go completely berserk and leap down the throat of the man she'd just discovered she deeply cared for.

Claire peered up through the trees to the barely visible deck railing. Now it was getting dark, and her brother's cat—if still alive—could be at the mercy of rogue raccoons for a second night. He had only one ear left after his first tangle with them. The pitiful thought brought on a second bout of tears as Claire pictured those flyers with Smokey's lopsided face and realized she might never have the chance to hear him purr. The thought made her unbearably sad and made her want to feel Logan's arms around her, to lose herself in that sweet comfort she'd only begun to discover.

It also made her regret saying those awful things to him today and wish that she could do it over again. But she couldn't and she . . . wouldn't. Because everything she'd said was true. She and Logan were completely different in ways that were far too important to ignore. He'd never understand the only way she'd functioned in the trauma room today was as a result of prayer, a direct appeal to God to help her save Sarah's life. And that she'd been praying for Logan's skill as he maneuvered the lifesaving needle into their teammate's injured chest. He'd never buy that what happened in the ER today had less to do with being tough and soldiering on and all the other noble attributes he seemed to demand in himself and his favorite nurses and far more to do with the grace of God.

Claire's brows drew together as she wondered once again if she'd missed signs of stress in Sarah—way back, at the Little Nugget interviews—and if there might have been some way to prevent today's tragedy. She had so many questions. Was what she'd told Logan right? Had Sarah taken sleeping pills to cope with the stress of her work? Had a desperate need to please Logan caused the nurse to take risks that nearly took her life? *Does Logan really care about any of that?*

Claire stood, brushing the dirt from her jeans and knowing there was another question eating at her as well. A big question. How was she going to stop having feelings for a man so obviously wrong for her and who figured nowhere in the plan?

+++

Sarah laughed and gripped the edge of the dining table; she had to hold on to keep from bobbing above it like those balloons . . . a rainbow of shiny colors. And look how the silver one reflected the light from the candles. She laughed again, pinching the edge of the big wooden table as the seat of her angel scrubs hovered above her chair. She was an astronaut at a birthday party. So crazy. Floating and laughing and . . .

Emily had frosting in her hair and all over her sweet face, pink and sticky and dotted with candy sprinkles. She tried to wipe it away even though stretching her arm out made her side hurt. But it only hurt a little and she didn't care. She was happy, so happy, because . . . there he was, sitting next to Emily at the table, smiling and still wearing that long bathrobe. A bathrobe at a birthday party—too silly. His hair was long, but he looked familiar and so very dear.

His eyes reflected the candlelight even more than the silver balloon did, and somehow they stayed focused solely on Sarah. No matter how far she drifted sideways, how many times she lost her bearings and slid completely off the chair, and how foolish and inept she must have seemed, he watched her every move with a loving and gentle expression on his face. And with profound patience. It made Sarah feel as if she were the special child at this table somehow, that she would always be precious to him no matter what. It filled her with an unimaginable joy.

She smiled and reached toward him, ignoring the pain in her side. "Daddy? Daddy?"

"It's me, Sarah. It's Logan."

+++

Logan lifted himself from the lumpy vinyl chair, realizing he'd dozed off. He rubbed his eyes and squinted at the clock on the darkened wall. Nearly midnight? No wonder his back was sore.

He glanced out toward the nurses' station and saw at least three heads turn hastily away. No doubt he'd be the subject of hospital gossip over the next several shifts. *"Did you hear how McSnarly spent the night in . . . ?"* But he didn't care. He was here because he had to know the truth.

Logan stepped close as Sarah finally opened her eyes. "Hi there, sleepyhead."

"Umm . . ." Sarah turned toward him, blinking; one eye was swollen closed and purple. "Sorry," she said after swallowing. "Hard to talk . . . mouth's . . . so dry."

"Well then, I can fix that." Logan lifted a can of Diet Coke from her bedside stand. "Got the official word from your surgeon that your belly's good. So let's party."

He popped the pull tab and inserted a flex straw into the can. Then held it while Sarah took a sip, reminding himself of the better times when he'd seen her doing this same thing. Too many times to count. In the ER, taking a quick swig of her cola and hustling to keep things organized, coming in early and working through her lunch break to make certain he had everything he needed. Was Claire right? *Am I the reason Sarah's here?*

"There," he said, pushing the thoughts aside. He lifted the can away. "Feel better now?"

"Better but still stoned," she said, lifting her arm to let the IV tubing dangle. "Morphine. Enemy of caffeine. I can't stay awake."

"You don't have to. Sleep is exactly what you need." Logan nodded, trying to forget what Claire had said about that bottle of sleeping pills, that Sarah had been trying to sleep so she could work. All because he counted on her to be there. "Doctor's orders," he added. "And it's working. I saw the latest X-ray; your lung's expanded nicely, and there was only minimal bleeding into the tissues."

"I don't remember much, but the nurses said you did a needle decompression."

"That's right. To relieve the pressure around your collapsed lung. Then I inserted the chest tube."

"I had the needles in stock, the full-size range of chest tubes, at least two water seal units, and . . ." Sarah's voice drifted off, her eyelids closing.

"Yes," he said, smiling with a growing sense of relief. This was proof positive that Claire was wrong. Because he and Sarah—absurd as it might seem—were having the same sort of conversation they'd be having if she weren't lying in that bed. About equipment, about procedures, about getting the job done. Things they both believed in. They were simply two teammates rehashing a tough shift, logically and unemotionally. Almost as if Sarah hadn't been the patient and Logan hadn't had to—

"You saved my life," she said softly, gazing up at him again. Her bruised chin trembled. "If you hadn't found the lung injury so fast . . ."

"No. Not me. Claire spotted it. We . . ." He hesitated, wondering if thinking of Claire in terms of *we* was a thing of the past. "Claire and I handled it together. She was sharp to suspect the tension pneumo so quickly and call me in there."

"She did great. And it was a good thing she was there." Her puffy brows drew together under the edge of her bandage. "But she was assigned to urgent care."

"Right. And we lucked out that she'd come in early. So when we were short a nurse—" Logan stopped himself but not in time. *Idiot. I'm an idiot.* For the first time Logan regretted that his favorite nurse could always read his mind.

"Short a nurse because I was late. Because . . ." Tears filled her eyes. "I set two alarms. I always do. Ten minutes apart, in case one fails. So I can be there early. If I'm early enough, I can check everything—all the stock, all the resuscitation equipment. Have it exactly the way you want it. Ready. No foul-ups, no weak links anywhere along the chain. Like you always say. But . . ."

Weak links? Logan held his breath, uneasiness rising. "Sarah, I know. I know how hard you—"

Sarah clutched his arm, stopping him. Tears streamed down her bruised face. "I'm sorry," she continued, her expression stricken and childlike. "I've been so sad lately, and I couldn't sleep. I took those sleeping pills; then I overslept. I drove as fast as I could to get there so I wouldn't be very late. So I wouldn't . . ." She closed her eyes for a moment as a mournful sob rose from deep in her throat. When she looked up, Logan knew she was about to say exactly what he didn't want to hear. "I did it all for you. Because I know how much you count on me. But now I've let you down. I'm so . . . sorry."

"Ah, Sarah, hey. Don't . . . don't." Logan leaned over the bedrail, sliding his arms around Sarah as best he could without disturbing the equipment or causing her any more pain. He stooped down and carefully rested his chin against the top of her hair.

He stood for a long while, silently holding Sarah while she cried. And completely frustrated by a confusing rush of feelings— hating the pathetic part of him that wished he'd never turned his motorcycle around, hoping he could think of some way to help Sarah, and finally realizing that he'd stepped with both feet into the very truth he'd come here to find. This time there would be no easy escape.

CHAPTER SEVENTEEN

Sarah pressed the button on the medication pump, and within seconds a metered dose of morphine began to ease the searing pain brought on by her sobs. *Oh, Logan, don't look at me that way.* He'd pulled the chair close to the bed, and she could see his blue eyes in the dim light that spilled through the open door. She shouldn't have said anything about not being able to sleep.

"Why were you sad?" Logan asked, his voice low. His dark brows drew together as if puzzling over a critical diagnosis. "You said you took those pills when you hadn't been able to sleep because you've been so sad. Why?"

Sarah closed her eyes, partly due to the floating effect of the medication but mostly because she could see how tough that question was for Logan to ask. The man didn't do feelings, not out loud anyway. He fixed things, got it done, all the while avoiding the messy sinkhole of emotion. So for Logan to ask something that personal . . . Tears welled under Sarah's lashes. He was one of the few people she had left who cared. *I have nothing left to lose—he deserves the truth.* Sarah opened her eyes and took a deep breath. Her throat squeezed around words she'd never said aloud before. "Today is my baby's birthday."

"Your baby?" Logan blinked, confusion in his eyes.

"Emily . . . Emily Grace would have been two today," Sarah explained, the morphine making her voice sound as soft as angel wings even to her own ears, making her daughter's name seem to leave her lips and float overhead. Almost like that silver balloon in her dream, the one that reflected all those candles. And she was surprised that saying Emily's name felt good. Joyful even.

"Would have been two years old?" Logan asked.

"Yes. She died. When she was twelve weeks old. SIDS," she added, feeling a familiar ache deep in her chest, pain that had nothing to do with fractured ribs. "She was perfect. From the moment I first saw her face. Healthy. I watched her so carefully." She met Logan's eyes to be sure he understood that. "I tried hard to do everything right. Then one morning, I had to wake her for a feeding. Which was unusual, and then I saw that . . ."

"And her father?" Logan asked, his voice husky and low. "Your husband?"

Nothing left to lose. "Husband? No. He had other plans. I knew him for only a few months. I'd barely graduated from nursing school down in LA. First time living away from home. I made a horrible, horrible mistake. So I took my broken heart back home. When I found out I was pregnant . . ."

Logan raised his brows as if he'd remembered something. "That's the problem between you and your parents?"

"My mother threw me out."

"But you're close to your father. You told me you worked at his body shop." He smiled. "And you always had his tools ready, knew exactly what he wanted, just like you do for me in the ER."

Not anymore. Not after I messed things up so badly, caused an accident that injured people. Sarah's eyes filled with tears again. "I let him down, just like I did you. I did something completely unforgivable and I paid the price. I'm still paying that price."

"No," Logan said, "I can't believe that after two years, after all you went through, your parents would still—"

"Believe it," Sarah interrupted. Her breath stuck in her chest, and she swallowed against a lump in her throat. "When I told my mother about what happened to Emily, she said it was my fault. That my baby was taken away because of my sin. And I would never be forgiven. Ever."

Logan's eyes narrowed and he clenched his jaw. "Your father feels that way too?"

Sarah recalled the strange and wonderful dream she'd had about her father and the birthday party. Her father in the robe with his hair way too long but with all that loving acceptance in his eyes. "No. I've talked to him a few times, but it's hard for him to go against my mother. And since she's the secretary at his shop, she screens his calls there."

"But he knows you're here now," Logan said, nodding. "Your father knows about the car accident, right?"

Sarah shook her head, feeling the gauze bandage brush against her pillow. "I can't put him in that position. My mother's not going to change her mind. I gave up hoping for that a long time ago. I gave up praying for it . . ." She paused, the dream image returning even stronger than before. The candles, the sense of joy, seeing her father after so long. "I've given up, that's all. I don't expect you to understand."

"But I do," Logan said barely above a whisper. "I do understand."

Sarah turned her head to get a better look at Logan's face and saw an expression there she'd never seen before. Sadness and pain. Then something that looked a lot like anger.

"Your mother abandoned you," he said, his tone flat. "I know how that feels. Mine left when I was only a kid. I'll bet I could match you prayer for prayer. Didn't work for me, either."

Sarah waited, unsure of what to say. The room was silent except for the hum of the automatic blood pressure cuff as it inflated around her arm and the bubbling of the water seal container attached to her chest tube. "I'm sorry, Logan," she said finally.

He shrugged. "It was a long time ago. What matters now is you. Getting you well. Helping you feel better about things. How can I fix it?"

The lump rose in Sarah's throat again. "You can't. It's something I have to learn to live with. Emily was the most wonderful thing that ever happened to me. I carried her under my heart for all those months." She pressed her hand to her chest above the bandages. "She's still here. I loved her and I wanted her from the first moment I knew I was carrying her, even though everyone said she should never have been." Sarah smiled through a blur of tears. "I had my daughter for only a short time. But she was a miracle, a joy. And to lose her . . ." She felt a tear slide down her cheek. "If you had a baby, you could understand how it feels. How the loss—" Sarah stopped as she saw the pained look on Logan's face. "What's wrong?"

"My wife was pregnant," he said quietly. "She miscarried at five months. A boy."

+++

Claire hit the End button on her cell phone and disconnected from her voice mail. No messages there or on the answering machine.

Logan hadn't returned her call during the twenty minutes she'd wandered around outside, calling for Smokey. She wondered if his phone was still turned off, if she should try again. Claire glanced at the clock. Nearly quarter to one in the morning. She wasn't going to call him. And after the scene in his office this afternoon, there was every reason to believe he'd turned his cell phone off so he wouldn't have to talk with her.

She sank back against the couch. What was she going to say, anyway? The message she left on his voice mail said it all: "Logan, it's Claire. I don't feel good about how things ended with us today. Will you call me?"

Ended with us. Ended. Had they? She glanced at the daffodils sitting on the coffee table in front of her. Hope in a glass vase. It was funny how the sight of those yellow flowers had made her feel hope. Stretching up, lifting their petals to the sun, and swaying in the breeze, they'd seemed like a miracle after so much darkness.

The daffodils made her feel hopeful for the first time in so long. It had scared her because she couldn't imagine it, couldn't trust her heart to ever feel anything more than grief and pain. And she didn't believe anything could fill the void left after Kevin's death. So she'd thrown her old vase of dusty silk daffodils away to keep herself from remembering that brief glimmer of hope at Daffodil Hill. Logan replaced them with this bouquet of real ones. Then kissed her, made her laugh, and asked if she could fit him into her life . . . helping her feel better than she had in so long. Until today. When she destroyed all that by letting doubts crowd in about Logan's compassion.

Claire's gaze dropped to the stack of flyers on the table next to the daffodils. The photo of Smokey, who'd finally ventured outside with the raccoons and was gone now. Lost. Or worse. Claire shook her head. They were in the same boat, she and Kevin's one-eared cat. Both gathering shreds of courage to square off with what they feared most and ending up lost. She looked across the room to the framed photos on the fireplace mantel. "Kevin, your cat's in the woods and your sister's wandering aimlessly." If ever she'd needed his advice, it was now.

She stared at the hammered tin frame next to Gayle's cross-stitched Scripture and the leather-strung pewter cross draped once more across the photo. Kevin's cross. She smiled, her heart tugging as if she'd felt her brother's big hand lovingly ruffle her hair. Almost as if she'd heard him say what he'd told her a thousand times: *"Give it to God, Sis."*

Claire sat upright on the couch, bowed her head, and prayed for Smokey to come home, for Sarah to be healed, for Logan to find his heart and his faith, and finally for herself. She peeked at the vase of daffodils. *Let me find room for hope in my master plan. Amen.*

+++

Logan regretted saying the words the moment they left his mouth.

"You lost a baby too?" Sarah asked, her hand hovering over her heart again.

Logan glanced toward the door, wishing he were outside it and already past the nurses' desk and all those curious faces watching his every move. He turned back to Sarah and saw the sympathetic look on her bruised face. "A miscarriage. Not at all what you went through. I'm sorry. I don't know why I brought it up."

Sarah smiled gently, her face reminding Logan of a broken doll. "Because you understand how it feels to lose your baby. And because you and . . . What was your wife's name?"

"Beckah," Logan said, wishing more and more that he could get up and leave. Grab his jacket, head outside to the bike. *Today is the wedding.*

"You and Beckah loved that little baby boy. . . ." Sarah's voice faded, her eyes closing.

Logan exhaled, aware now that he'd been holding his breath and that his stomach had twisted into a knot. He'd been a fool to mention Beckah's miscarriage; it wasn't anything like what happened to Sarah. Even if Beckah had been far enough along to feel movement and had held Logan's palm against her swelling abdomen so he could feel it too. Even if she'd already picked a name from her endless lists of boys' names.

"I was so blessed," Sarah said, opening her eyes again. "I had Emily for only a few weeks, but I got to hold her, feel her soft skin . . ." Her chin trembled. "I wish Beckah could have held her baby."

Ah, no. Don't. Logan's stomach wrenched again, and he reached out to touch Sarah's arm. Stop her. "Hey, shh. Don't worry. Everybody's okay. Let's get you well now. You need to sleep." He glanced toward the nurses' station. "And I need to get out of here before I generate any more rumors."

"Rumors?" Sarah wrinkled her brows.

Logan smiled, feeling a rush of relief that the subject had changed away from Beckah and babies. "Sure," he said, tipping his head toward the door. "It's probably already going around that you and I are involved."

"You? If they only knew you remind me of my father."

Logan frowned, feigning insult. "Hey," he said, watching Sarah's lids close again, "don't say that to anybody. You'll ruin my reputation."

She smiled without opening her eyes, burrowing her head

against the pillow as best she could with the bulky bandage. A broken, abandoned doll.

"Your dad owns that body shop, doesn't he? In Pollock Pines? It's his?"

"Mm-hmm . . . ," she answered, her voice barely audible.

Logan stepped closer and saw that she was asleep. The morphine was working. Good. He'd grab his jacket and slip out. But before he could turn, Sarah's hand rose, batting aimlessly at the air above her head and nearly hitting him. "Easy, kid," he said, grasping her arm gently and lowering it to the bed. "You'll pull on that IV tubing." He smiled down at her as she opened her eyes. "I'm going home now, Sarah."

"I . . ." Sarah's heavy-lidded gaze drifted overhead. "I keep seeing this silver balloon and my father in that bathrobe. It's so crazy. My father's almost bald, but I keep seeing him with long hair and . . . oh." Her eyes opened wide, even the injured one, like something amazing had happened. "Logan?"

"I'm here."

"I'm not sure I can do this, but I think I need to. We should . . . pray. For our babies. Will you help me?"

Logan's breath caught. If he left right now, she'd probably forget the whole thing. The morphine was making her see balloons. With a little luck she'd forget he was even here. That he'd mentioned Beckah and the . . . His stomach twisted again, perspiration rising on his forehead.

"Please?"

He looked at her, considering all she'd been through. And that much of the reason she was lying here today was due to him. How could he walk away? How could he tell her he didn't believe in prayer? "Okay," he said, taking her hand and bowing his head.

Sarah squeezed his fingers. "Jesus, thank you for being here. For coming on Emily's birthday. Please watch over her and also over . . ." She hesitated. "What was your baby's name?"

His throat closed. "Matthew Logan."

+++

Logan swiped the sleeve of his flannel shirt across his forehead before sweat could drip into his eyes. Not that he had anything to show for it. He squinted at the oak stump illuminated by the headlights of his Jeep, scarred by ax marks, surrounded by wood-chips, rooted deeply into the floor of his future bedroom—and not budging a lousy inch in any direction. Even though he'd been whacking at it for hours. He rotated his wrist toward the light to check his watch. It was 5:40 in the morning.

He leaned the ax against the stump and walked through the darkness toward the overlook. Below him, only a scant few lights shone near the river. Saturday morning and most of the people in the houses were still sleeping, no doubt. Sane people who hadn't been swinging an ax in inky darkness for three solid hours. He'd never seen anything so blasted stubborn as that stump, except himself. *And God?* There it was again. God. Pretty much the pattern since he'd driven up here—chop the stump, think about God, chop the stump, God again . . . chop, God, chop, God. Logan *was* nuts. Or suffering from sleep deprivation.

Logan rested against the granite boulders, still warm from yesterday's sunlight, and breathed in the pungent scents of mossy oak and loam. His land, his home. He'd worked hard to make this come true, the one promise that filled him with hope, but now . . . Logan thought of Sarah again, about how she'd asked him to pray with her and the look on her face afterward. Peace? Was that what he'd seen? Peace, after all she'd been through?

How could that be? For years Sarah had known nothing but pain. And loss. Rejected by her boyfriend and her mother and even her father for all intents and purposes. Logan clenched his teeth; the thought still made him angry. Then she'd lost her baby to crib death, and yesterday morning she'd nearly lost her life. She was lying in intensive care in horrific pain, with a hole in her chest, yet she'd bowed her head and thanked Jesus for being there and asked him to watch over their babies. *My baby.*

What Sarah said about carrying her daughter under her heart, about being blessed to have had a chance to hold her even for a few short weeks and how she wished Beckah could have had that too—it shook Logan to the core. It brought back images of Beckah after the miscarriage, her pale skin and the tragic look in her eyes, and his failed efforts to console her. His failure all around. He kept thinking of Sarah pressing her hand over her heart and saying, "She's still here," the same way Jamie had touched Logan's chest and talked about Jesus. Jamie, who was three years old. The same age that . . . *Ah, no. No.*

Logan closed his eyes against the unfamiliar sting of tears as he remembered holding Sarah's hand in prayer. And the question that stunned him: *"What was your baby's name?"*

Stunned him because it was a truth he'd never allowed himself to feel. Beckah hadn't only had a miscarriage; she'd lost a baby. *My son, Matthew Logan Caldwell.* Who would be nearly three years old now. Logan had failed to help Beckah, failed everyone since. Sarah and Claire too. He'd worked his whole life to single-handedly fix everything and he'd accomplished nothing. Failed like he'd failed with that stump. That blasted stump that refused to move. Stubborn as he was, immovable as . . .

Logan raised his gaze to the sky. Dawn was coming, light piercing what had felt like unending darkness. He ran his fingers through his sweat-dampened hair, walked slowly back to the Jeep, and turned the headlights off. Then he sat down on the oak stump and bowed his head. Tears slid from his eyes.

"You've been chasing me for a long time, Lord. Well, I've stopped running. The truth is, I can't do this by myself anymore. I need you."

+++

Claire raised the collar of her fleece pullover, then lifted her cup and scooted back into the deck chair. She sighed, her breath mingling with steam rising from the hazelnut coffee. Kevin's weather-station thermometer beside the kitchen door read barely forty-two degrees, a chilly Gold Country dawn. A Saturday meant for snuggling under a down comforter, sleeping in. Except that Claire was missing Smokey . . . and Logan.

She looked over at the cat's blue enamel food dish, now topped with crumbled bacon and chunks of cheddar cheese. Irresistible, hopefully, for a cat who escaped the clutches of monster raccoons. But as for Dr. Caldwell, it was obvious Claire offered no such temptation. He hadn't returned her call.

It seemed impossible that yesterday's dawn found her filled with hope and the discovery she might be falling in love with Logan. Now all that joy was gone. Like a burst balloon, candles extinguished before a wish was made. What would she have wished? Easy. That her master plan would succeed, providing the well-orchestrated answer to her constant prayer. She'd made it simple for God, done all the legwork and left him only the official stamp of approval. Monday the hospital would announce the choice for clinical educator, and Merlene's endorsement boded well for Claire's chances.

There was one more thing she was wishing for. Something outside that carefully checkmarked spreadsheet. *I wish Logan could be part of my future.* But there were too many obstacles. Not the least of which was her tirade against him yesterday. And the fact that it was unlikely he'd ever share her faith.

It kept coming back to that. Dr. Logan Caldwell was as apt to pray as Smokey the cat was to purr. Foreign acts to both of them. The cat's quirk she could work around, but a man who wouldn't trust in God . . . Claire's chest constricted. Then she leaned forward in the deck chair, tipping her head to hear. *The doorbell?* She set her coffee down, sifted her fingers through her hair, and walked through the cabin to the front door.

Logan stood on the doorstep, unshaven and rumpled, with woodchips clinging to his flannel shirt—and a look of undeniable urgency in his eyes.

CHAPTER EIGHTEEN

Claire stepped back so he could come in, battling a wave of déjà vu. Logan Caldwell on her porch at sunrise. But this time there was no deli bag and coffee, no eager smile. Today felt different. Scary different. Her stomach knotted.

"I'm sorry," he said, brushing at his shirt. "It's early and I'm a mess."

"It's okay. Come in." Claire waved Logan toward the couch and went to get coffee, rehearsing all the while what she would say. *Why is he here?* It wasn't due to a problem with Sarah; she'd checked with the hospital this morning and Sarah's condition was still stable. So it had to be her voice mail. What had she said? *"I don't feel good about how things ended with us today."* Ended. There it was again. Claire's fingers trembled as she lifted the coffeepot. Was Logan here to make that ending a reality?

By the time she returned to the living room, her mouth was dry with dread. She set his cup on the coffee table next to the vase of daffodils and sat near him on the couch. He asked about Smokey, and she told him she'd had no luck finding him.

There was a stretch of awkward silence; then they both spoke at the same instant.

"Claire, I . . ."

"About yesterday . . ."

Claire managed a weak laugh. "Go ahead." She watched Logan search for words, her heart thudding dully in her chest. *Go ahead and tell me it's not going to work out. That it's best we end this now. You're sorry, but . . .*

"I'm sorry. You were right about me. I'm an idiot." He exhaled, his lips curving in a tentative smile. "You're not going to faint, are you?"

Claire opened her mouth, closed it, then shook her head.

"Good." Logan cleared his throat, his expression growing serious. "Because I need you to listen. You were right about Sarah. She had that accident—" he winced—"partly because of me. She was trying to please me. She took those pills because she was hurting from some tough things that happened to her, and she knew I was the kind of man who could never understand that. That I would consider it an excuse, a weakness. But you know what? You know what's so ironic?"

Claire shook her head, holding her breath. She hadn't a clue about anything.

He gave a short laugh. "It was me all along. I'm the weak link. Not Sarah or Keeley Roberts or even . . . McMuffin." His eyes softened. "And certainly not you. Not you in a million years. You're the bravest woman I've ever met. You came back to the ER and had the guts to stand up to someone like me after all you went through with your brother. After everything that happened afterward. I'd like to get my hands on that Sacramento doc for what he did to you." He grasped her hand. "I'm sorry, Claire."

Claire's eyes filled with tears, and the ache in her throat made it impossible to form words. Then somehow she was in Logan's arms, her face nestled against his beard-rough jaw. He was warm and solid and smelled of salty skin and chopped wood.

She finally found voice enough to whisper against his cheek, "Where did all this come from? What's happened?"

His hands slid down her arms, and he held her away while he answered. "Sarah and an oak stump, I guess. That would be the easy answer. But the fact is, I went to the ICU last night to talk with her. To prove you were wrong about my causing her accident. I wanted the truth, and I got a whole lot more of it than I'd planned. Talking with Sarah made me face things I've been too stubborn or too angry to deal with. For as long as I can remember. From my mother to my marriage with Beckah. I didn't tell you she'd been pregnant the year before we broke up."

Oh no. Claire struggled for words.

Logan raised his palm before she could speak. "Wait. There's more. The truth is, I was disappointed when Beckah told me she was pregnant. I told her the timing was wrong, my career wasn't established, and my student loans were too high. I couldn't deal with it."

Claire remembered Jada Williams, and her stomach quivered. "Oh, Logan, you didn't ask her to—"

"No," he said, cutting her off, "I'd never do that. But Beckah knew how I felt, and when she miscarried, she was sure I was relieved. I wasn't—I really wasn't. I couldn't convince her of that, and I couldn't seem to comfort her either. I did it all wrong. She was suffering and I quoted statistics about miscarriage. She couldn't sleep and I wrote a prescription. At the worst time in her life, I didn't give Beckah anything she really needed. She got more and more depressed and I told her to buck up, that counseling was worthless. When she wanted us to start going to church together . . . I scheduled myself to work Sundays."

Claire touched his hand. "I'm so sorry."

"The point is, I'm the one who should be sorry. I'm the one

who fouled up. When Sarah was talking about all those rough things she'd been through, I started feeling like she was telling me about myself. And when she asked me to pray with her . . ." Logan smiled at Claire's audible gasp. "Another thing you were right about, it seems."

Thank you, God. Oh, thank you. Claire watched Logan through a shimmer of tears, her heart taking flight.

"Somewhere between the ICU and three hours with an ax in my hands, I realized I was so angry about people leaving me that I'd started pushing everyone away—even God." He frowned. "Especially God. I wasn't going to talk to someone who knew the truth about me." Logan shook his head. "Of course, the real truth was that God's been there all along, waiting for me to finally figure out that I need him in my life."

Claire swiped her fingers against the corner of her eye. Then she waited while Logan sat there in silence, noticing how tired he looked. More than tired. He looked vulnerable despite those big shoulders and that strong, beard-shadowed jaw. Vulnerable and raw and . . . so very dear. *I'm falling in love with him. I care for this man with my very soul.* Claire smiled, her heart so full she could barely breathe. She was going to tell him how she felt. Right now.

"So we had a talk," Logan said before she could speak. "On the stump."

"We?"

"God and me. But mostly I just listened. It seems I've got a lot of things to make up for. Like—" He stood up suddenly. "Wait, it's Saturday!"

"Right." Claire patted the couch. "Sit back down; you're exhausted. I'll fix some breakfast and . . ." *Tell you how I feel about you.*

"Ah, blast." Logan checked his watch. "I'll have to hurry. Thank

you for listening, but I need to go or I'll never get there in time."
He bolted forward, his leg bumping the coffee table.

Claire grabbed the vase of daffodils before it could topple over.
"Wait."

"Can't. I'm sorry. I have to do this," he called over his shoulder.
"I'll call you."

+++

Logan fastened his helmet strap; he'd make better time on the
bike than in the Jeep. Two hundred twenty-four miles to Carmel,
according to MapQuest. Three hours and forty-five minutes. He
could shave some time off that. Traffic on I-5 wouldn't be too bad
on a weekend, except that you never knew how it would go near
the Bay Area.

Logan kicked the starter, put the bike in gear, and pulled out
of the condominium carport. He'd get there before Beckah's wedding. He had to. He needed to tell her he understood why she left.
That he'd driven her away, done everything wrong even though
he hadn't wanted to. She needed to know that even though he'd
made it impossible for her to stay, he'd never wanted her to go.
It was all his fault. There wasn't much time, but he had to try to
finally make things right.

+++

Erin peered through the wavy window glass of Gold Strike Coffee
and toward the road lined with old-fashioned streetlights, wishing
it were warm enough to sit at one of the little tables outside. But
midmornings in April were still parka weather in historic Placerville. It was called Old Hangtown back in the 1840s because of the
way justice was carried out at the end of a rope.

She frowned and reached for her coffee cup. No, she wasn't going to think about Brad. Yet. She'd deal with him later today. This morning she was meeting with Claire to talk about Sarah. *Ah, there she is.* Erin returned Claire's wave and watched her cross the street toward the coffeehouse, thinking once again how radiant her friend looked lately. That the flush on her cheeks had to be from more than the chill morning air.

"Hey there," she called out as the old door's bell announced Claire's arrival. "They have cinnamon rolls this morning. Still warm—I got you one. Grab your coffee."

She did and a few minutes later joined Erin at the window table. Claire thanked Erin for the pastry, then unwrapped her marled lavender scarf, her eyes shiny as she settled into her chair. Erin smiled knowingly as Claire laid her cell phone on the table. *Who's the lucky guy?*

Claire smiled back before lifting her cup. "Obviously you couldn't sleep either."

Erin shook her head. "I still can't believe yesterday. If this keeps up, I'll be wallpapering the nurses' lounge with those awful critical stress pamphlets. Oops, sorry."

"No problem. Trust me, none of this was in my master plan. Not one bit of anything that's happened over the past two weeks, bad and good . . ." Claire's voice faded away, and soft color rose to her cheeks again.

Well, well, well. Every symptom in the book.

"Thankfully Sarah's condition stabilized," Claire said. Her dark brows drew together, and she lowered her voice. "But what about the accident investigation—could that jeopardize her nursing license?"

Erin set her cinnamon roll down. "Good question. I was awake half the night thinking about it." *And about thieving Brad.* "Sarah's blood screen was basically clean. Alcohol and drug levels nearly nonexistent. So the police won't have anything to hang their hats on there. But there's still a chance she could be charged with speeding or reckless endangerment, I suppose. Driving without sleep is as dangerous as any drug." Her stomach tensed. "I may as well be herding cats for the way I managed this one." *And my love life.*

"You? Why are you saying that?" Claire lifted her spoon from her coffee, staring.

"I should have seen how troubled she was. Here I am, spending all this time organizing Faith QD to offer support for the staff, and I miss something like that? I've already signed up for the next CISM peer counseling class, but maybe that's not good enough. I mean, what kind of charge nurse am I, if I'm so blind I can't see something like this coming with one of my nurses?"

"You're the best kind of charge nurse. Don't do this to yourself." Claire reached across the table and grabbed Erin's hand. "I'm glad you're taking the counseling course. That'll be great. But you can't blame yourself about Sarah. I counseled her after the day care disaster, remember? I keep going over that, but she seemed so tough, so together. And now in hindsight we're all thinking about things we missed in her behavior and feeling guilty about it." She paused as a waitress in a fringed doeskin vest refilled their cups, her gold nugget earrings swaying as she moved.

Erin watched as Claire took the opportunity to peek at the display on her cell phone. She felt a twinge of envy; was she ever going to feel that way? ever find anybody she could trust? "Expecting a call?" she asked with growing curiosity.

Claire's gaze lifted. "Not exactly. Well, I'm . . . hoping."

Erin raised her brows, but Claire shrugged. The mystery man would stay a mystery for now, it seemed.

"Anyway," Claire continued, "what I meant was that we're all pretty much undone by what happened with Sarah. If you'll pardon my quoting certain unpopular stress pamphlets, we shouldn't put unrealistic pressures on ourselves. We need to—"

Erin wrinkled her nose. "You're not going to mention petting sheep and eating corn dogs, are you?"

Claire groaned at the reference to the chaplain's rodeo therapy. "No. But we need to watch out for each other."

"And try to do things that feel good," Erin quoted, smiling as Claire peered at her cell phone yet again. She tapped the phone. "So when are you going to break down and tell me who's suddenly making you feel so good?" She grinned. "Come on now. It's not like I can't tell something's going on."

Claire's eyes lit up. "Oh, Erin, I don't know if I should say anything. But I'm dying to tell someone how I feel."

"Spill it. Please. You have no idea how much I need to believe in happy endings right now."

A phone rang, startling them both. But it wasn't Claire's; it was coming from Erin's purse. She dug it out, rolled her eyes as she recognized the number, then faced Claire, mouthing that she was sorry for the interruption. Erin turned her chair away, leaving Claire to her cinnamon roll.

+++

Claire chuckled after taking a sip of her coffee. The way Erin's voice carried, everyone in the coffee shop could likely hear.

"What?" Erin asked as if straining to hear. "Yes, I hear you. . . . Really? I can't believe you did that. How'd it go? . . . Her last name's

Roberts. Keeley Roberts. Staffing should have her phone number. . . . What? . . . Yes, I checked with ICU an hour ago. They were taking another X-ray, but she's doing fine. . . . Well, then, you'd better hang up. All we need is for you to have an accident too. . . . Okay. Talk to you later. Bye." Erin disconnected, then turned back to Claire. "Forget petting sheep. After that call, I'm sure the flying pigs will be distraction enough."

Claire licked the icing off her fingertip. "Who was that?"

"McSnarly."

Claire lowered her roll, a raisin falling to the table.

"He wanted to tell me he'd found a way to reach Sarah's father in Pollock Pines; apparently there's some issue with his phone messages. So Logan sent the police to his body shop to tell him to get over to Sierra Mercy because his daughter needs him. Can you believe that?" Erin took a sip of her coffee. "And guess what else our doc is doing on his day off?"

Claire opened her mouth and then closed it without saying a word.

"Calling Keeley Roberts to apologize." Erin raised her palms. "I'm serious. He's on some strange campaign today. If I dared to hope, I'd say that sometime between yesterday and today Logan Caldwell met God on a mountaintop." She stared at Claire. "What?"

Claire shrugged and feigned innocence but couldn't help smiling. "So," she asked, her grin spreading, "did Dr. Caldwell say anything else?"

"Only that he was planning to check on Sarah when he got back into town."

Claire's smile faltered. "Back into town?"

"Yes, and that's the weirdest thing of all. He was on his bike on Highway 1, a few miles outside Carmel."

"Carmel? Why would he . . . ?"

"His ex-wife's wedding. He said something about having to talk to her and 'finally make things right.' Imagine it: your guests are all gathered, you're wearing this great dress, and the organ starts to play. It's your second chance at happily ever after. Then up roars your ex-husband on a motorcycle, and—" Erin halted. "Claire?"

"I . . . ," Claire whispered, rocked by confusion. She'd seen Logan just a few hours ago, and he said he'd call her. Yes. He had. *And now he's with Beckah?* Her stomach lurched. She'd almost told him she was falling in love with him.

Erin leaned across the table, her eyes filled with concern. "What's wrong?"

"You're sure?" Claire asked, telling herself Erin could have misunderstood. Even if Logan had been talking about Beckah, even if he always talked about Beckah, even if . . . *No, don't let this be true.* "You're sure he was going to Carmel?"

"Yes," Erin said, and then the confusion on her face slowly changed to understanding. She pointed to Claire's cell phone. "Uh-oh. . . . *He* was the call you were expecting? I can't believe this. You and Logan?"

Claire nodded, then shut her eyes to quell the flow of tears. She wasn't going to cry; this was humiliating enough without sobbing in public. "We've been going out, and it's been great." She opened her eyes. "*Was* great. Now I don't know what's happening. Logan showed up this morning just after dawn and—like you said—was talking about mistakes he'd made and how he needed to make up for them. Actually you weren't too far off about God and the mountain." She smiled despite a second rush of tears. "So that part's all good."

"That part's great. But you mean he didn't say anything about going to the wedding?"

"No. He was talking about his marriage and how he'd fouled things up. All of a sudden he just took off. Said he had to do something, had to hurry to get there in time." Claire decided not to say Logan promised to call. Right now it sounded like a bad line from a soap opera.

Erin was quiet for moment. "I don't know what to say. Except that in the time I've known Logan, he hasn't gotten close to any women. Despite what some people say, deep down I honestly think the man has a wonderful heart. So if he's opened up to you . . ."

Claire took a slow breath. "He has about a lot of things. And he is wonderful. More than wonderful. He brought me daffodils, showed me the sunset on his building site, took me fishing, and made me laugh. He said I make him feel optimistic about things, that he wants to be in my life." She bit her lower lip. "Remember when you were talking about finding a guy who gets it?" She tapped her fingers over her heart. "One who understands that it's what's in here that counts?"

Erin nodded. "Absolutely."

"I think Logan's one of those. And Lord help me, I might be falling in love with him." She sighed, her throat aching. "I'd started feeling hopeful for the first time in so long, but now . . ."

"Oh, sweetie." Tears welled up in Erin's eyes. "Maybe it's no big deal that Logan went to Beckah's wedding. Maybe he . . . um . . ."

Claire tried to smile, touched by Erin's support. "Maybe he likes those little bags of candy-coated almonds?"

"Yes!" Erin laughed, swiping at a tear sliding down her cheek. "Now you're talkin'. And goose pâté, organ music, all that fancy Carmel la-di-da. Logan's a fool for that stuff. Plus, he'd never pass on the chance to get dressed up. Coat, bow tie, paisley cummerbund, patent leather loafers . . . the whole *GQ* thing. Right?"

Despite herself, Claire smiled at the ridiculous image. *Thank you for sending me this amazing friend, God.* "Except that when Logan rushed out of my house this morning, he was wearing plaid flannel, work boots, and was completely covered in sawdust."

Erin grinned. "Well, that settles it. They'll never let him in!"

Their chuckles faded and they were silent for a few moments. Then Erin reached over to pick at Claire's cinnamon roll, catching her eye. "His will be done," she said very softly.

"Yes," Claire whispered, trying not to look at her cell phone.

+++

Sarah squinted at the clock on the wall, trying to orient herself. Eleven forty-five . . . in the morning? She glanced out toward the nurses' desk. Yes, day shift staff. She understood now why patients got confused in hospitals. It all seemed Alice-in-Wonderland surreal: fluorescent lighting, medication, sleep disturbance, eerie sounds, and strange dreams.

Despite the pinching pain in her side, Sarah smiled. She'd stopped having the dream about Emily's birthday party. The one she'd had over and over since her car collided with the guardrail, the dream with all that candlelight, the silver balloon floating overhead, and the man with the long hair who was watching her so intently with such loving and forgiving eyes. She finally realized that he reminded her of every picture she'd ever seen of Jesus.

Sarah looked at the Bible Chaplain Estes brought early this morning. She hadn't opened it, and she doubted she would anytime soon. But having it here made her think about Logan and how they'd prayed together last night for the babies they'd each lost. It felt right, and she hoped he'd found as much comfort as she had. That their babies were being watched over, and . . .

Who is that? Sarah blinked, staring through the doorway at the man talking with the nurse at the desk. He was middle-aged and a bit overweight, wearing work twills and a nylon Windbreaker, not completely bald. *But so much grayer than I remember.*

Tears filled her eyes and she waved, calling out with every ounce of her strength, "Daddy!"

CHAPTER NINETEEN

Claire sprinted the last quarter mile of Gold Bug Loop, welcoming the burn in her legs and lungs, far more tolerable than the painful confusion she'd struggled with since leaving the coffeehouse an hour ago. A complete jumble of thoughts. Images of Logan holding his ex-wife in his arms, replays of the conversation they'd shared at dawn, and endless analysis of his expression and tone when he'd said, "I'll call you."

She sucked in a breath and pushed harder, pumping her arms, lengthening her stride, and telling herself to let it all go. Except that Logan hadn't called, of course. And worse, he seemed to have turned off his cell phone after he'd reached Carmel. Did he find Beckah before the wedding?

She didn't know the answer. Maybe she never would because Logan had shut Claire out. *And now . . .* She slowed to a stop in front of Kevin's oak tree, gulping air and fighting another alarming wave of nausea. She breathed slowly through her nose to dispel the queasiness that swept her since the other awful thought had surfaced. Her confusion hadn't only been about Logan Caldwell. It was about God too. Claire needed to face the very real possibility that God was also shutting her out, that he had no intention of answering her prayers about Logan, her future, or even her brother's poor lost cat. It was the only explanation for everything that had happened these past weeks. God had stopped listening to Claire as certainly and deliberately as Logan had switched his cell phone to voice mail. *"Logan Caldwell. I'm not available . . ."*

Not available. *Is that what you're telling me, Lord?*

Claire swept her fingers across her dripping forehead, then dropped onto the cool grass, wiggling backward until she rested her back against the oak's deeply creviced trunk. She blinked up through its branches at the noon sun, realizing that the familiar hollow ache in her chest had returned with a vengeance. That empty hopeless hole left by Kevin's death. It wasn't fair. None of this was in Claire's master plan; it wasn't supposed to happen. She'd been so careful to protect herself, her future—her sanity— since her brother's death. She'd prayed for that every single day. But now she'd run smack into the worst irony of all: God chose to answer Logan's prayer instead of hers. He met Logan at that oak stump and inspired him to search his heart . . . and find his wife.

Claire sighed. She shouldn't be surprised; she'd suspected that Logan still had feelings for Beckah. Even if he'd said all those things about wanting to be included in Claire's life, about wanting to see her again. Even if he'd held her, comforted her as she talked for the first time ever about Kevin's death, kissed her so passionately, made her believe that her heart could feel love again. Even if he'd given her daffodils . . . and helped her to feel hope.

Oh, Lord, why? The ache in Claire's chest became unbearable, and she blinked against a rush of tears. *Why are you doing this to me?*

She stood and crossed her arms, trembling as goose bumps rose on her damp skin. Chills, without the wonderful sense of well-being and peace that always came at the end of her runs. No endorphin rush—she hadn't felt it the last several times she'd run either. God was denying Claire this small comfort too. The same way he'd ignored her desperate prayers. When she'd made plans to move forward with her new career, God allowed her to be sent back to the ER, a place he knew would fill her with pain and fear. And when she'd prayed for her heart to be healed, he let Logan come into her life instead. To mislead her into being hopeful again, make her feel safe enough to fall in love. Then God let it all end, leaving Claire as lost as her brother's one-eared cat. Why? Had it been too much to ask?

Her gaze drifted to the carved numbers and letters on the tree above her. The Scripture, her brother's initials, Gayle's initials. A future that never would be. Her throat squeezed tight and tears came again. Kevin was gone, Smokey was gone, and Logan was gone. God wasn't sticking around either. He didn't care about her plans or that her hopes were dying like that vase of daffodils back at her brother's cabin.

All she had left was the new job, a decision to be announced on Monday. It was the reason she'd come to Sierra Mercy Hospital in the first place. She'd wanted nothing more than to be clinical educator back then. Everything else and everyone else—Merlene, Logan, Erin, Sarah, and Jamie—had somehow come into her life and confused it. They'd steered her away from her plans, knocked her off track. And it all happened because God stopped listening to her prayers.

Claire hugged herself to still the shivers and tried to take stock. Merlene put in a recommendation for her regarding the educator position; she was on Claire's side. They had a new nurse in the ER, so her obligation there had ended. The timing was right to move ahead with the plans she'd made for herself. A clean break from the painful confusion of these past weeks—past years. There was no reason Claire couldn't do that. It was what she'd wanted from the beginning, wasn't it? The only difference now was that she'd be doing it all by herself. *I can do it.*

If that was true, why did the thought make her feel so unbearably lonely?

"Where are you, Lord?"

+++

"You look absolutely radiant, Sarah. But then, I heard you have a special visitor."

Sarah smiled at Erin through a blur of tears. She might as well get used to that; they just kept coming. "Yes. My father. He should be back in a few minutes. He wanted to hunt down my favorite ice cream—eggnog. I tried to tell him it wasn't going to be easy in April. But right now I believe anything can happen. Did you hear Logan sent the police to his shop?"

"I did," Erin said, a faraway look coming into her eyes for a moment. "Our doctor's on quite the mission today." She pointed at the hospital-issue Bible lying on the table next to a bandage roll and a Diet Coke can. "And it looks like Chaplain Estes is thinking along those same lines."

Sarah nodded, feeling a twinge of guilt for all the times she'd passed on Erin's invitations to join Faith QD. "Even though I told him I wasn't ready for that. Because I don't deserve . . ." She sighed. "The truth is, I did some really bad things a few years ago. Hurt my parents. You can't imagine how much. I've been so ashamed."

"You're not sure God's forgiven you?" Erin asked as she reached for Sarah's hand.

A tear trickled alongside Sarah's nose. "I only know he's intent on making me a complete crybaby." She squeezed Erin's fingers.

"I'm not sure where I stand with God yet. But I hope you and Logan and Claire and everyone can forgive me for the trouble I caused. I'm so sorry."

"Now hold it. Listen to me." Erin leaned forward, her expression intent. "I'm the one who should be sorry. Me. I'm in charge of that ER. It's my responsibility to look out for my staff. My friends," she added, her voice warm. "You're a coworker and a friend, Sarah. And I should have noticed you needed help."

"Don't apologize." Sarah shook her head. "You've been great. I'm a tough nut to crack."

"Still, I think I've let too many things outside of work distract me. Stupid complications I've been trying to deal with."

"Like Brad?" Sarah asked, calculating by Erin's immediate frown that she'd guessed right.

"Yes. You can't even imagine what problems he's causing. I'm meeting him for lunch. Trust me, I'll be loaded for bear. But before that, I have to finish straightening out my grandmother's credit card account. I'm furious at the billing errors I'm finding. Like eleven hundred dollars' worth of charges at some Nevada horse farm? Can't wait to do battle on this one."

Sarah grinned. "Go get 'em, boss. I'll bet you've been blistering that punching bag."

"Of course. And speaking of battles—" Erin lowered her voice— "don't worry about your job. If the accident investigation creates problems, we'll figure out a way to deal with it. And help you with a plan for counseling if you need that, write letters of recommendation. . . . We'll make it all happen. A team effort. We're not letting go of you."

Sarah lifted her chin and met Erin's gaze. "Don't bend any rules for me. I want to do the right thing. Finally."

"I know you do, and I'm going to bounce some ideas around with Logan when he gets back." She pulled at a strand of her ponytail, her expression troubled.

"Gets back?" Sarah asked.

"It's a long story." Erin glanced toward the nurses' station. "And right now I see a man holding what looks like a big Baskin-Robbins sack." She pretended to sniff the air. "I think I can smell eggnog—you believe in miracles, girlfriend?"

Sarah smiled, her eyes misting yet again. "I'm starting to."

+++

Claire finished towel drying her hair and ran a big-tooth comb through it, deciding to let it dry naturally. She had nothing but time today. Accent on *nothing*.

She frowned at herself in the bathroom mirror. No, she wasn't going to think that way. She'd wallowed in self-pity all the way back from Kevin's tree, half-jogging, half-walking . . . mostly crying, and marched straight through the cabin door to the vase of withering daffodils. She'd tossed them out, along with the congealing mound of treats in Smokey's untouched food dish. Then she'd showered until the hot water—and her tears—finally ran out. Hope. When had that pesky element crept in and become so important?

Claire set the comb down and turned away from the mirror, not wanting to read the answer in her eyes. *It all began with Logan.* It was time to get back on track. Back to the original plan.

She padded barefoot to the bedroom closet and pulled out a long sweater, tugging it on over her jeans and T-shirt, and slipped into her pink flip-flops. The sweater and a mug of tomato soup would keep her warm while her hair dried and she worked on her lists. In essence, she was right back to where she'd started a few weeks ago and hadn't really lost anything. "Only God and Logan and my brother's cat," Claire muttered. She headed for the living room, telling herself to get a grip.

The point was she'd still be waiting for the announcement of the clinical educator job regardless of what happened in the past few weeks. Even if she hadn't been blindsided by the ER and its director. She'd hear the official word on Monday, and there was still every reason to believe her original plan would be moving forward. She'd had some distractions, sure. But she would put them aside the same way she'd tossed away the wilted daffodils. It was good, actually. Her mind could be clear now, focused on her future.

The phone rang and Claire's heart leaped to her throat. *Logan—it must be. Oh, thank you, God!*

She caught it on the third ring, snatching the cordless phone from its cradle and striding toward the fireplace. "Hello?"

"Claire? It's Merlene Hibbert."

"Um . . . oh. Yes." Claire's legs weakened, first with disappointment, then with sinking dread. Another disaster in the ER? A complication with Sarah? "Is something wrong?"

There was silence, followed by Merlene's foreboding sigh.

Claire sank onto the ottoman, her hands beginning to tremble.

"I thought I should tell you before you heard it through the grapevine," Merlene said. "The board has decided on Renee as clinical educator. I tried to convince them to make it a flex position shared with you, but Renee wants her full-time hours back. I'm sorry."

Claire stared at the phone, stunned for a moment. "But you mean . . ." She gripped the phone until her knuckles went white, struggling for words. Why was this happening?

Merlene cleared her throat. "Unfortunately, as of Monday we

won't have a position in the ed department for you. Renee may need you to help her for the next couple of weeks, but after that I'm afraid Sierra Mercy can only offer clinical shifts. I know it's not your first choice, but with Sarah Burke out, we'll have an opening in the ER. That would have to be approved by Dr. Caldwell, of course." She sighed. "Although I've just learned that he won't be coming in for his shift tomorrow. Out of character for him, but if he's back on Monday, I'll ask—"

"No." Claire rose, despite a crippling rush of dizziness. *Logan's staying in Carmel?* "Don't. Please don't ask him. Dr. Caldwell doesn't want me—I mean, I don't want . . ." Her voice faltered as she battled tears. "I know you mean well, but please don't make any plans for me. I need time to figure things out."

"Very well, but I want you to know I tried my best to get you hired. Your effort on behalf of the ER staff during the day care incident was a godsend, and I have to wonder if you hadn't been there for Sarah Burke, well . . . you were clearly an answer to prayer."

Answer to prayer. "Oh, I . . ." Claire shut her eyes for moment, trying to think of something to say, then turned toward a sound in the kitchen. A scratching and a plaintive, hoarse . . . meow? Was that a meow? "Oh . . . oh!" Claire's voice cracked with emotion as she caught sight of Smokey at the pet door. "I have to go now. My cat was lost, and he just came home!"

Twenty minutes later, after a can of tuna and a leisurely sniffing tour of the cabin, Smokey was curled up in his favorite spot on the back of the couch, dozing. Claire felt like she'd run a Denver marathon. She was too exhausted for tears of happiness or disappointment. She was numb . . . mostly just numb. She gingerly stroked Smokey's back. Despite his matted tail, some missing fur on the top of his head, and a scabbing wound on his remaining ear, her cat looked like a survivor.

A lump rose in Claire's throat. "You did it, boy. Who'd have thought . . . ?" She gazed toward the fireplace, then rose slowly and quietly so she wouldn't disturb Smokey and walked over to stand in front of the mantel.

She touched the frame of Kevin's photo, the one of him in the silly Superman shirt, and shook her head. "He did it, Kev. Smokey finally faced his raccoons. He went out there and squared off with the one thing that scared him most in the entire world." She nodded. "Trust me, I know exactly how that feels, and—"

I do know. She stared at Smokey, her thoughts swirling aloud. "My cat and his raccoons. Me and the ER—we both did it. We did what we had to do, and it was okay. More than okay." *I helped save Sarah's life.*

"We're winners, Kev. We're . . . champs!" She grinned at her brother's picture, noticing for the first time how happy he looked in the photo. Completely full of joy. And then she noticed that her chest didn't feel hollow anymore. For the first time since Kevin's death, she was thinking of him and remembering him and not . . . hurting. How could that be?

Claire's gaze moved along the line of photos—Kevin; she and Kevin with their parents; and the snapshot with Gayle in Mexico, the one draped in the leather-strung cross she'd worn that first day in urgent care. Crazy as it seemed, it was true; looking at the photos wasn't painful. In fact, it made her happy and strangely peaceful and warm. Clear down to her soul . . . like that sensation she'd been missing after running. Only better. Much better.

Goose bumps rose as she realized it went further than that. Because the fact that she'd lost the job didn't feel all that bad now either. Even knowing that her carefully crafted plans for her future . . . Claire's breath caught as her gaze lingered on the last frame in the row on the mantel. Gayle's hand-embroidered linen. Her engagement gift to Kevin, his favorite Scripture.

> *"For I know the plans I have for you,"* declares the Lord,
> *"plans to prosper you and not to harm you, plans to give you hope and a future."*
> Jeremiah 29:11

Claire reread the words she'd lived with for two years, the same verse carved by her brother's hand on the oak tree in Gold Bug Park. She held her breath, the words leaping out at her like she was seeing them for the very first time: *To give you hope. And a future. I have plans.*

His plan. Claire raised her hands to her mouth, tears stinging her eyes. Hope. By God's plan. The answer had been there all along. Had been inches above her this morning when she'd cried out, asking God, "Where are you?" God's plan, not Claire's plan. And he *had* answered her prayer. *Heal my heart. Move me forward.* He'd moved her forward by sending her *back* to the ER to face her fears.

"Oh, Father." Claire sank to her knees beside the hearth and bowed her head, tears spilling down her face. "You had a plan for me, and I got in the way. All I had to do was trust you. You are my hope. I see that now. Thank you, Lord."

+++

Erin leaned back in her computer chair and checked her watch. Still too early. She was meeting Brad at the park for a picnic, and he said he'd pick up some deli sandwiches. But she wanted far more than pastrami and dill pickles today. She wasn't settling for anything less than the truth. About the Little Nugget Victim Fund envelope and what he'd done with the money. Gambling? Had he taken it to Tahoe the night he'd left her behind? He'd brought a pizza over the evening before—after Erin put the envelope in her tote bag. Was that when he stole it?

Were there any more lies? betrayals? Erin's stomach churned. After all those years with her father, she already knew much more than she wanted to about dishonesty. Today when Sarah talked about making mistakes, Erin almost repeated something she'd heard over and over from her mother: "We can't out-sin God's ability to forgive." Well, regardless, Erin doubted she had what it took to forgive Brad. She'd wanted to try. She'd prayed about it countless times since she'd found those torn checks, but . . .

But now she still had twenty minutes to kill. She'd do a bit more work on her grandmother's credit card mess. Over a thousand dollars to a Nevada horse farm. How could they make a mistake like that? Ridiculous. Erin smiled, thinking of Iris Quinn. Redheaded like Erin, tall and willowy, and Kate Hepburn feisty. Or was, until the exhaustion of caring for her sick husband took its toll. Followed by the unrelenting stress from a mountain of medical bills left in the wake of his death. Erin hated seeing the spark dwindle in Nana's eyes, and if she could do battle with the credit card company . . . *ding-ding*, round one!

Erin reached into her desk and pulled out an envelope neatly labeled, "Credit Card Statements, Iris Quinn." Then typed in the name of the creditor, Betcher Horses, and clicked to start the Internet search. She grinned, relishing the thought of explaining that the only livestock her seventy-six-year-old grandmother owned was a goldfish named Elmer Fudd and the last time she'd been on a horse was on the carousel at the Santa Cruz boardwalk.

Her eyes widened. *Wait. What?* She double-checked the spelling on the credit card statement and the Web site URL. Betcher Horses was a horse-racing Web site? Online betting? How could that be possible?

Erin picked up the statement showing the disputed balance and the Web site URL. Printed, of course, with Iris Quinn's name and credit card number. Similar to many other statements Erin had stored in her desk for at least a year. Her grandmother didn't gamble. But if someone had managed to get ahold of her credit card number . . .

Oh no. Erin closed the Web site and propped her elbows on the desk, pressing her face into her palms. No. It couldn't be. But her roommate didn't gamble, and as far as Erin knew, her roommate's fiancé didn't either. And the only other person who'd had access to this desk—to Iris Quinn's credit card information—was Brad.

Betcher Horses? Erin growled, her hands balling into fists. *Betcher sweet backside, I'm going to . . . try to stop short of killing him.*

+++

Claire poked at the logs in the woodstove, closed the glass door, and latched it. The afternoon had turned rainy, and the oak-scented fire, along with the sweater, mug of soup, and her cat's safe return, warmed her inside and out despite the day's turmoil.

She glanced up toward the sound of raindrops pelting against the steep metal roof of her cabin and smiled at her thoughts. *My cabin. My cat.* It was the first time since Kevin's death she'd thought of them that way. She'd surprised herself earlier when she'd said those words to Merlene on the phone: "My cat was lost." It always seemed like she was a kind of caretaker here, preserving all that had been her brother's—his house, his cat, his SUV, his firehouse sweatshirt, his running trails.

Maybe because she'd felt too guilty to let him go and too terrified to face her fears head-on. So she'd jogged her brother's trails, run from the ER, turned away from her friends and her church, and printed off spreadsheet after spreadsheet of painstaking plans for her future. Doing everything she thought would protect her heart. And then expected God to put those plans into effect. Claire shook her head. She'd been a stubborn fool.

She peered out the rain-streaked window to see the pines moving in the wind and the sky still dark with clouds and then rejoined Smokey on the couch. Her Bible lay open on the table next to a lone daffodil petal that had dropped when she dumped the vase. *Hope.* She'd reread Jeremiah 29:11 and her study Bible's explanation of the verse: ". . . as long as God, who knows the future, provides our agenda . . . we can have boundless hope. Not that we will be spared pain, suffering, or hardship, but that God will see us through to a glorious conclusion."

And then she remembered what Erin had said this morning at coffee when they'd talked about Logan: "His will be done." That's what Claire should have been praying all along. She knew that now. God had a plan, and she had to trust it for her career, for her life, for . . . Logan Caldwell? Claire's throat tightened. Was it God's plan that Logan go back to Beckah?

She sank into the couch, remembering the look on Logan's face this morning and the urgency in his eyes when he'd told her about praying with Sarah and talking with God on that oak stump. Praying. A man who'd once been a brokenhearted boy clutching a picture of Jesus and praying for his mother to come home. A man who'd lost a baby, a wife . . . and now found his faith again. Tears rose in Claire's eyes. "Your will be done," she whispered, her voice blending with the steady drumming of rain.

The truth was that despite Claire throwing out every roadblock she could, God had gifted her with a number of blessings these past weeks. He'd called her back to the ER to provide the very counseling she needed herself. He'd given friendship—and vital missing fellowship—with Erin and the Faith QD ministry and presented that beautiful, healing moment with her patient Jada Williams. Then he'd stood beside her to save Sarah's life and in the process restored Claire's trust in her skills. And he'd sent Logan. *To show me my heart is healed enough to love again.* That was good, so good, to know.

Claire hugged herself, aware of that achy-good sensation in her chest, the same feeling that started when she'd begun to realize she was falling in love with Logan. *"Plans to give you hope and a future."* God had brought Logan into Claire's life so she could feel hope again. As for her future . . . she'd have to have faith. If it didn't include working at Sierra Mercy, she'd be okay with that. If that future didn't include Logan Caldwell, then she'd somehow have to accept that too. Because as much as it hurt to lose him, she believed now that God intended to see her "through to a glorious conclusion." Meanwhile, she still had Erin and Smokey and—

Claire sat up suddenly, not sure if the insistent pounding sound was rain or thunder or . . . the door? She listened again. Yes, knocking. She crossed the room, afraid to breathe. Then prayed as she turned the doorknob. *Your will be done. Your will be done.*

Her knees barely held her when she saw him.

Logan's hair was wet; whether from a shower or the rain Claire couldn't be sure. He'd changed from wood-sprinkled flannel to a fresh white shirt and khakis but hadn't shaved. And that simple ruggedness, combined with his obvious fatigue, made him look as raw and vulnerable as her wayward cat. His blue eyes caught hers and Claire's heart stalled.

"Hi," he said softly. "I'm back."

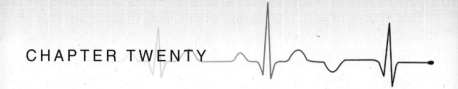

CHAPTER TWENTY

"Logan," Claire managed, "come in. You're getting soaked."

He glanced through the rain toward his Jeep, and for one awful—*awful*—moment, Claire's stomach sank. *He's going to say Beckah's with him.*

"Great. Thank you." Logan smiled. "But I left the Jeep running because I didn't know if you'd be here. My cell phone battery died, and—stay there. Don't move an inch. I'll be right back."

That's why he didn't call. Claire's heart soared as she watched Logan jog to the Jeep, but she reminded herself not to press him with questions. She'd let him say what he came to say. *Your will be done.*

In mere moments, Logan returned and stepped through the front door. He took Claire's hand and led her toward the couch, declining her offer of coffee. His voice, despite his obvious fatigue, took on the timbre of urgency it had early this morning. "I was afraid you wouldn't be here," he said, tugging her forward. "I need to talk to you about—" He stopped as he spied the bedraggled black cat asleep on the couch. A grin lit his face. "Hey, Smokey's back!" Logan turned and gave her hand a squeeze. "That's so great. He's okay?"

"A few nicks here and there, but it looks like the one-eared cat versus raccoon came out just fine." She smiled, that sense of amazement washing over her once again. *Smokey and his raccoons, me and the ER.* Now Logan. What had Logan battled today? And who won?

"Good," Logan said, sitting and drawing Claire down beside him. He continued to hold her hand, his gaze on her face. "Plenty of good things today, then." He glanced down for a moment. "And I . . ."

Claire held her breath. She told herself that whatever would be would be, what came of Logan's day in Carmel she'd accept. She'd be happy for him. She'd still feel love for him no matter what he said, but she would let him walk away if that's what had to be done.

"I went to see Beckah today," he said, raising his eyes to hers again. "In Carmel."

She started to feign vague surprise but then decided against it. Today was about truth. Nothing less would do. "I know."

Logan raised his brows.

"I mean, I heard you went. I was with Erin when you called this morning. But I didn't know if you'd found Beckah. . . ." Her voice faltered.

"I did. I found her."

"Oh." Claire struggled against a lump that threatened to choke her.

"Not that anyone was thrilled with a Harley pulling up to the wedding chapel, believe me. Especially that guy with the cages of doves." He chuckled at the confusion on Claire's face. "Beckah's bird thing. But at least I caught her before the ceremony started."

Claire tried to smile, but her teeth were clenched too tightly. If Logan didn't cut to the chase pretty soon, she was going to jump out of her skin. She summoned a whisper. "And?" *You stopped the wedding? You told her you still love her? You . . . ?*

Logan sighed. "I told Beckah what I told you this morning. That I handled everything wrong from the beginning. With our marriage and especially with the baby." His brows drew together, the look in his eyes achingly honest. "The truth is, I let my wife down when she needed me most. I told Beckah I didn't expect her to forgive me, but I had to come tell her how sorry I am. Because I know she deserves so much more."

She tightened her fingers against his, her chest cramping. *Yes. She deserves who you are now.* Claire cleared her throat. "And what did she say?"

Logan smiled, shaking his head. "She said, 'God is good.' That she'd been praying for me since we broke up and that my coming there today was her answer."

Claire's heart thudded. "Her answer?"

Logan nodded. "No surprise Beckah was light-years ahead of me on figuring things out. Figuring *me* out. She knew I wasn't going to get a clue until I finally got things right with God."

"You told her?" she asked, genuinely surprised. Then realizing, of course, that Beckah would have seen that Logan had changed. It was so beautifully apparent. So awesomely perfect. Beckah would know Logan was becoming the man of faith she'd wanted all along. Claire's throat constricted. What woman wouldn't want him? But had Logan felt the same way about his ex-wife? Had he told her—?

"I told her about you, too," Logan said, beginning to grin.

"About me?"

"Yes, all about you." Logan brushed his thumb gently across the top of her hand, his eyes warm. "She got an earful."

Claire's voice emerged in a pathetic squeak. "How did she react to that?"

Logan laughed. "Well, first, she said I'd given her the best wedding present she could have hoped for by coming there to talk with her. And that I should stop feeling guilty, because she's completely happy now. Then she said there was nothing to forgive." He smirked. "Unless I'd managed to scare her precious doves to death."

She felt suddenly dizzy with a warm rush of hope. "What did she say about me?"

Logan took both of Claire's hands in his. "Beckah said she was glad . . . I found someone to love."

Love? Claire's eyes opened wide and then immediately filled with tears. Her heart swelled until there was barely room to breathe. Was this possible? Love?

"It's true, Claire. Even if it's been only a few weeks, I know how I feel. I'm falling in love with you. You're everything I've ever hoped to find in a woman. You make me believe anything is possible." He frowned. "I know I'm not easy, and I've got a lot to learn about relationships. About God too. But I want all of that now. I'm hoping you'll be willing to help me. . . ." Logan hesitated, his eyes searching hers. He reached up to brush a tear from her cheek and let his fingers linger along her jaw. "Please say I'm not scaring you with this. Say you're not going to tell me to get lost. Tell me it's possible you could feel the same way."

Claire smiled through her tears. "Yes. Oh . . . yes. Of course I'll help you—we'll help each other." She trembled with the sudden rise of a million goose bumps. "I'm sure that was God's plan all along." She exhaled, her heart full beyond measure as she gazed into Logan's eyes. "I feel the same way about you, Logan." *Thank you, Lord.*

Logan took her face in his hands and touched his lips gently to the side of her face, then to each of her closed eyelids, her brow . . . and finally her mouth. He wrapped his arms around her, kissing her with warmth and tenderness. And then continued with a second deeper and more lingering kiss that threatened to take Claire's breath away—until Smokey leaped from his perch on the back of the couch to land on Logan's shoulder. They both jumped and burst out laughing.

"Hey, careful there." Logan lifted the one-eared cat cautiously into his lap. He stroked the top of Smokey's head. "What's the matter, champ? Feeling left out?"

Claire chuckled at the sight of the infamous McSnarly making nice with her finicky cat. God was indeed good. *Wait.* She leaned closer, listening in disbelief. "Do you hear that?"

Logan grinned, the crinkles appearing beside his eyes. "Miracle day. He's purring."

+++

"Aha," Logan said a few minutes later, watching from the doorway as Claire filled a large earthenware mug with coffee. "Real cups. I almost got impaled with that toy tea set."

She looked up and laughed, completely at ease, and he remembered the first time he'd seen Claire in this kitchen, the night he'd driven her home from the Denim and Diamonds fund-raiser. She'd been so nervous, pacing around the room in those same pink flip-flops.

Logan exhaled softly. Claire looked so beautiful in that long sweater and jeans, her silky hair spilling loose around her shoulders. She was an incredible mix of intelligence, strength, and rare innocence, a woman who'd endured so much heartache yet somehow remained warm, sweet, loving. . . . *She might love me. Me.* Logan's breath caught, still trying to get his sleepless brain around the staggering thought. He'd do anything he could to make it work, to protect this woman and make her happy. *Help me do things right this time. Help me be the man she needs.*

He crossed the kitchen to stand behind her and slipped his arms around Claire's waist as she searched the silverware drawer. "Need some help?" he asked, brushing his lips against her ear.

She sighed and turned in his arms, looking up at him, her eyes . . . troubled. *Troubled?*

"No, but . . ."

"What?" Logan's brows drew together with concern.

"You must be starving and I don't have anything to offer you." She shook her head. "Smokey got the tuna, the coconut cookies are gone, and I had the last of the soup. All I can find is jalapeño pickles, chai tea, some birdseed, and—"

Logan laughed, pressing a fingertip against her lips. "Don't say another word. I was hoping you'd let me take you out somewhere nice tonight. Someplace that doesn't require a fishing pole." He narrowed his eyes. "As a matter of fact, I was planning this great date when you stormed into my office to tell me I was a heartless loser."

"I didn't," Claire said, her face turning pink.

"You did. And I'll admit it knocked me sideways." He raised his brows. "No one's had the guts to take me on face-to-face before."

Her lips curved into a half smile. "I noticed you didn't fight back."

"No," Logan said, thinking how long ago that seemed and how it felt like he'd traveled so much farther than the miles to Carmel and back. "Probably because I knew on some level what you were saying was true. People had every right to complain about me.

But the fact is—" he paused, glancing down to where Smokey had curled himself around his pant leg—"I was making myself even more miserable than I was making everyone around me. And I probably would have kept right on doing that." He bent down, kissed Claire's lips gently, and smiled at her. "If it weren't for you. You started the whole ball rolling, and now look, we've got miracles. Kind of like your cat."

"Hold it, McSnarly. You're not going to start purring, are you?"

Logan slipped his arms around Claire's waist again. "Maybe." He kissed her, enjoying her sweet response, and leaned back. "But I'm trying to control myself. Because I want to take all the time in the world to get to know you—to get everything right. You're too important to do it any other way." He stepped back and rubbed his hand across his eyes. "Plus, I'm so blasted sleepy I can't see straight. I crashed for a couple of hours last night in the ICU, then swung that ax until dawn."

Claire grinned, her eyes lighting. "And talked with God."

"Yes. That'll wear you out for sure." He smiled. "I rode my bike forever and then hauled on back here. I haven't even shaved. I must look—"

"Wonderful," she said emphatically. "I've never seen anyone look so wonderful. But you really should go home and get some sleep."

While Logan hated the thought of leaving her, Claire was as right about this as she'd been about Sarah's condition yesterday in the ER. "Okay, I'll finish my coffee and do that. Get some sleep, clean up, and then I'll be back. I was thinking we'd have a late dinner at Rio City Café on the Sacramento River. Get dressed up and have candles, soft music . . . all those romantic things," he added, certain he was sounding corny but knowing he'd do anything that made Claire happy. Balance a tiny coffee cup, make a fool of himself doing country line dances, buy a hundred bouquets of flowers, hang the moon if she asked him to. "Anyway, we'll make a real night of it. I don't have to be up early for work. Do you?"

"Work? Well . . ." Claire sighed. "No. Work definitely won't get in the way. And your romantic dinner sounds perfect." She handed him his coffee mug, then beckoned for him to follow her to the living room. "But if the rain lets up, I might want you to take me somewhere else first."

"Where?"

She stopped and smiled mysteriously. "You'll see. Deal?"

"Deal," he agreed, trying to suppress a yawn. "Nap. Mystery detour. Dinner. Sounds like a plan."

They drank their coffee sitting close to each other on the couch. Watching the fire, listening to a new country music CD, and saying very little. It felt warm and peaceful and . . . *good*.

Logan propped his chin on his palm, watching as Claire lazily petted Smokey, then let his gaze drop to her Bible on the table. For some reason, it made him remember Jamie's hand on his chest. Logan smiled. *It all feels good.* A lot like . . . coming home. He set his empty mug down, content to sit here forever but fighting a losing battle to keep his eyes open. If he didn't get moving, he'd wind up sprawled out and snoring—nothing romantic about that.

"I'm going to leave now," he said, standing and pulling Claire up beside him. He folded her close in a hug. "I'll power sleep," he whispered in her ear, "and get back here as soon as I can. I miss you already."

He walked to the door, thinking aloud the things he needed to finish up. "I'll call Erin on the way home. Tell her I've crossed Keeley Roberts off my apology list and make sure she has enough staff scheduled for tomorrow." He shook his head. "Erin's working overtime to help pay her grandmother's mortgage. She's one incredible woman. And scary—do you know she works out with a punching bag?"

"I do," Claire said, glancing at her watch. "Which reminds me. You should sleep first and call Erin afterward. Right now, she's having a late lunch with Brad." She grimaced. "I got the feeling your incredible charge nurse was spoiling for a fight."

+++

Erin yanked her elbow from Brad's grasp and spun around to face him. "You're denying this?" She pointed at the credit card statement and carefully taped-together checks atop the picnic table, seething at his nerve. "I found those checks in your car!" She crossed her arms over her chest to still her trembling. And stall her fists. "Do you think I'm stupid?"

Brad glanced toward the small group of people at the next picnic table and then smiled at Erin. The sun, finally peeking through thinning clouds, glinted on his blond hair as he reached for her again. His voice was deep, soft, and smugly confident. "Whoa there. Easy, girl."

"Don't. Don't tell me to whoa, and don't touch me." She pulled her cell phone from her jacket pocket. "Just give me one good reason why I shouldn't call the police."

Brad's smile disappeared. "Because you don't have proof."

"What do you call that?" Erin asked, slapping the checks and knocking a package of potato chips off the table.

"Your word against mine." A smirk tugged at his lips. "Do you have any idea how many of the boys in blue get great car deals from me? Besides, you haven't lost anything. You said it yourself; the checks were stopped by the banks."

"But there was also over four hundred dollars in cash. Cash. Including nickels and pennies donated by Merlene's granddaughter. Money for charity, to help a precious boy who was burned. I don't understand how you could take his money and gamble with it. Is that what you did?" Erin blinked against a rush of tears. *How could I have been so blind?*

"You're forgetting I gave you a donation. A check for two hundred and fifty bucks. Not to mention flowers that set me back more than a few."

The roses. Erin grimaced against a wave of nausea. How could this be happening?

"So, even if I borrowed the cash—which I'm not admitting to— what's the big deal?" He gestured at her grandmother's credit card statement. "As for your wild accusation about online betting, I'm guessing the police would smell the obvious there."

Erin scrunched her brows. "Meaning?"

Brad raised his palms. "That you're looking for revenge, of course."

"Revenge?" Erin's eyes widened, new dread churning her stomach. "What are you talking about?"

"Give me a break. Do I have to spell it out?" He studied her face for a moment. "Look, you're a beautiful, desirable woman. Fun, too, the few times I can get you a decent distance from work. And away from that church, but—"

"I met you there," Erin interrupted, frowning. "We met at church."

Brad shrugged. "I meet a lot of women at a lot of churches. Other places too." He shook his head. "Fortunately they don't perch on an iceberg like you do. A guy can only be so patient. Three months with no more than a few little kisses? What do you think I am, a monk? You can't blame me for having something else going."

"I . . ." Erin fought a rush of dizziness, her face flooding with heat. Brad's brows rose, a look of amusement spreading across his face. "I can't believe this. You really did expect me to be that patient. Well, then, I guess we need to talk about—"

"Wrong." Erin lifted her chin. "We're finished talking. Forever." She snatched up the checks and credit card statement and stuffed them into her purse, holding it against her like a shield. "If nothing else, at least I know now that you're nowhere near the kind of man I'm looking for. Nowhere even close. I was a fool to trust you."

Brad was silent for a moment and then pulled the Corvette keys out of his pocket, his eyes watching hers. For an instant, his expression seemed almost regretful. He sighed. "The man you're holding out for doesn't exist, Erin Quinn. You can trust me on that 100 percent."

Erin watched him walk away, not sure what made her soul feel sicker—that Brad was a liar, a cheat, and a crook. Or the bone-deep fear he was right: she'd never find someone to love.

+++

The best part was that she wasn't afraid anymore. Sarah straightened in the bed and took a breath, grateful she needed very little pain medication and that Inez had helped brush her hair and pull it back in a clip. She could almost see beyond the swelling in her left eye. In a few days the doctors would remove the chest tube and she'd no longer be confined to this room.

But the real freedom, the wonderful sense of peace, had little to do with her remarkable clinical improvement. She glanced at the Bible on the overbed table. Even if she wasn't ready to face God, she now knew with amazing certainty that her sweet, innocent Emily was safe in the arms of angels. That she'd be watched over for eternity. Nothing scared Sarah in the beautiful light of that. She could survive it all—long weeks of recovery from her rib fractures, the accident investigation, her already-scheduled counseling, and even the possibility of a disciplinary review by the California Board of Nursing.

She sighed, pressing a flower-embossed get-well card against the front of her hospital gown. She looked up as a student nurse arrived at the doorway with a food tray. Sarah smiled. "Hey. Come on in."

"Here's your supper," the bright-eyed woman said, smiling back. "Bread pudding tonight." She regarded the card in Sarah's hands with a knowing look. "Someone special?"

Sarah nodded. "It's from my mother. Daddy signed her name." She took a soft breath, remembering her father's awkward but earnest explanation when he'd brought the card at lunchtime. *"I bought it for your mother to send along to you. She wouldn't sign it, but she read every word. Every single word. Then she said, 'Oh, go ahead and take it to her. Can't hurt.'"* He'd winked at Sarah, then said, *"That's something, pumpkin. That's our start."*

Sarah chuckled at the student nurse's puzzled expression. "It's much better than it sounds," she said, the ever-capricious tears springing to her eyes. "This card gives me hope. And there's nothing better than that."

+++

Claire stood, leaning against a tree and watching Logan as he surveyed the vista, that wonderful new warmth filling her chest to brimming. He'd dressed for their date in slacks, a crisp shirt, twill jacket and tie, arriving rested and freshly shaved. And at peace with himself finally. So different from the man who'd rapped on her door at daybreak, scruffy, intense, and so frantic to talk. Claire smiled at the memory. McSnarly in flannel and woodchips, all fired up from a long-overdue meeting with God. It still seemed surreal. So much had changed in such a short time. They were like two new people meeting in a familiar old setting. She sighed as Logan moved close, his lips brushing her cheek.

"So what do you think?" Claire asked, loving the way the deepening sunset glinted on the flecks of gold in his blue eyes. "Are you glad I brought you back here?"

"Mm-hmm," Logan answered, slipping an arm around her shoulders and returning to the view. Daffodil Hill, three hundred thousand fluted blooms dancing in the breeze, lifting their buttery faces to be kissed pink by the setting sun. A few yards away, the last straggling picnickers loaded baskets and blankets into cars parked along the rural roadside, one of the children tossing chips to a ragtag clutch of chickens.

Logan chuckled. "And I'm glad you're not wearing hiking boots this time." His gaze traveled appreciatively past the hem of her spring dress to her ribbon-tied sandals. "If you take off running in those, I might have some hope of catching you."

Claire smiled, feeling the breeze lift a tendril free from her upswept hair. *Hope.* There it was again, the reason she'd been drawn to this spot the moment she'd first seen it and the reason she'd wanted to come here again tonight. The sight of those daffodils, even when she'd been so anxious and confused, buoyed her troubled spirit with a promise of hope. She had no doubt it was God's plan from the very beginning, and he was making good on that promise. More than good. "I'm not running away. I'm completely happy right where I am."

"Even with your career sort of . . . sidetracked?"

"Even with that. I finally figured out I need fewer spreadsheets and more prayer along the lines of 'your will be done.' I'll be helping Renee for a while, but then I have a few new ideas I want to run by Merlene."

Logan laughed, drawing her closer. "I'm sure you do, Nurse Avery." He glanced toward the deserted roadside and turned back to Claire, the tenderness in his expression making her heart melt. "Right now I have an idea of my own."

"Like?" Warmth rushed to her face as Logan tucked a finger under her chin, lifting it.

"Like kissing you," he whispered, his lips an inch from hers. "If . . ."

"If?"

"If you're not going to leap away and sit on a chicken."

"Not dressed for it," she murmured, smiling and closing her eyes.

"Good." Logan cradled her face and kissed her thoroughly, then leaned back, his hands still warm on her face. "Remember when I said I'm falling in love with you?"

Claire nodded, smothering a grin. Like she'd ever, ever forget. Silly man.

"Well, it's true." Logan inhaled slowly, his eyes earnest. "This feels so right, Claire."

"To me too," she whispered, feeling that truth to the corners of her soul. "I've never been so happy in my whole life, and I—" She stopped, wincing. "Ouch. I think I got pecked." Claire stepped away from Logan, squinting at a clucking shadow near her sandals. She frowned. "Chickens."

"Ah . . . good. That's a relief. For a second there, I thought you were complaining about the kiss."

"Never." Claire laughed, taking hold of his hand. "I'd love to prove that to you over and over. But don't we have a dinner reservation?"

"We do." Logan led her the short distance to the road. "Which is good, since I'll need plenty of strength for tomorrow," he added as they reached the Jeep.

"Tomorrow?"

"I was hoping to talk you into spending some time with me."

"Oh. Nice sales job, McSnarly."

"Thank you." Logan grinned. "I'm still going in to check on Sarah and Erin, but mostly I needed the morning to tackle that blasted stump again. No more stalling around. No more ax. I'm getting a heavy-duty tow cable, attaching it to my Jeep, cranking it into low gear, and ripping the thing out. I was hacking at that stump all night using my Jeep's headlights." He shook his head. "The answer was right there all along."

Claire smiled, remembering how, at one of her lowest points ever, she traced Kevin's tree carving inches above her head. *"For I know the plans I have for you . . . plans to give you hope and a future."* Could anything be more wonderful than that? "I know exactly what you mean. And a thought just occurred to me."

"What?" Logan asked, leaning against the Jeep's door.

"Maybe you could save that stump. Have it made into a table base or something. It's a good reminder of what happened there this morning." She raised her brows, and Logan's expression—at once both solemn and joyful—touched her heart.

"Yes, you're right. Let's do that." Logan looked toward the hills of blooms barely visible in the fading light, then grasped both of Claire's hands in his own. "Come with me tomorrow, and we'll look at those house plans together. I'll buy deli and we'll have a picnic right in the middle of the building site. I want to hear what you think about everything. Every detail. Because once that stump comes out, I'm telling the contractor to move forward with things. Fast as he can."

He wrapped his arms around her, hugging her close enough that she could feel the soft thudding of his heart. "I think we should plant some daffodils," Logan added, his lips against her ear.

Claire's breath caught. *His oak stump. My daffodils. Faith, hope . . . love.*

"So what do you think?" Logan asked. "About the flowers. Good idea?"

"The best idea I can imagine," Claire whispered, smiling despite a rush of tears. Happy, hopeful, amazing tears springing from joy beyond anything she could have planned. She was never surer about anything in her life.

Heal my heart. Move me forward. . . . Oh, thank you. Thank you, Lord.

EPILOGUE

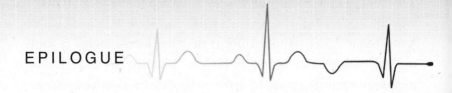

October

Claire licked frosting from her finger and glanced at Erin, sitting across from her at the nurses' lounge table. "I can't believe we're eating cake at nine thirty in the morning." She chuckled at the look on her friend's face. "Okay, scratch that. Of course I can—we're nurses." She picked up the card she'd been reading and studied the enclosed photo. A chubby, smiling two-month-old African American baby dressed in a 49ers jersey—and the obvious center of attention at a housewarming party.

"Who is this baby?" Erin asked, peeking at the photo as Claire set it down.

"Charles Avery Williams. Future fullback."

"Avery? As in . . . ?"

"As in . . . an honor from a grateful patient." Claire smiled at the memory of Jada Williams that day in urgent care when they'd joined hands and bowed their heads. "And proof of the power of prayer."

"Well, amen to that." Erin leaned back and propped her feet on another chair, grinning and sifting her fingers through her hair. "I can't believe you showed up today. It seems like you've been in classes, studying for classes, or on the road to a gazillion more classes ever since they crowned you Disaster Queen."

Claire snorted. "Emergency preparedness coordinator, thank you. And I'm hardly the queen. More like royal lackey. Yesterday I actually inventoried the county's entire stockpile of biodegradable toilet tissue." She wrinkled her nose. "But Sierra Mercy is footing the bills for my classes, and—" she pinched her fingers close together—"I'm this close to getting the CISM trainer's certificate. Then I can start teaching those peer-counseling workshops myself. Get a few more nurses trained besides you and improve staff resiliency against critical stress. Plus, I'm still working on that plan to make Faith QD part of it all."

Claire's smile faded as she glanced at the message piped in pink buttercream across the remains of the sheet cake. *Good-bye and Good Luck, Erin.* Her throat tightened and she told herself not to cry. "I still can't believe you're leaving."

Erin nodded. "Monday. Right after we clean up from the garage sale and get Nana's goldfish cozy in his new travel tank. I don't want my grandmother within a hundred miles when they pound that Bank Owned sign into her lawn." The familiar mix of anger and pain flickered in her green eyes. "As far as I'm concerned, the loan company that got her into this subprime mess is as guilty of scamming her as . . ."

"Brad?" Claire asked, knowing Erin's heart had to be hurting from that betrayal, no matter how many times she shrugged it off.

"Except that I'll never prove it. But he sure does put a face on all this ugliness. At least we got those credit charges reversed."

"And thank goodness your grandmother still owns the home in Pacific Point."

"Cottage." Erin clucked her tongue. "Meaning it's so small I might have to sleep with my feet out the window. I'm not even sure where I can hang my punching bag, but I'll figure it out. On the plus side, there's a view of the ocean . . . if you use binoculars and squint at this teeny space between Arlo's Bait & Moor and the surfboard shop." She laughed, then nodded. "Iris Quinn needs to be there. So we're going."

"She must have great memories of that house."

Erin's expression grew wistful. "Me too. I spent summers there for as long as I can remember. Fishing with Gramps, collecting shells, falling asleep on the sofa bed while listening to the ocean, and . . . hiding a starfish in my pillowcase." She grimaced. "Don't try it; they get pretty ripe."

Claire smiled, missing Erin already. "Sounds like good times."

"They were, especially during all the upheavals with Dad. Being there with Gramps and Nana felt safe, you know?" Erin twisted a strand of hair, her gaze drifting. "Peaceful. Like I could finally trust everything would be okay, and . . ." Her words faded and she shrugged. "Maybe we both need that now." She brightened. "God did pretty well by you. Maybe he has a plan for me too."

"I'm sure he does."

"Meanwhile," Erin continued, "I've got that job at Pacific Mercy Hospital, where Nana worked when she was a student nurse. And since it's the same hospital system, my pay and benefits stay the same. There's still a second mortgage to pay on the beach cottage and—"

Erin and Claire turned toward the sound of the door opening.

Sarah peeked in. Her blue eyes were bright and she looked rested, with only the barest hint of a forehead scar remaining from the trauma she'd survived. "Hey, great. You made it, Claire. But get a move on, ladies. Urgent care's due to open in twenty minutes,

and there's already half a dozen people in the chapel. You're late."
She disappeared through the door, leaving Claire and Erin shaking
their heads.

"I'm still pinching myself that we've got her back," Erin said
with a sigh. "It's so great that the driving citation didn't affect her
nursing license."

Claire nodded. "And the counseling's been helpful. She seems
much happier."

Erin grinned. "Yeah, well, some things haven't changed—the
woman can still pitch a Diet Coke can twenty yards. Let's get a
move on before we rile her."

+++

Claire walked toward the front of the refurbished chapel, sneaking
a glance back at the hallway door. No more stragglers, it seemed.
But this group, on Erin's last day to lead Faith QD, was already
the largest to gather before a midmorning shift. Included were
Merlene Hibbert, Keeley Roberts, Inez Vega, and almost a dozen
other employees from several departments—most of them wearing
Erin's lamp logo T-shirts. And though Sarah was currently holding
down the fort in the ER, even she had come to a Faith QD gathering recently. "Only observing," she'd told Erin. "Seeing what all
the fuss is about." Claire smiled, thinking about the far-reaching
possibilities. Hope was a wonderful thing.

She looked toward the altar, her heart tugging as it always did
when she caught sight of the hand-painted tile plaque depicting a
sweet-faced angel holding an armful of purple flowers: *Amy Hester
Memorial Chapel.*

Erin gathered the group into a circle, and Claire took one last
peek at the chapel doorway . . . then her heart leaped. He made

it. Logan, standing on the threshold wearing his blue scrubs. And holding little blond Jamie in his arms. The boy's mother, Carly, stood beside them, waving.

"Got room for a few more?" he called out, grinning. "Guess who had a doctor's appointment today?"

When the hugging and laughter ended, they all took their places, joining hands around the circle and bowing their heads. Logan grasped Claire's hand and she closed her eyes, feeling once again there was nothing as wonderful as hope, love . . . and the awesome power of the Healer's heart.

+++

Logan settled into his deck chair and lifted his sunglasses to gaze out over the acreage, its trees turning burnished copper, red, and saffron gold in the late afternoon light. He turned to Claire. "So how many do you think that makes? We've been planting for hours, and—" He laughed. "Wait. Hold still."

"What?" Claire asked, sitting upright, batting at the air around her head. "Another wasp?"

Logan smiled. "A smudge of dirt. Hold still, Gopher Girl. I've got it." He brushed his thumb across her cheek and let it linger there, stunned once again that this warm and beautiful woman loved him. Even after six months, it still amazed him.

"Gopher Girl?" Claire wrinkled her nose and swatted him with her gloved hand. "Very romantic, McSnarly. And highly unappreciative of the woman who just dug more than six hundred holes for . . ." She smiled, her eyes lighting. "Oh, Logan, we're going to have the most unbelievable hill of daffodils in the spring."

He gazed upward at the nearly completed cedar home. "And maybe the rest of the roof too."

Claire laughed, tugging the brim of her ball cap down to shade her sun-pink nose. "You're so picky," she pronounced, spreading her arms wide. "We've got this gorgeous weather, leaves that knock your eyes out—" she grinned and tapped the glass tabletop in front of them—"an awesome oak stump table, the promise of daffodils, leftover pizza in the cooler—"

Logan touched his finger to her lips, quieting her. He watched her for a moment, his heart crowding his chest until it was hard to breathe. "So you're saying that you want for . . . nothing?" He smiled slowly. "Because I happened to pick something up today, and—"

Claire's delighted squeal cut him short. "It's ready?"

"Ready and—" he reached into the pocket of his denim jacket— "right here." He lifted the lid on the velvet Mother Lode Jewelry box, loving the sound of Claire's gasp when she saw the ring. "I think they got it exactly the way we wanted. See how they set those little gold nuggets around the diamond?" He looked up and saw her eyes filling with tears. "I know I already asked, but I want to hear you say it again. Will you marry me, Claire?"

She nodded, tears spilling over her dark lashes, then flung her arms around his neck. "Yes, yes, and yes," Claire murmured against his ear. "I love you, Logan."

He wrapped his arms tightly around her for a moment and then pulled away, holding her face in his hands. He kissed her tenderly. "I love you too."

Logan helped Claire pull off her gardening gloves and slid the ring on her finger. Then watched her hold it up to see the diamond sparkle in the sun, saying she couldn't wait for them to show everyone at church on Sunday. And that they should take photos to e-mail to their parents, and . . . He laughed as she peppered his cheek with kisses, then told her, sure, go ahead and call Erin—he'd finish installing Smokey's electronic pet door, then get the pizza out, and they'd sit around the oak table and watch the sunset.

When he returned with the pizza box, she was still talking to Erin about wedding plans, about having Erin and Sarah as bridesmaids, asking if Erin thought Sarah might want to rent her cabin in the spring, and promising she and Logan would visit in Pacific Point.

He pulled his chair close to Claire's and took hold of her hand, listening to her laugh and chatter with Erin, getting a kick out of her excitement and knowing he'd never been happier in his life. Right here, where he'd found his faith and where he was building a house and a future with this very special woman. A friend, a soul mate, a helpmate—he smiled at the sight of Claire's dusty work gloves on the table with his—soon a loving wife, and one day the mother of his children. Without any doubt, it was the answer to prayer.

ABOUT THE AUTHOR

Candace Calvert is a former ER nurse who believes love, laughter, and faith are the best medicines. A multipublished author of humorous mysteries, she begins an exciting new direction with the debut of *Critical Care*. A mother of two and native Californian, she now lives with her husband in the beautiful hill country of Texas. Visit her Web site at www.candacecalvert.com.

BOOK DISCUSSION GUIDE

Use these questions for individual reflection or for discussion within your book club or small group.

Note: Book clubs that choose to read *Critical Care*, please e-mail me at Candace@candacecalvert.com. I'll try to arrange a speaker-phone conversation to join your discussion.

1. In the opening scenes of *Critical Care*, nurse Claire Avery must counsel ER staff after a heart-wrenching disaster. This might be viewed as step one in God's plan for her own healing. Why?

2. Dr. Logan Caldwell is initially seen as critical, controlling, heartless. How does this impression change as the reader sees more scenes through his eyes? What motivates his behavior? Discuss.

3. *Critical Care* utilizes symbolism through various motifs. For example, daffodils signify hope. In your opinion, what does Logan's oak stump represent?

4. Claire and the ER, Smokey and the raccoons—why are these conflicts strangely similar?

5. Claire prays with her patient Jada Williams. Many hospitals today attempt to provide for patients' spiritual needs. Have you

(or a friend or family member) ever had a medical care worker offer spiritual support? offer to pray with you? How did (or would) you feel about that?

6. The Sierra Mercy ER staff participates in a voluntary debriefing after the Little Nugget Day Care tragedy. The facilitators recommend several ways to combat symptoms of stress, including exercise, eating well, journaling, and doing things that feel good to you. What have you found effective in helping you de-stress?

7. Nurse Sarah Burke's near-fatal accident becomes a catalyst in the healing of both Claire and Logan. How does that happen for each of them? Discuss.

8. In a climactic scene, Claire confronts Logan regarding his treatment of newly hired nurse Keeley Roberts. Why do you think that defending this nurse becomes so important to Claire?

9. Sarah, during most of her hospital stay, has recurring dreams about a birthday party. The elements include the blazing light of candles, a silver balloon reflecting that light, her daughter at age two, and the appearance of a man she thinks is her father but who has long hair, a bathrobe, and eyes full of love, acceptance, and patience. Even though he is attending a child's birthday party, this man seems to have eyes for only Sarah. Though confusing, it fills her with "unimaginable joy." How does this affect her? What hope do you see in this? Discuss.

10. ER nurse Erin Quinn finds it difficult to trust. She forces herself to try, despite red flags warning her about the sincerity of her boyfriend, Brad. Have you ever had that experience? What are signs you might be heading down a wrong path—anxiety, a

sinking stomach, sleeplessness? How easily do you trust? How readily do you turn to God to provide the answers to these nagging doubts?

11. Jeremiah 29:11 sets this book's theme, and Claire must learn that God is the ultimate planner for her life. Can you identify with this struggle? Are you a planner? How difficult is it for you to "let go and let God"? Discuss.

12. The prominent message of *Critical Care* is one of hope. The book's epilogue offers both elements of closure and hints of struggles to come. Claire, Logan, Sarah, Erin—how far has each come in personal growth? their faith journeys? What do you see for their futures? Why?

Please visit my Web site at www.candacecalvert.com for more information on upcoming books in this series.

Thank you for reading *Critical Care*.

Warmly,
Candace Calvert